Helen Harris is the prize-winning author of five novels and many short stories, published in a wide range of magazines and anthologies. She teaches creative writing at Birkbeck College, University of London.

Sylvia Garland's Broken Heart

"This passionate, yet perfectly-controlled novel … is beneath the surface a smouldering furnace … It is a book with depth and resonance and pace."
                                                    Jane Gardam

"Harris turns out to be a virtuoso when it comes to understanding family. She is superlative – I can't think of anyone better – at describing just how irritating everyone can be. She even-handedly lets us see how her characters get on one another's nerves. The result is sympathetic, funny and truthful."
                                        Kate Kellaway, *The Observer*

"*Sylvia Garland's Broken Heart* is a sensitive portrayal of the complexities of modern family life…This absorbing reflection on the joys and sorrows of marriage and parenthood comes highly recommended."   The BookTrust

Playing Fields in Winter

"So well ⸻⸻⸻⸻⸻⸻⸻⸻⸻ :ingly and
passiona⸻⸻⸻⸻⸻⸻⸻⸻⸻ hero and
heroine,⸻⸻⸻⸻⸻⸻⸻⸻⸻ ished first
novel."⸻⸻⸻⸻⸻⸻⸻⸻⸻ *isekeeping*

"The relationship between Sarah and Ravi is very nicely, perceptively and credibly handled. Miss Harris has got a real subject, she can tell a story and create character."

Alan Massie, *The Scotsman*

"Helen Harris has command over her language ... there are passages which are rich in suggestion and imagination."

Punch

Angel Cake

"The old woman is a totally convincing, rather surprising character and Alison is immensely likeable ... *Angel Cake* ... consolidates her reputation as a young writer of talent ... well worth reading." Susan Hill, *Good Housekeeping*

"A story of immense beauty and sadness, written with a rare compassion." *Jewish Chronicle*

"Few novels I have read give a better picture of the confusions of an old age where the world has shrunk to one room and the only events in life are the visit to the grocer, the battles with the brisk social worker and the skirmishing with the home help."

David Holloway, *Daily Telegraph*

The Steppes of Paris

"A breath of spring, although with two acclaimed novels already to her credit Helen Harris's talents are well past the budding stage ... wry, beautifully exact and bubbling with life."

Christopher Wordsworth, *The Guardian*

"I have never read a novel which describes so well the plight of the ex-pat in Paris ... the fraught progress of the affair is described with sharply wry observation."

Clare Colvin, *The Sunday Express*

"An attractive, well written portrait of a young man and an elderly Russian family ... well worth reading." *The Bookseller*

THE BRONDESBURY TAPESTRY

the Brondesbury tapestry

HELEN HARRIS

**Illustrated by
Beatrice Baumgartner-Cohen**

HALBAN
LONDON

First published in Great Britain by
Halban Publishers Ltd
22 Golden Square
London W1F 9JW
2018

www.halbanpublishers.com

A CIP catalogue record for this book is available
from the British Library.

ISBN 9781905559909

Typeset by AB, Cambridgeshire

Printed in Great Britain by
CPI Group (UK) Ltd, Croydon CR0 4YY

For Ian

"There was never yet an uninteresting life. Such a thing is an impossibility. Inside of the dullest exterior there is a drama, a comedy and a tragedy."

Mark Twain

THE SECOND CHANCE CENTRE

Autumn Term 2012 Register

Course: Life Story Writing			Day: Thursday Time: 2pm			
Instructor: Dorothy Woodward			Room Number: G3			
Student Name						
Pearl Barter						
Iris Bennett						
Enid Harkin						
Sabine Moreton						
Esther Solomon						
Renée Thorpe						
Edgar Whistler						

Dorothy

IT WAS A MUTED September day when Dorothy entered the Second Chance Centre for the first time. You couldn't exactly say the sun was shining but it was bright through the clouds. She had a gracious smile ready for whoever was sitting at the reception but when she walked in, there was no one there. A strong smell of something curried filled the building and it seemed that everyone had gone to lunch. Never mind: she would find her room on her own, which she did pretty quickly because the Second Chance Centre turned out to be quite small – and also rather scruffy.

She sat down before the circle of empty chairs and wondered who would fill them. She was half an hour early but soon a procession of strangers would arrive and she would welcome them kindly. As she waited, her mind returned to the disastrous sequence of events which had brought her here and the thought of her kindness made her sit a little more comfortably on the hard plastic chair.

Out of the windows, to her left and to her right, she could see two completely different views as if each one looked out onto a different city. To her right, she could see a stretch of the smarter side of Larkrise Road: white stucco houses with steps up to front porches and single door bells. To her left, one of the few trees on the Larkrise Estate was just starting to turn yellow and looking particularly pitiful.

Dorothy wondered what she was doing in this forlorn place and, feeling palpitations begin again, she reached for her Rescue Remedy, always somewhere in her bag.

Its' reassuring warmth had barely begun to spread when the door was violently thrown open. A short but evidently dangerous man with a shaven head shouted at her, "What you doin' 'ere?"

Dorothy flushed. "I'm running a group," she said.

"What group? No one told me anything 'bout a group." He glared at her. " 'Oo said you could sit in 'ere?"

Dorothy felt herself starting to panic. Had she got something wrong? She couldn't remember the funny name of the person with whom she had exchanged emails on and off over the summer, organising everything. She had no idea who this awful man was but it was obvious he would take great pleasure in evicting her. And now, suddenly, she was desperate to stay.

She told him firmly, "The manager said so."

He laughed. "Which one? We got too many of 'em round 'ere."

Dorothy floundered. It had been an unusual name. "Oh, goodness – it began with La —"

The man's face darkened. "I knew it. Lavonda. That one. It 'ad to be 'er."

Dorothy held her ground. She sat straighter.

The man's face took on an expression of exaggerated scorn. "So this group o' yours, what's it 'sposed to be doin'?"

Dorothy answered, as loftily as she knew how, "Life stories," and she was horrified when the man began to roar with laughter.

"Life stories? Blimey, if I told you my life story —"

Still laughing, he made to turn and leave. "I'll 'ave to speak to someone 'bout this. Not tellin' me – it's way outta line."

The door banged shut. Dorothy felt trembly and she knew she had gone all blotchy too. Instead of sitting calmly and preparing herself, she was a wreck.

A few minutes later, the man came back, again throwing the door open so hard it banged against the wall where, Dorothy noticed, the handle had made a deep groove before.

"I spoke to 'er. Lavonda. You can stay in 'ere. But next time don't come in 'ere wivout tellin' someone you're 'ere. I thought you'd come in off the street. We get a lot of 'em round 'ere."

He went out, again banging the door brutally behind him.

Dorothy was beside herself: someone off the street? Was that really what he'd thought? How dare he? Couldn't he see she was a respectable person? But then she began to worry that maybe there was something about her now, since the disaster, the way she held herself maybe or a look in her eye which did make her look lost, cast adrift, just like a homeless person.

In less than fifteen minutes, people would start to arrive. She had to pull herself together. She looked around the bare room but there was nothing to lift her spirits here. Nobody had put the clock forward in the spring and it was still an hour behind. If she was in charge, she would have sharply reproved whoever was responsible. She stood up and began to walk around the room, breathing deeply. She would walk around it six times, her special number and afterwards she would feel calmer. On the fourth or fifth time round, she lost count. She was starting to feel giddy too which wasn't helping. She paused by the window which looked out onto Larkrise Road and held onto the windowsill. The street seemed deserted; everyone in the world apart from Dorothy was at lunch.

Out of nowhere, a face loomed into the window, only inches away from her. Dorothy recoiled in shock: it was a ghastly face, gaunt, staring, contorted with the effort of peering inside. For a second or two it stayed there, grappling with some trick of the light which made it hard to see in through the pane. Then the face made out Dorothy staring back, it cracked into a dreadful grin and, just as suddenly, vanished.

Dorothy stood there, quaking. What, who was *that*? She wasn't even sure if it had been a man or a woman although, along with the staring eyes, the awful teeth and the wild hair, she was sure there had been an eccentric pair of multi-coloured glasses which most likely only a woman would wear. Was it one of the people who came in off the street? Should she alert someone? Was she even *safe* in here?

She retreated from the window. She went and sat back down on her chair and tried in vain to compose herself. It occurred to her that maybe the face was on its way in to her group, sneaking a look at the new teacher before coming in. Surely not? She couldn't be expected to have someone like that in her group, could she? Panicking, she realised that from now on everything was out of her control. It wasn't meant to start like this at all.

In the library, Dorothy had been in charge. It was only a branch library, not the main one with the imposing Victorian premises and the extra resources. But it was her library and, as Head Librarian (always capitals), she had over the years made it utterly and completely her own. You made the best of a bad

4

job of course. Her premises, which she had learnt in time to call "infrastructure", were two cavernous rooms and a sort of storage cupboard which she had turned into the Head Librarian's office. The library was in a wing of neglected Mercy House, a grand private home bequeathed to the Council in the Fifties and, she believed, not maintained since. Of course the Council could hardly have turned down Mercy House but it had been an elegant burden for them ever since and regularly the subject of rumours in the local press.

When Dorothy walked up the sweeping gravel drive of Mercy House in the morning, she felt she owned the place. The library shared the building with Sports and Leisure but they had so-called flexible working arrangements and never started before ten. For twenty-seven years, Dorothy had come in at half past eight. For the first half hour, until her deputy, poor Pam or later Parvaneh, arrived around nine, she was the lady of the house. She made herself a cup of tea and chivvied the urban foxes off the lawn. She collected the contents of the library's letterbox from the main front door. Of course it was too early for the postman; he only sloped up around midday. But there was always a lot in her letter box: overdue books returned under cover of darkness, the occasional hand-written, hand-delivered letter from some local trouble-maker as well as a heap of quite fascinating junk mail. She would usually take a look in the main letterbox too – they never bothered to lock it – and make small incriminating notes of what she found there. Then she would carry her own post back to her office, treading carefully on the slippery path in the morning dew and she would settle to read it all, sipping her tea. Looking back, it seemed she had been perfectly happy.

Some mornings of course, there were more urgent tasks: emptying the buckets which they put out under the leaks in rainy weather before they overflowed or mopping up if they already had. Everyone who visited the library was used to the steady tapping sound of the drips and some even claimed it enhanced concentration. They agreed that it was part of the library's dilapidated charm, along with its devoted librarian.

One of the things Dorothy was often complimented on were her signs. She took great care with them, they were always perfectly spelt and punctuated and at certain times of year they went up everywhere, a visiting wit remarked, like seasonal foliage. "Please let the librarian know at once if you find any evidence of mould or mildew in a library book." Or "WET UMBRELLAS – Please leave wet umbrellas in the urn provided for this purpose beside the front door and do not bring them into the library where they risk inflicting water damage on the books which are already under threat from our leaky roof!"

Often, Dorothy worked late; there was always something to catch up on. In the evenings, she had time to read the new acquisitions – although over the years there were fewer and fewer of them. She chose books and decorations for her seasonal themed displays and she snooped on the various strange people who frequented Mercy House at night.

The catastrophe did not come unannounced. For several years, they heard rumours that the Council was going to sell Mercy House. Look at the state of it, it cost far too much to maintain. But the period of nebulous rumours went on for so long that no one really believed them. The rumour of a new sports centre had also come and gone. Besides, how could you move a library if there was nowhere for it to go?

The answer to that came with cruel simplicity in a letter sent by the Council to all Head Librarians just before Christmas, the last but one Christmas. All the branch libraries were to close down. It was unthinkable. The letter claimed it was because they were no longer being used as much, they were uneconomical but the Head Librarians all knew that was untrue. They gathered for a protest meeting at Unitarian library – Dorothy, Barbara, Brenda and Gerald Shrimsley – and Dorothy was pleased to see that Unitarian was even more rundown than Mercy House. They all agreed there was no way this could possibly happen and afterwards they felt much better. Dorothy said that some days she had twenty or twenty-five people visiting her branch and Gerald said his library was a place of great inter-faith significance for the community. They reminded one another that the letter was called a consultation document and that, whatever the council might have in store for them, it would certainly take them an awfully long time to get round to it.

There was no consultation about it at all. By April, it was signed and sealed: all four branch libraries were to close down in twelve months' time and the future of the librarians would be decided on a case by case basis. Barbara and Brenda both took early retirement; they had grandchildren and, in Brenda's case, a husband with the beginnings of Alzheimer's. Gerald's branch was to remain open independently, staffed by a team of inter-faith volunteers. Mercy House was to be sold.

Dorothy was offered early retirement too but the thing was this; over so many years the library had become Dorothy's life. She had no other. Early retirement was out of the question; sooner the bridge over the Archway Road. Even if they redeployed her, ugly word, it would be no good. Without Mercy

7

House, without the foxes and the leaks, without above all the company of her few regular library users and the thrill of her night-time espionage, she did not see how she could carry on.

She had first come to work at Mercy House in her early thirties after the Peter Gentry fiasco. Although there was no reason to suppose then that it would be her last romantic involvement, that was how it had turned out. She remembered a faint flurry in her forties when she started receiving declarations on postcards left in the library letter box but that had come to a sorry end with a crudely illustrated postcard which she had to tear up. She suspected one of the shabby men who spent too much time in the library in bad weather.

She had lapsed, she supposed it was a lapse, into a life which consisted of her library. On the days when the library was closed and, with the passage of the years and the cuts, there were more and more days when the library was closed, she would wait at home for it to re-open. Was she unhappy? Her life did not seem to her significantly worse than that of people she knew with husbands and wives and children. Certainly, they always had plenty to grumble about. There was a cleanliness to her life which she found pleasing. But without her library, she knew it would be a wasteland.

Someone at the Council must have felt sorry for her. She was invited to a meeting with a vast sweet-faced woman in Human Resources called Anne. Anne gave her tea and biscuits, lumbering about the little booth that was obviously used in sensitive situations and then sat down and faced her, sighing.

"I wish it didn't have to be like this Dorothy," she began, looking appropriately distressed and opening a file. "But these are tough times and we simply don't have the resources to keep all our libraries open anymore. Now I understand so far you've refused the Council's offer of early retirement, although it's a very good offer you know and if I was fifteen years older I'd jump at it."

Dorothy had to suppress a smile at the thought of this immense woman jumping at anything. She answered, "What I want is to work, not to be got rid of. You have no right to treat me as if I'm finished just because I'm sixty."

"Oh Dorothy, Dorothy," Anne exclaimed, looking anguished. "We don't think you're finished by any means. The council values the contribution of our older workers." She paused. "There are a number of really worthwhile voluntary roles on offer in a whole lot of different sectors. If you accepted our offer of early retirement, we would love to consider you for one of those."

Dorothy gave her a look. "So you're happy for me to carry on working, is that it, just not to pay me?"

Anne was completely unruffled. She had obviously done this many times before. "Shall I tell you about some of the voluntary roles?" She asked. "Maybe something will appeal to you?"

When Dorothy understood at last that there was no way out and the library was due to close in April, she agreed to come along to a meeting where she would find out more about the voluntary roles. The experience of the extra-long Christmas and New Year closure was so dismal that in the end she went to the meeting almost gladly.

She disliked the name of the Second Chance Centre but the most suitable so-called roles seemed to be there. Although someone explained that the Centre was supposed to be a second chance for deprived local residents, Dorothy did hope that no one would imagine it was a second chance for her too. She volunteered to run the local history group since she was pretty knowledgeable about local history, her years as a librarian had familiarised her with all the local archives and societies.

She was baffled and distressed when, a few weeks later, she received a letter, congratulating her on being appointed to run the new life stories group. The letter came directly from the Second Chance Centre and was signed by a Ms L Clarke, programme coordinator. Dorothy considered the letter scornfully: the name, the Second Chance Centre, was printed across the head of the paper in squat chubby letters shading from dark grey on the left through to an especially nasty mauve on the right. The paper was pulpy, ostentatiously recycled. As for Ms L Clarke's knowledge of punctuation, it left a lot to be desired.

Dorothy telephoned the Second Chance Centre. An answering machine told her to leave a message. She left a short, rather snappish one but Ms Clarke did not ring back. A couple of weeks later, sitting brooding in her cubby-hole at the library, she sent an email to the address in the letter and immediately Ms L Clarke, Lavonda, replied. She told Dorothy that, far from being a mistake, her appointment was a unanimous choice about which everyone at the Second Chance Centre was thrilled. Dorothy answered that, having applied to run the local history group, that remained her preferred choice. Lavonda replied that one of the local archivists whose hours had been cut had already been appointed to that role. Dorothy sulked. After asking around all the other soon to be unemployed librarians, she understood that no one had applied to run the life stories group.

Then it was April and her library closed. In early May, she emailed Lavonda and told her that, after consideration, she was willing to run the life stories group. She did not hear back. A week later, frantic, she emailed again and this time Lavonda replied that she was glad to hear it and could Dorothy please send in immediately an outline of all the group's proposed activities so that they could carry out a risk assessment.

The classroom door opened a fraction. Round the edge of it, a nervous bird-like face appeared. It was two o'clock on the dot.

"Hello," Dorothy called out in a kindly voice. "Can I help you?" For the first time since April, she noticed that she sounded like a librarian again.

The door opened a little more and a thin woman with a frightened expression edged in. She asked hesitantly, "Is this the life stories group?"

"Yes," Dorothy said. "It is. Come in, come in, you're the first one."

The woman stayed in the doorway, still looking uncertain. Dorothy saw her take in the semi-circle of empty chairs and Dorothy herself, no doubt still looking blotchy. Dorothy picked up her register. "Do come in dear," she said. "What's your name?"

"Moreton," said the woman. "Sabine Moreton" and Dorothy thought she heard a French accent.

Reluctantly, the woman came forward and took her time choosing a chair. She perched on one some way away from Dorothy and waited, looking uncomfortable. Dorothy had a horrible feeling that she had only come in to be kind to her.

"Have you come far?" Dorothy asked.

The woman shook her head. "I live five minutes away." She gestured at the window with the view of Larkrise Road. "That side."

For a few moments, they sat in silence. What, Dorothy thought, if no-one else turns up? The woman checked her watch and Dorothy turned to look at the clock, still an hour slow. They faced each other again. With dreadful misgiving, Dorothy realized that she had no idea at all how to begin.

Pearl

WHEN PEARL CAME home from the Second Chance Centre, she found her grandson had gone back to bed. It was just gone four and she was livid; he had no business, a healthy young boy, being in bed at that time of day. He hadn't washed up his lunch things either, just shifted them from the kitchen table to the counter as if assuming that in due course Pearl would do it for him. Without knocking, she erupted into Kai's room.

"What the *hell* — ?"

Under the duvet, a huddled shape, from an invisible source, a low steady drumming.

"Kai!" she yelled. "What the *hell* d'you think you're doing?"

No response; he must have his earphones in.

Pearl yanked the duvet back furiously. Kai recoiled, blinked at her, he obviously hadn't heard her coming. Not only did he have his earphones in, even in bed he had his hood up too. No wonder he hadn't heard a thing.

Pearl gestured angrily at her own ears. "Out. Up."

Kai pulled out his earphones but he didn't move. "What's up Nan?"

Even though she wanted to go on being angry, even though she knew that for Kai's own good she had to, Pearl felt her fury subside a little. He looked so sweet lying there in his baggy clothes, the thin gangly length of him, his gentle vague-looking expression. He wouldn't hurt a fly. Her soft side whispered to her that she ought to be grateful; so many boys on the estates had turned out really bad. Not her Kai. He had never been in trouble with the police, to her knowledge never harmed anyone, never nicked anything. He was just a bit dozy that's all; he didn't do a whole lot. Maybe she should go easier on him, her gentler side suggested, let him take it easy in the holidays?

Her rage returned; it wasn't the holidays anymore, was it, school had started again this week, just like the Second Chance Centre, but Kai hadn't gone back.

Louder than she intended, she demanded, "It's after four Kai, why are you back in bed again?"

He scrambled into a sitting position, folding his long legs under him as if he felt that the less space he took up, the less offence he would cause.

Even though her heart bled for him, Pearl carried on glaring and waited for an answer, looking daggers.

Kai shrugged. "I don't see what's wrong with being in bed. It's not as if I've got anything else to do, is it?"

"You could be at school," Pearl shouted. "You could be doing your *A levels*."

Kai squinted at his phone, in bed beside him. "School's finished now," he said cheekily. "Chill Nan."

"Get up," Pearl ordered him, beside herself with rage and indignation and also fear for this lovely *useless* child. "Go into the kitchen and make us both a cup of tea please. Now."

Kai struggled out of bed and headed for the kitchen,

barefoot. Pearl thought about telling him to put some shoes on but knew, from long years' experience, to pick her battles.

She stood alone in Kai's small room for a moment and took advantage of being in there without him to have a quick look round. She thought of the things some other boys on the estates were said to have in their rooms – knives, drugs, unmentionable things – which she knew she would never find in Kai's. Still, it was always worth checking.

By the time she came into the kitchen, Kai had made the tea. Hers was perfect, just how she liked it, with milk and two sugars and, in a clear effort to smooth things over, Kai had put the biscuits out too.

Pearl sat down, started to drink her tea and tried not to look pleased. "We need to have a talk, you and I," she said.

Kai slurped his tea and shrugged.

Pearl was about to launch into a long lecture when, as if it had only just occurred to him, Kai asked, "Where did you go this afternoon Nan?"

Pearl frowned. He was just trying to change the subject, wasn't he? When had he ever shown any interest in what she got up to?

She gave a small exasperated snort. "We're not here to talk about that now Kai."

But he persisted, bless him. "Yeah but tell me: where did you go? I been wondering."

Pearl flushed. She didn't want to discuss where she'd been or what she'd been up to with Kai or with anyone else for that matter. She wasn't exactly sure herself why she'd gone along and until she'd worked that out, there was no point discussing it full stop.

15

"Kai," she said crossly. "It's *you* we need to talk about not me."

Kai sighed deeply. "Don't see why. I've not done anything wrong."

Pearl was on the verge of bursting out, "You've not done anything *at all* is the point Kai," when, in a gesture clearly intended to win her over, Kai flipped his hood off. He looked at her appealingly.

"Go on Nan. Tell me."

"Whyever d'you want to know?" Pearl blustered. "What's it to you?"

"Well," said Kai, "you always say where you're off to when you go out, don't you – I'm off to the shops, I'm going over to see Mavis or whatever – and today when you went out you didn't say anything so I figured you were up to something."

Despite her annoyance, Pearl felt flattered that her comings and goings had attracted this much of Kai's on-off attention.

"Up to something," she repeated indignantly. "What did you think I might be up to?"

Kai said, "I thought you might have gone up to school to talk about me to Mr Robinson."

Pearl was astounded; she had been thinking of doing just that all summer but she hadn't summoned the courage. An instant later, a wave of indignation swept over her; did Kai think she had no life of her own at all? Was it so unthinkable that she might have gone out quietly to do something *for herself*?

"Well I didn't," she said crossly, "although if you carry on this way I well might." And then, not really intending to, she said, "I went to the Centre if you must know."

Kai looked surprised. The Second Chance Centre was the biggest joke on the estate. "Why?"

She had gone too far already. "I'm thinking of joining a group."

"A group? What sort of a group?"

Pearl tensed. "A life story group."

Now Kai looked amazed. He considered his grandmother as if it had never crossed his young mind that she might have either a story or a life.

"Wow," he said, "that's cool."

Pearl preened. That was not a word she had ever thought to hear Kai use about her.

"So go on – tell me about it. What did you do? What was it like?"

Pearl looked at his face, alert now, interested, alive. For Christ's sake, he really cared about this.

"I don't know why you find it so fascinating," she began grumpily. "It's just a load of old women, that's all. And one old chap. There's nothing cool about it at all."

Kai grinned. "A load of old women and just one guy?" he asked cheekily. "How's that going to work?"

Pearl rolled her eyes. "I don't know what you're thinking Kai. It's a *course*, not a social group."

Even as she said this, she knew it wasn't the whole truth; when the old man came in, late, you could actually feel the excitement. A ripple passed over the group of women like a wind blowing across long grass.

"We're going to tell our life stories," she said. "Some

people are going to write them down, some people are just going to tell them and one woman – she's a complete head case – she says she's going to tell hers in pictures."

Kai was agog. "You mean like a cartoon?"

Pearl said, "I've no idea. She's off her head as far as I can see. You know who she is; she's that funny woman with the hair and the glasses who lives in Meadowcroft, the art teacher."

Kai gave a throttled squawk. "Miss Harkin? She's in your group? That's crazy."

"Crazy's just about right," said Pearl. "She's a real case. I don't remember, did she teach you?"

Kai exclaimed, "Yes, she did. In years seven and eight. Then she left. Or maybe she was fired, I don't know. She went. She was *insane*."

Pearl couldn't remember when she had last seen Kai look so animated.

"So there's her," she went on, "and a few others. And it's run by a funny little woman who used to work at the library before it closed down." She paused. "She's a bit of a one too."

"How?" Kai asked.

Pearl was wondering just how to describe Dorothy when Kai leant forward. "Nan," he asked urgently, "what about *you*? You haven't really got like a big story to tell, have you?"

Pearl looked at her grandson: so much he didn't know. She paused. "Yes I do actually Kai," she said slowly. "But I'm not sure I'm going to tell it. Certainly not there, with that lot."

Kai seemed desperate. He clutched her hand across the table. "You've got to!" he insisted. "Please Nan, you've got to."

Pearl stood up and started clearing away the tea things. "There's no *got to* about it at all," she said. "*I'll* decide if I'm going to go along or not. And most probably I won't."

After a moment, she added, "You know, there's things I'd like *you* to do Kai which you don't."

In the sulky silence which followed, she sneaked a look at him. His face, so alive and animated just a moment before, had resumed its' zoned out look.

Pearl's heart sank. She realized that, for Kai's sake, she was going to have to go to the group whether she wanted to or not.

Mechanically, she started to do the washing up. She hadn't enjoyed the first session and now she felt resentful that she was going to have to go back when, actually, she wasn't at all sure she wanted to. She wasn't even sure why she'd gone along in the first place.

Almost everyone was from the other side. Although the Centre had been built supposedly for the people who lived on the estate and the other worse estates round about, the truth was very few of them went there. The people who came to the Centre's fancy courses – aromatherapy, meditation, chocolate cookery and the like – were mainly from across the road, taking advantage of the council-subsidized prices. Even when they started steel band and rap to attract the young people from the estates, it was the richer teenagers who came along, with their expensive hoods up, pretending to be street smart.

Pearl scrubbed angrily at a burnt pan, another of Kai's late night brew ups gone wrong. What was she going to *do* with him? Maybe she really should go up to school and talk to Mr Robinson? He was the only one at that school who had ever got through to Kai. They hadn't done anything for her Tracy either. Pearl could feel tears coming on. She stamped over to the kitchen doorway and yelled at Kai's closed bedroom door, "You here tonight Kai?"

There was no answer.

Pearl started to cook anyway; Kai could always eat his later when he was prowling around in the middle of the night.

Frying onions, she tried to imagine telling her life story to the group. Never. They wouldn't even understand what she was on about. Probably the worst thing that had ever happened to some of them was losing their handbag on the bus.

Iris

Iris DITHERED ON the kerb. When you had got as slow at walking as she was, crossing Larkrise Road was no joke. It used not to be so busy but nowadays you had to wait forever for a break in the traffic and then, when one came, you barely had time to dash over to the other side. Dash wasn't really the word anymore. But Iris wouldn't use a stick. She knew the way it went; first a stick, then a walker, first a walker, then a wheelchair. So long as Iris was still upright, she would not stoop to a stick.

Crossing Larkrise Road was an exertion in more ways than one. Iris contemplated the drab low rise blocks of the Larkrise Estate and braced herself. Going over there was an act of charity – one she performed gladly in memory of dear Subhamoy and Mina Chatterjee – but it was still an effort. Iris lived in one of the smartest roads to the north of Larkrise Road, right up next to the park in fact and, in the normal course of events, she never came this way at all. But every year she would sign up for a course at the Second Chance Centre – silk painting, Over 50s Keep Fit – and that was her contribution to society. Iris believed that by joining the unfortunate inhabitants of the estate in their dingy Centre, she was doing her bit to raise standards. Having someone like her in the classroom, braving the cooking and other smells, improved the quality of the classes for everyone and that was the spirit of the Chatterjee bequest.

Iris had only known the Chatterjees, Subhamoy and Mina, slightly. They lived in the biggest house in Iris's street, they were rumoured to be fabulously wealthy and their Indian origins gave them an exotic, spiritual allure. They ran a chain of chemists. Iris had been surprised that you could apparently make so much money out of selling corn plasters and haemorrhoid cream. Of course by the time she met Mina and Subhamoy – at pre-Christmas drinks and mince pies at a mutual neighbour's – their days of standing at the counter were long behind them. There were branches of Karma Chemists all over North West London and Mina and Subhamoy, the prosperous heads of a prosperous clan, were much in demand at parties. They were that rare thing: a wealthy, self-made couple who truly cared about others. For all their wealth, their lifestyle was not lavish, they were fervent vegetarians. Their leisure pursuits were all high-minded: music, the arts, improving theatre. You regularly saw their names in programmes in the lists of patrons whose financial help was gratefully acknowledged. Subhamoy and Mina told people they wanted to give something back to the country which had taken them in when they fled from East Africa with nothing thirty years ago.

They were distressed by the state of this country too. Growing up in East Africa, Mina had once told Iris, they had studied from textbooks which showed Great Britain as a shining example to less developed nations. They had been shocked when they arrived here by the dingy down-at-heel reality.

Since settling in Brondesbury, they had been constantly troubled too by the poverty and despair on their own doorstep. Iris couldn't help bridling a little at this; surely the poverty in East Africa had been much worse than anything you saw on the streets of North West London? It seemed Mina and Subhamoy meant a different sort of poverty; a poverty of the soul. They were deeply troubled to see around them so many unfortunate people living idle, directionless lives, not working, on benefits, having children whom they could not then be bothered to bring up properly, drinking, gambling, taking drugs. They wanted to help raise them up – and that was the inspiration for the Subhamoy and Mina Chatterjee Centre.

The Centre, at its inception, was to be a place where poor people living round about could come to enrich their lives. It was to be a community arts centre where people could learn painting, music, pottery, possibly yoga. It was not to be a place where people sat around and chatted, played table football or bingo. They must not consume alcohol on the premises either. Everything about it was to be improving, uplifting.

While Mina and Subhamoy's vision had in due course come to be, and their Centre had eventually been built, unfortunately a number of things had not gone to plan along the way. Inevitably, the Council had become involved. Since they were going to have to cover the running costs, once Mina and Subhamoy's philanthropic centre had been built, they had a say in how everything was done and they were every bit as benighted as you would expect.

The first thing to go had been the name; unpronounceable, someone high up at the Council had ruled and put their foot down. The Chatterjees had been deeply hurt, things had almost come unstuck over that. But over time, taking various factors into account – and first and foremost the fundamental goodness of the Chatterjees – a compromise had been reached: the centre would have an ethnically neutral name which would be equally pronounceable by all the diverse communities of the borough and a very large plaque would be put up in the front hall to acknowledge the inspiration and generosity of Subhamoy and Mina Chatterjee.

Iris yanked open the heavy front door and noted with disapproval a new crack in a pane. She must speak to one of the managers about that. Since the Chatterjees' dreadful and untimely death, she had felt a little proprietorial about the centre – which she still thought of privately as the Chatterjee Centre; she liked to keep an eye on it for poor Mina and Subhamoy's sake.

In the hall, she paused beside their plaque. She did this every time she came in. She told herself it was so as to pay homage to Mina and Subhamoy's memory. But at the same time it drew everyone's attention and reminded them of Iris Bennett's link to the Chatterjees.

She cast a glance at the sullen young woman sitting at the reception. She had not yet looked up, oblivious to Iris's stance beside the plaque. So Iris had to clear her throat loudly and call out, "Life stories – which room is that?"

Barely lifting her head, the girl said, "G3."

"And which way," Iris asked, "is *that*?"

Now the girl looked up. She appeared to take in Iris: her carrying voice, her imperious manner and her high and mighty hairdo – a high bun, held in place with tortoiseshell combs – and she replied rudely, "Straight down there, you should find it."

Iris was on the verge of answering back, putting the ill-mannered girl in her place. But she knew she was already late and, while she liked to arrive a little late, to make an entrance, come in too late and you risked looking hopeless. So she turned away and noted the rudeness for future reference. She knew just whom to have a word with.

Outside the classroom door she paused briefly, adjusted her scarf and combs and checked her watch: ten past two – perfect. Then she opened the door wide and made her entrance.

When she saw how few people there were sitting inside, she wondered why she had bothered. There had been more than twenty of them last term in Over 50s Keep Fit, a jolly, mixed, if sweaty group. She might have guessed that life story writing would not be a crowd-puller on the Larkrise Estate. She should have signed up for silk painting again instead.

"Do come in," the teacher called out. "Take a seat."

She gestured at the ring of empty chairs. She sounded irritated, as much by all the empty chairs, Iris guessed, as by Iris's late arrival.

Iris considered where to sit; she knew that where you sat the first day, you would most likely be stuck all year. So, even though it meant walking the whole way round the semi-circle, she opted for a chair at the opposite end from everyone else. Start as you meant to go on.

"Where were we?" the teacher continued, looking hot and bothered. "Introductions. We were just doing introductions."

Iris said, "I am Iris Bennett" but the teacher interrupted her, "No, no, we had started at the other end. We were just making Esther's acquaintance. Do carry on, Esther. I'm sorry about the interruption."

A dark, much younger woman squirmed uncomfortably. "So, where was I, my name's Esther Solomon and I've come along because I want to tell my Mum's life story but I'm having trouble getting it down. It's sort of complicated —"

She hesitated, grimacing, and the teacher said soothingly, "Just tell us as much as you want Esther."

Esther wrung her hands and recited, as if she had rehearsed it, "My Mum's name was Rita Solomon and she had a really hard life. Not hard in the sense of hard up but personal stuff."

She crossed and uncrossed her legs and finished off, "Yeah, that's it."

The woman sitting closest to Esther – two chairs away – turned towards her. She was a frightful-looking person, Iris thought, with a mass of wild grey hair and wearing some very ill-judged patchwork trousers on her scrawny legs.

"Why," she asked Esther – and her voice had a disturbing grating quality – "do you want to tell your mother's story instead of your own?"

The teacher intervened. "Let's stick to introductions for now please." She looked awfully tense.

"Your turn," she said to the woman in the patchwork trousers. But the woman more or less ignored her and said to Esther, "Well, I'm looking forward to finding out why. It's a very unusual thing to do."

She turned back to face the others. "Enid Harkin," she

said. "I'm an artist and I'm planning to tell my life story in pictures."

Iris couldn't resist it. "Well, that's pretty unusual too," she said and she and Enid glared at each other across the semi-circle.

Next came two unassuming plumpish women sitting side by side: Pearl and Renée. Until they spoke, Iris assumed they had come together but Pearl lived on the estate, she said so and Renée rather obviously didn't. It was just a coincidence, Iris supposed, that they shared the same taste in M and S cardies.

After Renée, there was another woman with a French name, Sabine, except she really was French – or rather Belgian. Then it was Iris's turn. She was disappointed that most of the women seemed to come from the better side of the borough and not from the estates at all. It would make it harder to stand out – although of course Iris would manage. Her introduction wasn't quite as polished as she would have liked because, truth to tell, she had been too taken up with what all the others had to say. Not that any of it was so frightfully fascinating of course but still; it was a window onto other people's lives, wasn't it? It was that curiosity which had drawn her there.

Iris gave her name and told the group about her connection to the Chatterjees.

The teacher asked, "And are *you* planning to write *your* life story?"

Iris gave her what she hoped was a withering look. She had just remembered that the teacher used to be that officious little librarian at Mercy House before it closed down. What on earth was *she* doing here? What possible qualifications did *she* have to run a life story group? And did she remember that Iris had not returned her last book when the library shut?

"Yes," Iris said grandly. "I am." But she said nothing else, creating, she hoped, an aura of mystery.

"Good," said the little librarian. "Good. Because, after all, that *is* what we're here for."

Iris was seething at this put-down when Enid the artist spoke up again. "What about you?" she asked the teacher. "Will *you* be telling your life story?"

The librarian went red. "Well," she said, "well."

"Oh go on," said a couple of the women, Iris thought fawningly: future teacher's pets.

The librarian said, "We'll see about that," and she made a great to-do of handing out a sheaf of photocopies. It seemed to Iris that her hands were shaking.

"I don't believe you've introduced *yourself*," Iris said as she took her own copy.

But the librarian got the better of her again: "I did actually, before you joined us. I'm Dorothy, Dorothy Woodward."

Iris was about to reply, "Of course you are. You were the librarian at Mercy House, weren't you, before you were closed down." She was going to ask, "How did you turn into a life story teacher?" when something entirely unexpected happened which distracted everyone. The door opened again and a man entered the classroom.

28

Edgar

IT WAS MADELEINE who had persuaded Edgar to go along to the life stories group. She was always telling him to get out and about more, to take part in more stimulating activities and one day she had come in and smacked the brochure from the Second Chance Centre down on the table. "There you go," she said, "take your pick."

Edgar hadn't really wanted to go. He had skimmed through the brochure, hadn't liked the look of anything (maybe the pictures of the women in leotards in the Keep Fit classes). But clubs and classes had always been more Joan's thing than his and it made him feel strange to have Madeleine pushing him to do something which he knew Joan would have wanted too.

After she had made their tea, Madeleine sat down and put her tired feet up. She browsed through the brochure, oohing and ahing and reading aloud the names of all the classes she would love to go to if only she had the time: choir, relaxation, slimming.

Edgar said firmly, "You don't need slimming" and Madeleine laughed comfortably.

Then she said, "Listen to this." She read out to him about the new life stories group and commented, "You should go to that one Edgar dear. You're a lovely storyteller."

29

Well, there was nothing he wouldn't do for Madeleine. Madeleine had come into his life when he expected nothing more from it. Joan had been gone for five years but he had not stopped missing her. It was true he did not go up to the Garden of Rest as often anymore. But that was more a question of stamina than anything else. His feelings for Joan, his wife of thirty-seven years, were undiminished. For five years, he had woken every morning to Joan's absence. Their small maisonette on the Larkrise Estate, which Joan had always kept spotless, felt dark and neglected nowadays. Edgar did his best but housework and all that had never been his forte. Joan wouldn't let him in on the mysteries of how it was done. When she knew she was on her way out, she had said to him, "You'd better get someone to take care of you Edgar. Otherwise there's going to be one hell of a mess." She was in hospital when she said it, lying flat in bed, almost the same colour as the sheet. From the anxious look on her face, Edgar couldn't tell if she was more worried about him or about the mess.

"Don't be silly love," he'd told her. "No one's ever going to step into your shoes."

Thinking about that now, he felt guilty. Except of course Joan had told him to find someone to take care of him. And Madeleine, strictly speaking, had not stepped into Joan's shoes.

The way it had come about was nothing short of miraculous. A little over a year ago, he had his heart attack. Truth to tell, he had suspected it was in the works but he hadn't done anything about it; he hadn't been that bothered. Even before Joan had passed away, retirement had not suited him. The idea of the lights going out was quite appealing. He had taken no notice of the warning signs and, the night before it happened, he had met up for a meal with an old friend from his menswear days and purposefully ordered everything which Joan would have forbidden him, plus a bottle of wine.

He was in the queue in Karma Chemists the next morning when it happened: a crushing pain gripped his chest, he couldn't draw breath and then everything went dark.

He woke up in A&E with a pretty young lady doctor and a pretty young nurse bending over him. He thought, for a moment, that he had gone to heaven. But they were asking him who to call and he didn't know who to say.

He was in for a good few days. He had some sort of operation to fix things up and when it was time to go home and they realised he lived on his own, they arranged for a district nurse to call. The district nurse, God bless her, was Madeleine. Ever afterwards, Edgar thought it was too good to be true that he had got Madeleine on the NHS.

Although he had desired her the moment he first saw her, on the doorstep in her starchy blue and white uniform, carrying her big nurse's bag, it had seemed impossible to him that Madeleine might be attracted to him too. But, as she explained to him when they had got to know each other a little better, Edgar, at seventy-two, was one of her youngest patients. She spent her days looking after housebound eighty and ninety-year-olds who needed all sorts doing. Edgar, in his natty maroon dressing gown, needing nothing more than checking up on, a pep talk and a bit of dietary advice, was the bright spot in her week. Plus he had such lovely manners, she said. Well, that was his years in menswear. So, when his allotted number of house calls was up, when he was signed off, Madeleine had kept on visiting.

It had gone from there; to start with, just cups of tea and talking. Madeleine had told Edgar about her two children whom she was with difficulty putting through university and their father who had cleared off when they were still small. Edgar had told Madeleine about Joan. Madeleine put the kitchen to rights. When Edgar was well enough to go out and about again, he asked Madeleine if she would have dinner with him at his local Italian.

It was the first time he saw Madeleine out of her nurse's uniform. They arranged to meet at Brondesbury tube. When Edgar, who had got there half an hour early, saw Madeleine emerge from the tube station, he feared for a moment that his heart was going to go again.

It was a gentle late spring evening. Madeleine was dressed in a shiny dark red dress with a matching jacket and, instead of her nurse's bag, she was carrying a big dark red imitation crocodile-skin handbag. The idea that this beautiful full-figured black woman was walking out of the tube station towards *him*, that she had dressed herself up like this for *him* filled Edgar with a great wonder which had never gone away.

They greeted one another formally but, as they

walked away, Edgar asked, "May I?" and he took Madeleine's arm and she did not object. If he could have made that walk go on forever, he would. Strolling arm-in-arm along Kilburn High Road in the dusk, the pavements thronging as usual but apparently no one there but them. It was better than a wedding march because it was so unexpected. When they sat down in 'Da Luigi's' and Madeleine smiled at him across the table, Edgar felt as if a superb black sun had risen over his life and, in that moment, he knew that he would do anything at all to keep her there.

So going along to the Second Chance Centre – even though he didn't really want to – was no big deal. On the morning of the first class, Madeleine reminded him before she left for work and he doffed an imaginary hat to her and said, "Yes ma'am."

Madeleine's happy laugh as she went out seemed to linger all morning like the sweet aftertaste of a favourite dessert. Madeleine couldn't always stay over; sometimes her demanding children stopped her and sometimes there were work reasons. So, when she could, it always felt marvellous, a little get-away, just the two of them and Edgar was perfectly happy like that. He did not dare to hope that Madeleine might one day move in with him. He considered himself already the luckiest man alive and maybe it was better this way because Madeleine was not actually moving into Joan's home.

In the morning, he went to the drycleaners. Keeping his clothes nice was one thing he had always taken care to do. On the way back, he stopped for a coffee and to read the paper at the Pristina café. The owner Murat told him he was looking fifty again. Then it was time to heat up his lunch which was last night's Caribbean chicken leftovers. He was napping in his armchair when he heard Joan's carriage clock strike two and he remembered about the Second Chance Centre.

Distressed at the thought of being late, he hurried to get ready. Now it seemed to him that both the women in his life, Madeleine and Joan, were standing over him, chivvying him. Quickly, he put on his navy blue blazer and, after a moment's hesitation, a tie. It was a bit like going back to school, wasn't it? Then he took his felt trilby off its peg – he had only just swapped it for the summer straw – checked himself in the hall mirror and let himself out.

The Second Chance Centre was just round the corner but he had never set foot inside. Joan had been a regular, always coming home with cushion covers she had embroidered or cakes she had decorated and, once, some wobbly pieces of pottery which she had made. She hadn't liked pottery though; she found it too messy.

Edgar felt strangely inhibited when he walked inside. It was a combination of that "back to school" feeling and the knowledge that Joan had been here before him.

A kindly young woman at the reception asked him what he was looking for and, when he told her, she came out from behind the counter to show him the way. She was very friendly and chatty as they walked down the passage and didn't say anything at all about Edgar being twenty minutes late.

When he entered the classroom, for an instant he

wanted the ground to swallow him up. It was all women, sitting in a circle, talking nineteen to the dozen and, simultaneously, they all of them stopped talking and turned to look at Edgar.

He fell back on his manners. He said, "So sorry ladies," he raised his hat and from the group of women there came an appreciative murmur which made him feel straightaway more welcome.

Dorothy

AFTER THAT FIRST session of the life stories group, Dorothy's distress knew no bounds. What had she let herself in for? What in heaven's name had she been thinking of when she agreed to go ahead with such a foolish venture? Stories were one thing; after her long tenure at the library, she certainly knew a thing or two about stories. But life? What did she know about life? Her own had turned out to be so quiet and now, somehow, she was responsible for the safe narration of a whole lot of other people's which had doubtless been far messier and more lurid than hers. The whole thing was a nightmare. She couldn't possibly go ahead with it.

After tidying the chairs and turning out the lights, she went looking for Lavonda whom she had yet to meet. A grumpy girl sitting at the front desk, eating a garish kind of snack, pointed her towards Lavonda's office. Through a mouthful, she warned, "She may be in a meeting."

But Lavonda was in her room, reading a stack of files with an important look on her face which, Dorothy supposed, she must have had herself in the days when she had her own desk and files. Lavonda looked up when Dorothy appeared in the doorway and, switching to a look of professional concern, asked, "May I help you?"

Dorothy hesitated. She registered that Lavonda was black

and very much younger than she was. She did not look friendly. Even though Dorothy was particularly polite, when Lavonda understood that she wasn't an old dear attending class, her expression straightaway became less concerned. "I hope everything went ok with your group?" she asked. "Your numbers are very low."

Dorothy had been about to blurt out, "Excuse me but this is all a mistake. I can't go ahead with it. You'll have to find someone else." But perversely, as soon as she heard the implied threat in what Lavonda had said, she wanted to cling onto her class for dear life. Resigning was one thing, being pushed out again was quite another.

"It might grow though," she said, "mightn't it, if people bring their friends along?"

Lavonda raised her eyebrows sceptically. They were shaped and drawn in ferociously. She had an exceptionally high shiny forehead. She looked at Dorothy condescendingly. "There's not much diversity in your group either."

Dorothy had worked long enough in the library to know what "diversity" meant. Quickly, she answered, "It's more diverse than it looks you know. One woman is Belgian."

Lavonda's fierce eyebrows shot way up. "Belgian?" she repeated, laughing. "Belgian's not diversity."

Well, there were all sorts of things Dorothy could have said to that, weren't there: Belgium was a small country, Belgians were a minority too. Besides hadn't the Belgians been our allies in two world wars? But Dorothy knew that none of that would mean much to righteous Lavonda.

Instead she said, "I ought to be on my way. It's been lovely meeting you."

Lavonda shrugged. She said, "Bye" a bit dismissively and went back to her files.

Dorothy went home, a bus ride and a longish walk. When she let herself into her flat, she noticed that her cat wasn't there and she thought rancorously how typical it was that Whittington should choose to go off on one of his wanderings just when she would have welcomed his soothing presence. She made herself a cup of tea, cut a slice of ginger cake for the sugar and sat and looked out at the garden. A London garden on a muted September day did not offer much in the way of cheer. The garden was shared between the tenants of all four flats in the house but no one, apart from Dorothy, took much trouble with it and there was a limit to what she on her own could do.

She drank her tea and ate her cake, without much pleasure. Then she took out her register and looked wretchedly down the list of names:

Pearl Barter
Iris Bennett
Enid Harkin
Sabine Moreton
Esther Solomon
Renée Thorpe
Edgar Whistler

She shuddered as she read Enid's name. But the truth was her heart sank a little more with every name. That was how it had felt when they all came in too; as each new person entered the room, Dorothy's heart had taken a lurch as if at the revelation of a fresh complication.

It was not that anything had gone so awfully wrong. Everyone had introduced themselves and she had handed out some helpful photocopies to get them started. No, what troubled Dorothy was the feeling that each and every one of them had come along to unburden themselves and, it felt, overwhelmingly, as if the person left with all the burdens would be her.

There was something else upsetting too, something that frightful Enid Harkin had said.

"What about *you*?" Enid had asked. "Will *you* be telling your life story?"

As Dorothy contemplated the utter impossibility of such a thing, she felt on the verge of tears.

There was a series of hesitant taps at the door. Christopher – that was all she needed. But she had to answer; he would have heard her come in and waited politely for twenty minutes before coming up.

Reluctantly, she opened the door and Christopher said, "D-d-d-d-d-d-d-d-d!"

"Hello Christopher," she said rather briskly. "I warn you, I'm a bit busy. I've just come in from my life stories group" and, as she said it, she experienced the old familiar pleasure of having a job to do.

Christopher began, "H-h-h-h-h-h-h-h?"

"It went very well," Dorothy said. "Quite a big group actually."

"Gr," said Christopher. "Gr-great."

He gave a large but incomprehensible gesture with one thin arm. "W-w-w- won't k– keep you."

"Another time," Dorothy said. "Drop in for tea at the weekend maybe?"

Christopher gave another wild but incomprehensible gesture. "W—," he said and then, after a great gasp, suddenly, perfectly, "Will do."

Dorothy heard him go back downstairs to the basement flat. Poor Christopher. He was someone else who would never write his life story. He was youngish still, only in his thirties, but already living like an old recluse. He worked as a lexicographer, from home. He spent his days bent over his computer down in the basement, occasionally laughing at a dry lexicographer's joke, which he might share later with Dorothy but which never made her laugh. His life seemed blighted by his terrible stammer; he found any communication painfully difficult and had, through his choice of profession, presumably done his best to avoid it.

Dorothy had befriended him, in the days when she was still Head Librarian, because she felt sorry for him. But since the disaster, she was finding it much harder to feel sorry for Christopher. He did insist on behaving as if he felt sorry for *her*.

Spurred on by the sight of Christopher's hopelessness, Dorothy went back to her papers. "Begin by telling us something about your parents," she wrote. "What do you know about their lives before you came along? Set the scene for your arrival." She understood that, come what may, she had to make a go of this.

On the day of the second class, it was pouring. Dorothy caught herself wondering if anyone was emptying the buckets at Mercy House. They must be overflowing, if not. The books had all been taken away, it had broken her heart; some of them had gone to the main library and some of them, along with the computers, had gone to a charity which sent educational materials to Africa. In one of her wilder fantasies, Dorothy had gone off to Africa together with her books, to open a little library out there, somewhere in the middle of nowhere. Even though she knew full well she would never dare to do such a thing – and most likely they wouldn't want her either – she still enjoyed imagining it sometimes, particularly in bad weather. She saw herself in a small, simple, maybe mud-walled building, lending out the treasured remnants of her library to grateful Africans. Every now and then, like in an old Babar book, an elephant or a giraffe would poke its cheerful face in at the window.

She was ready well in time and set out for the Second Chance Centre with half an hour to spare. As she locked her front door, Christopher came bounding up the stairs from the basement, flailing his arms excitedly.

"G—" he began, "g-g-g-g-g—"

"Good luck?" Dorothy asked shortly.

Christopher nodded. "You'll, you'll be b-b-b-b-b—"

"Thank you," Dorothy said quickly. "Thank you."

Really, being patronised by Christopher was intolerable.

She got to the Second Chance Centre in plenty of time although awfully wet. In the front hall, she passed Lavonda.

"I hope your lot will still want to come out in this weather," Lavonda said discouragingly.

Dorothy said, "I'm sure they will" and when she got to the classroom, two of them, Pearl and Renée, were already there. Really, it was a bit much; it wasn't even quarter to. Dorothy glanced at the clock and gave them a reproving look but, truth to tell, Pearl and Renée were already deep in conversation and didn't seem interested in Dorothy in the slightest.

Pearl

IN THE END, Pearl decided there was nothing for it; she would have to go up to school and speak to Mr Robinson. She didn't want to but there was no getting round it; if she was going to do right by Kai and, as far as she was concerned, she would always do right by Kai, she would have to face up to the horrible feelings which setting foot in that school always stirred up in her and go and see Mr Robinson.

She had been in and out of the school all the time when Tracy started to go off the rails. But that was nearly twenty years ago now and probably none of the same teachers even worked there. Certainly, Mr Robinson hadn't worked there back then. Maybe, who knows, if he had, things might have ended differently. Kai seemed to be getting into a pattern of sleeping all day and being up all night. Mr Robinson might be her only hope.

One morning, while Kai was still asleep, she rang. The automated switchboard told her to press 3 if she was a parent and, although obviously she wasn't, after a split second's hesitation, she did. Kai wasn't even at the school anymore either. Maybe no-one would speak to her.

After a long wait, the person she least wanted to answer did: Prithi, the snooty school secretary. Pretending not to recognize Prithi's voice, Pearl said, "Hello this is Pearl Barter here. I'm Kai Barter's grandmother."

"Oh Mrs Barter!" Prithi said with false sweetness. "How are you? Kai's left, hasn't he? What's he doing now?"

"Cow," Pearl thought, "cow."

Practically every person for miles around knew that Prithi's Arun, two years older, had a place to study engineering at Manchester University.

"That's why I'm ringing," Pearl said. "He's thinking of coming back." This was of course an outright lie but certainly a white one.

"But Mrs Barter!" Prithi exclaimed, "Term started last week. I'm not even sure if we have any places in the sixth form."

Well, Pearl knew for sure that was a lie too. The sixth form had always been short of students; it was an uphill struggle convincing enough of the local kids to take the academic route.

"I'd like to make an appointment to see Mr Robinson please," Pearl said boldly. "I need to talk to him about Kai. I'm sure he'll want him to come back."

"Well," Prithi said, "I'm not sure he'll be able to see you. Now Kai's *left*."

Pearl contained her white hot rage. "He'll see me," she said furiously. "Thank you Prithi. I'll expect your call."

Well, that had been three days ago and she had not heard a thing. Now it was the day of the bloody life stories group too and she didn't dare go out in case Prithi rang while she was gone. Kai might wake up and take the call. Although, who knows, maybe it wouldn't be a bad thing if he did?

43

In the middle of the night, Pearl had heard something. She often woke in the night and lay and thought about stuff, mainly Tracy. Of course she thought about Kai too but, until the past few months, things hadn't been too bad with Kai and of course at night you always thought about the bad stuff, didn't you? Lately, she often heard Kai pottering about. She didn't know what he got up to, certainly a hell of a lot of snacking but he didn't seem to go out anywhere or have anyone over. In the morning, when he had finally gone to bed, his laptop was often left on the kitchen table and sometimes Pearl could bring it back to life by tapping any old key. But she couldn't make head or tail of what he was up to; swapping messages with people with strange names about stuff she couldn't understand. She couldn't even make out if they were boys or girls. None of it looked bad but then how would you *know*?

The other night, for the first time, she thought she heard someone else in the kitchen. Then she thought maybe Kai had the radio on really quiet. She lay and listened. No, he was talking to someone. But she was sure no-one had come over; she would have heard the front door go. He must be talking to someone on the computer. Who on earth could he be talking to like that at half past three in the morning?

Pearl had brought up two generations, God help her. She knew that, at Kai's age, you didn't ask questions and you didn't expect answers. But you could certainly get up and go to the loo in the night, couldn't you, at past seventy? No-one could accuse you of snooping if really you had a weak bladder.

When she opened her bedroom door, she could clearly

hear Kai in the kitchen, talking very quietly and then an even fainter voice answering, just a couple of words she couldn't make out.

Then Kai said, just audibly, "So d'you like hatebeak then?" Or was it hate speak?

Pearl went into the bathroom and shut the door behind her, not even quietly. When she switched on the light, the extractor fan came on and cut out everything else. Hatebeak? She caught sight of her face in the mirror; it had the same frantic look she had seen every day for years when Tracy was —. Please God, not again with Kai.

When she had finished in the bathroom, she thought about charging into the kitchen: "What the hell? This time of night?" – that sort of thing – but thought better of it. Wait until she had worked out exactly what Kai was up to. Anyway, when she came out, the kitchen had gone completely dark and quiet.

She felt tired today, as she sometimes did, from the broken night and the worry. The last thing she wanted was to go and face that group of women again. The only one she had taken to was Renée who, even though she came from the other side and had that nervous look they all had when they came over to the estate, was obviously a dear. Otherwise – she thought round the circle of chairs, lingering for a moment on Edgar – they really were a lot of head cases, weren't they? She didn't fit in there at all and it had been stupid to sign up and pay good money for it. The idea that she might actually share some of the worst times of her life with them was crazy.

But there was Kai, Kai whose sleepy face had come to

life when she told him about it, Kai who could be the willing family member Dorothy had talked about, who would operate the recorder and ask the questions while she told her story. Obviously, there were things she couldn't tell Kai about, like Tracy's —. But most probably she couldn't tell anyone about that anyway.

On an impulse, she barged into Kai's room and, to her surprise, he wasn't asleep at all. It was just gone one, he hadn't yet given sign of life but he was already up and on his computer. The fact that he was still wearing yesterday's clothes which he must have slept in *and* had his bloody hood up indoors, Pearl decided to ignore.

"Afternoon," she said menacingly.

Kai gave her a puzzled look, as though he genuinely had no idea what time it was.

"Hi Nan."

"D'you even know what *day* it is?" Pearl began.

Kai said, "No." He gave her a vague, curious look as if he couldn't work out why it mattered.

"It's Thursday," Pearl told him, "that's three days this week you've wasted already. What are you going to do so today's not the fourth?"

Kai looked hurt. "It's not really *wasted* Nan. I'm doing stuff online."

"Online!" Pearl shouted. "Online's not real life, Kai. And whatever it is you're doing there, it's not going to get you a qualification or a job, is it?"

It occurred to her that, for all she knew, maybe you could get all that online but Kai didn't argue with her. He just sat there, looking uncomfortable, waiting for her anger to blow over.

Before she had thought it through, Pearl blurted out, "I'm off to the life story group in a bit, you'll be pleased to hear, seeing as you're so keen on it. If the phone rings while I'm out, please answer it – nicely – and give me the message. I'm expecting an important call."

Kai said, "K."

As Pearl gave him a last glare before leaving, he asked, "Who's 'sposed to be ringing then?"

Pearl had already turned to go. She didn't answer. She was amazed when Kai asked, "Is it Mr Robinson?"

Pearl kept her face turned away. She pretended to be rubbing at a mark on the door. "And if it *was* Mr Robinson?" she asked. "How bad would that be? Someone's got to sort you out Kai. Seeing as you're not exactly getting anywhere yourself."

Behind her Kai said, "Cool" and then, just as she was leaving, "Thanks Nan."

She cried all the way over to the Second Chance Centre and when she got there, she told Renée, who was the only one there, that she had a bit of a cold. From her bag, Renée produced, as if by magic, a packet of Pearl's favourite lozenges. They sat companionably sucking and chatting until everyone else arrived.

Things didn't go nearly as badly as Pearl had feared. Renée hadn't recorded or written anything either – and neither had Iris – so she wasn't by any means the only one. The old man, whom Pearl was sure she had seen sitting alone in that scruffy café on the High Road, said he planned recording some stuff at home with the help of a lady friend and Pearl sensed everyone's hopes dashed at the revelation that he had a lady friend. But two of them, Sabine and Esther, had written reams. Dorothy said there was no pressure to read out what they had written but, incredibly to Pearl, they both seemed really keen.

Sabine went first, scared, her voice shaking but determined. She sat very straight, holding her papers tightly and read, it seemed to Pearl, as if she were giving evidence in court. Pearl found it fascinating; she had never been to Belgium and she loved hearing about the houses and the shops and the trams. It was like going off on a trip somewhere. It confirmed her belief though that nothing too terrible could ever have happened to someone from such a comfortable middle-class home that Sabine's first and worst memory had to do with cream cakes in a fancy cake shop. Nothing like that in the Co-op bakery on the Edgware Road. "Try some of my memories," Pearl thought rancorously. "Just try some of mine."

Esther read in a fast, rattling voice. It was hard to follow what was going on. She started off by saying she was going to tell her Mum's story but what she read was all me, me, me so it was rather confusing. Esther explained the "me" was actually her Mum. But right in the middle of a bit about a mother and a teenage daughter rowing – and Pearl still wasn't entirely clear who was who – Esther broke off abruptly. "That's as far as I got," she said and she began to cry.

Pearl took a quick look at Dorothy and saw that she was watching Esther with a horrified look on her face, not moving or saying anything.

"Oh love," Pearl said. She moved to sit next to Esther

and put her arm around her shuddering shoulders. "Don't upset yourself."

"I'll get you a glass of water," Renée said. "They must have that here."

When Renée came back with the water and Esther stopped crying and started apologising, Pearl returned to her seat. It would really be the limit, wouldn't it, if she was going to have to console these well-off women with their well-off problems. She would have to stop coming; that wasn't what she was after at all.

Sabine

SABINE'S HUSBAND MICHAEL had no idea she was going to write about Belgium. How he would have laughed if he had, with his mocking laugh she had listened to all these years. Long ago, when he met Sabine, when they got engaged, he had the idea Belgium was exotic, sexy because it was on the Continent. But when they went there it was a great disappointment to him because clearly there is nowhere less exotic than the suburbs of Brussels. Michael also objected to a lot of Belgian customs which Sabine thought charming: letting small dogs sit up at the table in restaurants for example or the chocolate effigies of the Mannekin Pis you sometimes saw in shop windows which pissed a stream of melted chocolate. Michael had a word for all that. He liked to say too, "Name a famous Belgian." He scoffed when Sabine told him there was much more to Belgium than he knew. But it was true, there were many things about Belgium which Michael did not know.

Sabine felt terribly nervous about reading her first chapter to the group. She feared they might react like Michael. But when she told them what she was going to read, "Memories of my Belgian Childhood" by Sabine Moreton (née Mertens), they reacted as if they knew absolutely nothing about Belgium at all.

"Ooh!" Dorothy exclaimed. "Lovely!"

The two plump women who sat side by side smiled blankly.

The old chap continued to look as if his mind was on other things.

Only the funny art teacher gave a surprising squawk. "Tintin!"

Sabine smiled gratefully at her. "Yes, Hergé, the creator of Tintin, he was Belgian, it's true."

The art teacher clasped her paint-stained hands. "Captain Haddock!" she exclaimed. "Professor Calculus! Thomson and Thompson! A graphic odyssey!"

Dorothy said, "When you're ready, Sabine."

For just a moment, Sabine wondered whether she could go through with this. Could she really tell her story in public? For there were things about Sabine's childhood too which Michael did not know.

1. *The Beginning*

Once upon a time there was a little girl called Sabine Mertens who lived in a tall thin house in Brussels with her two big brothers, Charles and Laurent, her father Alfred who was a doctor and her mother Bernadette who was a housewife and she was perfectly happy.

The house was situated in Woluwé Saint Pierre, a bourgeois suburb of Brussels on the edge of a big old forest. Like many Belgian houses of that epoch, it had a pretty pattern of coloured tiles on its high facade. It had steps up to the tall front door and to one side a steep slope down into the basement cellar. When it was icy this slope was excitingly perilous. The house had three tiers of small balconies going up, each one smaller and more fragile than the one below and the children were strictly forbidden to step out onto any of them. Everyone in Brussels knew a story of someone who had been standing on one of those delicate balconies when it had broken off, killing them on the pavement below – although no one ever actually knew the name of the person who had been killed in this way.

Sabine was born in this lovely home on 21 July, 1947, the Belgian national holiday. The family always joked that it was the excitement of the holiday which had provoked her mother's labour. In any case, having her birthday on the national holiday always seemed marvellous to Sabine when she was a child: there were fireworks and processions and the more patriotic neighbours hung out their flags. There was an atmosphere of celebration and parties and, even though Sabine knew that the celebrations were of course not really for her birthday, her father always teased her that they were.

Being born on the national holiday made Sabine feel a little special. Of course, she was loved and cherished at home in the normal way but being born on 21 July was something unique. Whenever she was asked for her date of birth – at school, at the clinic, registering to borrow books from the local library – the person who asked her would always smile at her, congratulate her and tell her what a splendid little Belgian girl she was.

When Sabine was a child, the pretty suburb of Woluwé Saint Pierre was her whole world. In those times, before the post-War building boom had transformed the whole capital, Woluwé Saint Pierre was still almost like a village. The city had already reached out its long fingers around the village, the tram lines joined it to the city centre but it was still a distinct community, separate from the city and superior to it.

The origins of this snobbish superiority were very ancient. The village of Woluwé Saint Pierre, named in historical records going back to the Middle Ages, had been built on land cleared from the great forest, the Forest of Soignes. It was named from the Woluwé, a small local river which by then ran mainly underground. The people who lived in the forest traditionally considered themselves somewhat special, separate. In the Middle Ages, they had their own forest court in Woluwé Saint Pierre where all crimes committed in the forest were judged and punished.

Their home was situated on the Avenue Parmentier, a steep street which led up from the main road, the Avenue de Tervuren where the trams passed. Sabine's brothers, Laurent and Charles, regretted that the noisy yellow trams did not go up and down the Avenue Parmentier too for they exhibited a bizarre obsession with all forms of transport from bicycles to spaceships. Sabine was very content that the trams did not go past their house. She was terrified of the trams ever since she heard the story of a small child who had been run over by one close by on the Avenue Orban.

The Avenue Parmentier was a quiet, respectable street. On one side was a small park, the Parc Parmentier where they loved to go and play. Several of the houses – including their own house – had a polished brass plate next to the front door advertising the *cabinet* of a doctor, a dentist or a lawyer. Their father was a doctor, he received his patients at home. This meant there were certain rules about not making noise in the house during the hours of consultation and certain ground floor rooms they were never allowed to enter. Sometimes there were nasty medical smells in the front hall and on the stairs. The worst of all was that they were not allowed any pets in case any of the patients was sensitive. But fortunately not far away on the Rue au Bois there was a fantastic pet shop whose kind owner loved little children and let them spend as much time as they wanted in his shop so they had plenty of contact with rabbits, kittens, puppies, turtles, guinea pigs and even a talking parrot who was not for sale.

In her pre-school years their lovely neighbourhood was Sabine's universe. It was so perfect, it was like a storybook. Within one kilometre radius of their house there was everything which a child could wish for: woods, lakes, parks, playgrounds, small shops with friendly shopkeepers, even a tram depot and, close behind their house, the local Brussels–Tervuren railway line for her brothers' games. In those days, children were allowed to play outside much more freely than today. Sabine was not allowed out by herself at a young age of course but with her two big brothers to protect her she was free to go anywhere. Unfortunately, Laurent and Charles did not always protect her, sometimes to the contrary. But three together they could go wherever they wanted, have all sorts of adventures, get into all kinds of troubles – so long as they were home in time for dinner, not too dirty or too injured.

They explored the whole area which seemed to them as fascinating and rich in discoveries as a region of Africa. In fact, they knew of some things in their neighbourhood which the grown-ups had no idea about. For example, they knew how to creep along the railway line and climb certain crumbling garden walls to look into the bedroom windows of the houses on the Avenue Parmentier from behind. They knew who got dressed at the window with the curtains open and who hugged a woman who was not his wife in his *jardin d'hiver* (glass conservatory). So long as they stayed on the streets – the Avenue Parmentier, the Avenue Orban, the long and curious Rue au Bois – everything seemed prosperous and respectable, clean and safe. But as soon as they left the pavements, began to explore the parks and lakes, the shady woods, they entered a different world, half wild, where all kinds of secret things might be discovered.

Sabine also loved to go shopping with her mother. She loved it for two reasons: firstly, she was a greedy little girl and the local shopkeepers always gave free snacks to the doctor's little daughter – habitually chocolates and sweets, sometimes sample mouthfuls of fatty sausage and pâté. She had a little shopping basket lined with a red and white check serviette and sometimes they would pop a treat into her basket to carry home. Sabine always devoured the treat before she got home so she would not have to share it with her brothers. Secondly, she loved the shopping trips because her brothers did not come.

In those days there were no supermarkets of course. Sabine's mother visited three or four small specialist shops every time she went to shop: the butcher, the greengrocer, the *charcutier* – nowadays I suppose you might call it a delicatessen – and the baker's. The baker's was Sabine's favourite. It smelt wonderful, in the morning when Madame Maes had been up baking since three, you could smell its exquisite smell from the corner of the street. When you opened the baker's door, a small bell rang like a cowbell on a country holiday. Madame Maes, who was without doubt the fattest woman in the commune of Woluwé Saint Pierre, would come out through the beaded curtains from her private back room. She would move forward, always delighted to see them, but sometimes a string of beads would catch embarrassingly across her giant bust and she would have to stop and untie herself. She would chat with Sabine's mother about the rain and the fine weather. Meantime Sabine would look in delight at the display of cakes. Her head was just at the same height as the shelves of cakes and she would stare at them with desire, imagining eating them all: the eclairs with chocolate or coffee icing, the slices of yellow custard flan, the creamy mille-feuilles, the strawberry tarts. In spite of the glass counter, she could almost taste them. Often, Madame Maes would see the greed in Sabine's face and slip a small cake into her basket. She knew Sabine's favourite was the strawberry tart.

But once Sabine noticed something horrible among the cakes. It was summer, the day was hot and the cakes under the glass counter were beginning to look a little hot too: the chocolate and coffee icing was sweating, the whipped cream was starting to sink down and on the strawberry tarts a wasp was crawling. No, not one wasp, two, three and their legs were getting stuck in the gluey glaze which was melting. Her favourite cakes were being eaten by nasty stinging wasps who were also drowning there. It was like the stories of bogs in the forest which could swallow children. The wasps were eating the cakes but simultaneously the cakes were eating the wasps. Little Sabine pointed horrified and began to scream. This was one of her earliest memories.

Esther

"Mine," Esther said resentfully, "isn't interesting and foreign."

When Sabine finished reading, people murmured admiringly.

The old lady with the tall hairdo said, "Very nostalgic. It reminds me of a trip I made to Brussels myself many years ago." She began to describe her trip with no reference at all to what Sabine had just read.

Dorothy made to intervene unsuccessfully.

When the old lady paused, lost for the name of a long-gone restaurant, one of the pair of quiet women spoke up. "It was beautiful," she said. "Well done Sabine. I'm looking forward to your next chapter." And she turned to her friend who nodded energetically.

Sabine thanked them. She looked around, as if she was hoping for more compliments but there were no more and then it was Esther's turn to read.

RITA'S STORY by Esther Solomon
Forword

I want to tell the story of my dear mother, Rita Solomon, who passed away two years ago this

58

November. She suffered so much in her life but because of the times she lived in and the community she belonged to, what she went through went totally unreconized. But as her only daughter I saw her pain close up and in many ways she passed it on to me too. In writing this I hope to hopefully shine a light in a few dark corners and maybe spare someone else similer suffering. Most important, I am writing this in memory of my darling Mum, may she rest in peace.

Esther thought she would never get past that part without breaking down and she barely did. But she gulped and paused and said, "Right, ok, right" and then she started to read again as fast as she could.

There is something wrong with me. I have known this ever since I was a small child but I have no idea what it is. No one tells me, no one ever says anything about it but I know. Even as a baby I knew, they say I cried so much. As far as I can tell, it is not an illness or a condition . But still I know I am not normal and the knowledge never lets me be. It is a feeling which follows me everywhere, it is like a bad smell but worse than a bad smell. It is always there, acompanying me but not exactly acompanying me because it is actually part of me, it is *me*. I am wrong and I know, however hard I try, I can never be right.

Where did this awful feeling come from? I have no idea. It will be years before I find out the answer and finding out won't make it any better, it will actually make it a zillion times worse.

To start with, I have no early memories and I don't know why. The first thing I remember is my mother walking me to school on my first day. I was just short of my fifth birthday and I was petrefied. I do not remember anything at all before that, there is just a really bad feeling.

But I have dreams, dreams which are so real they are almost like memories and sometimes I wonder if they are actual memories. Just because you only remember something when you are asleep does that mean it isn't real? My dreams come again and again, they are recering dreams, always the same, always terrifying and in the morning when I wake up they are so very real I am convinced they have actually happened.

At the beginning of the dream there is a sort of quick pink blur. It is gone so quickly, over almost before I catch it. It is like those lights you see before a migraine. It is a warning that the dream is about to start. I know the pink blur is a glimpse of something lovely but because I only ever see it right before my bad dream starts, it has turned into a warning sign instead of a comfort.

After the pink blur comes the nightmare. Everything which was warm before has turned cold. Everything soft has gone hard. Everything which smelt good now smells off. It is like being in an old photo negative where the people have black faces and white hair. I am in a back to front world. I am screaming. I hate the cold and the hardness and the bad new smells. I want to go back to what came before which I can't remember anymore. But I can't. In my dream, I am trapped in the horrible back to front world where absolutely everything is wrong and all I can do is scream. Sometimes I scream so much that my late husband Sidney shakes me awake. "You are safe Rita," he says gently as he has done so often before. "You are with me." I cry. I do not want my life to be like this: an allternating pattern of pretend days and nightmare nights. I do not want to keep on waking dear Sidney who works so hard to keep me and my little daughter Esther. I do not want not to have any baby memories. I do not want to have to keep dreaming my horrible dream. But there is nothing to be done so I am stuck with it.

Esther drew breath. "In those days," she said, "in my Mum and Dad's world, people didn't go to therapists and counsellors the way we all do now. If you had a problem, it was the stiff upper lip for you. It was bloody 'Keep Calm and Carry on.'"

The old lady said, "I have never been to a therapist in my life."

Esther shot her a dirty look and went on reading.

The suffering inside me swelled up more and more and eventually broke me apart like food which has gone off which bursts out of its container. My early life of not being normal, of knowing there is something wrong with me but not knowing what it is and then finding out but going on pretending that I still don't know, it took its tole.

One day I couldn't carry on anymore. I let down my dear Sidney and my darling little Esther. I couldn't care for them anymore, I had to be taken away to the terrible House on the Hill to be treated. Up there it was like my bad dream all over again. I was trapped in a back to front world, screaming to be let out.

After my stay there, my family say I was never quite the same again. I think in a way that is true. I was still myself of course, Mrs Rita Solomon, wife of Sidney, mother of Esther, cooking meals, keeping house, doing all the things that were expected of me. I had no more nightmares, there was no more screaming. But something was missing too. It wasn't that all my terrible torturing feelings were gone. They were still there but they were out of reach somehow, I couldn't relate to them, they didn't effect me. There was a kind of deadness in my heart. It was as if only the outside of me was still properly there functioning but nothing inside. When my daughter Esther became a teenager, going through the difficult years, she used to yell at me, "Where *are* you Mum? You're no different from a mother who's out at work all the time. You're just not *there*."

Iris

DESPITE THE VERY poor first impression, Iris was thrilled by
the first few weeks of the life story group. Of course some of
the other people were frightful but wasn't that always the way?
Enid, the artist, was unspeakable. But still there was something
very enjoyable about waking up on a Thursday morning now
and wondering what the week's instalment was going to be. It
was like following a soap on the television except much better
because you knew this was real. There was something else too,
something Iris wasn't entirely comfortable about admitting; if
you felt that your own life had, in some way, fallen short, it
was tremendously comforting to hear how very much worse
other people's had turned out. Not that, so far, any of the
others had shared any especially harrowing revelations. But
you could sense it was in the pipeline, oh yes, you could.

When Sabine read out about her Belgian childhood,
sitting ramrod straight, her voice shaking, you knew
something was in the offing. It might sound all hunky-dory –
fresh air and cream cakes and so forth – but Iris was ready to
bet on trouble ahead.

As for Esther, well, good God, when she read out her
torrent of words, tying herself and her sentences in knots, it
was hard to make head or tail of what was going on. But
something was amiss; that much was glaringly obvious.

Then there were all the others who weren't actually writing stuff down but recording it. Or so they claimed; privately, Iris had her doubts. They were all starting to drop hints too and it was simply fascinating. What was Renée's grudge against her father? What was the meaning behind Enid's bizarre drawings? Iris relished every session. She found Edgar, maybe the only one who didn't seem to have a whole family of skeletons in his closet, remarkably entertaining too. He turned out to be a natural raconteur, his tales of his years working in menswear had them all, as Enid sarkily remarked, in stitches. Of course, looming on the horizon, there was the awkward question of when Iris was going to make her own contribution. Dorothy had already insinuated as much; it was all very well sitting there listening to the fruits of other people's labours and so on. Iris wasn't the only one of course; neither Pearl nor Renée had said much. Well, Iris would make her own contribution, in her own good time. There was nothing to hide or be ashamed about in her early life. For Iris, the problem wasn't – by and large – the past, it was the present.

She considered telling her daughter about the life story group. Joanna, who was always so scathing about everything to do with her mother, surely couldn't disapprove of that? Mind you, she hadn't been exactly complimentary about silk painting, had she?

"What's the point?" she had demanded when Iris had shown her the term's handiwork, hanging over the chair backs in the dining room. "Haven't you got *enough* scarves?"

Hurt, Iris had answered, "They make the most marvellous gifts."

"Do they?" her uncharitable daughter asked. She had considered the strips of swirling colours which, under her scornful gaze, became self-indulgent and silly. "If you say so."

Iris had been thinking of offering Joanna to take her pick but then of course she didn't. Never mind, there were plenty of other people who would be only too happy to receive one of Iris's hand-painted silk scarves. Her cleaner, Mrs Mundy, was always very grateful and Mina, dear, lovely, *dead* Mina, had always been so appreciative.

Maybe Joanna would react the same way to the life story class: more indulgent self-expression, only this time turning out stories instead of textiles. Most probably she would; she had always mocked Iris's fondness for the Second Chance Centre, calling it "poverty porn". "Going to see how the other half lives?" she jeered. "Ooh, make sure you don't catch anything."

Iris found Joanna detestably mean. Privately, she acknowledged that there was an underside to her fondness for the Second Chance Centre; something perhaps not entirely creditable drew her there along with her charitable instincts. But that was really no one else's business, was it, least of all Joanna's who should learn that charity begins at home.

Iris had often regretted, even before Joanna turned against her, that she had only had the one child. That was something else to lay at her first husband's door of course. If Richard had not walked out on Iris when Joanna was only three, who knows, maybe, despite their differences, they might have had a second child. Even though, for years, Iris had thanked her lucky stars that, left on her own, she only had the one to worry about, there had come a time, as Joanna entered adolescence, when she began to dream about a devoted little boy who might have made up for his difficult sister.

Then of course Maurice had come along, marvellous Maurice, her second and best husband, who had swept her off her feet at a point at which she had almost given up all hope in that respect. Maurice had moved in, bringing with him great gusts of opera and cologne, he had transformed Iris's life, he had charmed everyone – except Joanna. When he and Iris announced they were getting married, Joanna made the most appalling scene. Aged sixteen, she wore black to the wedding. But, fortunately, despite her problems, she was clever enough to get herself off to university and, after that, only came home at Christmas. Iris and Maurice shared twenty-five beautiful years until he was carried away by cancer, aged only sixty-five. Iris knew she had sacrificed her daughter but, so long as Maurice was around, it hadn't troubled her all that much. Of course she wished it was otherwise but no-one's life was perfect, was it and, in every other respect, hers had gone pretty well. She began to see her untold life story as her opportunity for self-justification. Her third husband, Yusuf, would take some justification, it was true but, as far as the rest of it went, wasn't this the chance she had been waiting for to prove to Joanna that she was *innocent*?

No one thought as badly of Iris as Joanna did. "Dad was right to leave you, you're horrible!" That had been one of her youthful refrains. "I'd leave you too if I could."

Joanna conveniently ignored the fact that her father had walked out on her too, that, since the day he left, he had shown barely any interest in her, never saw her and only sent

66

intermittent, invariably late birthday and Christmas cards. Joanna blamed Iris for that too; she had allegedly alienated him. As for poor Maurice – whom everyone else thought was practically a saint – Iris simply could not bear to recall the vile things Joanna had said about him. Yusuf, strangely, she had tolerated rather better.

It was not as if Joanna's own life had followed a conventional path. She had announced at university that she was bisexual – which Iris considered simply a form of greed – and then, in her late twenties, she had come out as lesbian, with a series of successively scarier partners. Sometimes it seemed to Iris that Joanna's entire life was a lurid form of revenge.

Joanna's appearance had metamorphosed over the years. She had Richard's red hair although not his slender frame. She had gone from quantities of flying, unkempt hair as a teenager to a partially shaven head at university. Nowadays, she had a severe, greying military crew cut. Over the years, a quantity of piercings and tattoos had been added to make an absolute fright of her. On the rare occasions when Joanna and her mother were out together and Iris had to introduce her to an acquaintance, she was mortified. She knew that her mortification was Joanna's raison d'être.

It came to her painfully that Joanna would never read her life story. She would dismiss it like the silk scarves. It made Iris wonder who she would actually be telling her life story *for*. If Joanna, her only child, wasn't interested, then what was the point? Not only was Joanna utterly indifferent, even if she did read it, she would no doubt pour scorn on whatever Iris wrote. She would accuse Iris of falsehoods, of rewriting history, of trying to portray herself in a favourable light while vilifying others. Iris's life story would become another crime perpetrated with the sole purpose of wounding Joanna.

It was almost – but not quite – enough to put Iris off. For, as the weeks went by and she listened to the others, she came to understand that a life story could be many things and, in the long-running battle that was family life, it could be a trump card.

Edgar

MADELEINE ARRIVED WITH something no bigger than a cake of soap and put it proudly on the table.

"There you go," she said. "No more excuses now."

Edgar looked politely at the little device and wondered what it was.

Madeleine said, "It's a recorder. For your stories. I got it online."

They both contemplated the recorder. "We'll start tonight," Madeleine said, "after we've eaten."

Edgar asked, "Has it got batteries?" and received a look for his question.

Madeleine went into the kitchen and started clattering around. As she got into the swing of cooking, she began to sing, as she often did.

"Once more you open the DOOR
And you're here in my HEART
And my heart will go ON and ON."

Her powerful voice filled the little house. She was making fish, for Edgar's heart. Edgar sat in the front room and listened, while appetizing cooking smells filled the place.

It was one of the nights when Madeleine was free to stay over. Although it was a Tuesday and she had been at work, it still felt like a special occasion, a holiday almost. Edgar had been out in the morning and bought flowers and a fancy dessert. Coming back with the flowers, he had stopped as usual in the Pristina café and Murat had joked, "Who's the lucky lady?" No doubt he didn't expect a man of Edgar's age to have a sweetheart.

Edgar answered, "Her name's Madeleine. *I'm* the lucky one."

Murat looked impressed, Edgar couldn't help noticing, seriously impressed, and he topped up Edgar's tea for free.

When Madeleine arrived, some time after seven, Edgar was waiting for her, bathed and spruced up. The table was set, with the last of Joan's paper serviettes and the flowers arranged as best he could in Joan's vase. That did make him feel a bit queasy even though he knew he was doing Joan's final bidding. Besides, Joan would surely have approved of the orderly way Madeleine kept her kitchen.

There was one thing Edgar was not quite comfortable about. Before he sat down to eat, he always made sure to draw Madeleine's chair out for her, a bit showily, as if he were a waiter in a fancy restaurant. She teased him about this, calling him a charmer but he could tell she liked it all the same. It would never have crossed his mind to do a thing like that with Joan.

"So how did your day go dear?" he asked, once the food was on their plates (cod and fantastic potatoes and greens which tasted better than any greens Edgar had ever eaten).

Madeleine sighed. She was not at all a moaner but what she had to deal with in a day's work was an eye-opener for Edgar. The worst was when she called at the home of someone who was very ill and there was no answer. She had to call the key holder and when they let themselves in, the person was lying dead inside. Dead for a few days sometimes. Luckily that only happened once or twice a year.

"Something is really wrong with this country," Madeleine said, shaking her head. "Why are so many old people left all alone? They must have families and so forth. Where are they? What are they thinking of? You know, some of these old people I look after, I am the only person they see all week." She frowned as she ate her fish and Edgar agreed, "Terrible."

"I saw this one old fellow today, Mr Cheevers," Madeleine went on. "I been taking care of him for more than a year now, I guess. He's diabetic, he's got trouble with his feet. Well, he's got a daughter, so he says, but d'you know I've never ever seen her there? I don't know if she lives round here of course, maybe she lives a long way off. But he says he sees her twice a year, if he's lucky – at Christmas and when it's his birthday. *If* she can make it."

"Shocking," Edgar said. He felt shamefully jealous of old Mr Cheevers with his bad feet, who Madeleine had been taking care of for more than a year. It was less than a year since Edgar himself had met Madeleine. What if she had fallen for old Mr Cheevers first?

"He lives in a nice house and everything," Madeleine continued. "He's not hard up or anything, he talks beautifully." She chuckled suddenly. "He always asks me for a kiss."

"What?" Edgar said. His fish tasted dry in his mouth.

Madeleine laughed at his dismay. "There's plenty of them want that, you know. No need for you to be working yourself up about it. I know how to deal with them."

Edgar asked, "How?" He was assailed by horrible images of dirty old men, diseased, kissing Madeleine.

Madeleine looked at him – he was sure he had gone green – and shook her head. "Edgar," she said gently, "Edgar, what are you thinking? Do you imagine I don't know how to take care of myself?"

Edgar looked at her, well built, capable and, he had learnt, forthright. He felt embarrassed. He said, "I just don't like to think of people taking advantage of you. It's not right."

Madeleine saw that Edgar had stopped eating and she frowned. "I do appreciate appreciation," she said, looking pointedly at his plate.

Unhappily, Edgar forked up the remainder of his dinner.

"It's part of the job," Madeleine said, " – in a way. These old folks, they're on their own, most of them, they're lonely and of course they're not well – otherwise I wouldn't be there – and if it makes them feel a bit better to hold my hand for a minute or ask for a kiss, where's the harm?" She looked at Edgar reproachfully. "I do hope you're not going to make a song and dance about it."

Hastily, Edgar said, "No, I'm not." But he added, "I just don't like the idea of anyone being disrespectful."

Madeleine raised her eyebrows. "No one's being disrespectful." She paused. "Sometimes, it's true, someone who's not all that poorly tries it on, touching me somewhere or other and pretending it was an accident. I soon sort them out." She made a deft back and forth slapping gesture. "But, most of the time, you know it's just some poor soul reaching out for comfort. And if someone wants to hold my hand or asks me for a kiss, I think that's a sign of much more than respect, isn't it, it's more like gratitude."

Edgar looked at Madeleine in awe. In some ways she seemed almost saintly. No wonder her lucky patients adored her. But still he could not bear the thought of other men touching her. He knew he only had a share of Madeleine and for that share he was profoundly grateful. But he had never had to share like this before and it disturbed him. He and Joan had not had children, not deliberately, it just hadn't happened, although with the passage of the years Edgar did wonder whether Joan wouldn't actually have found them awfully messy. It had always been just him and Joan. Madeleine's life was so crowded: her children, her patients. Edgar knew he was incredibly lucky to have his share of Madeleine, he mustn't spoil things by wanting more but still he had done, ever since that first evening when they strolled down Kilburn High Road arm in arm.

Neither of them felt like dessert so they left Edgar's gateau in the fridge and moved to the settee. They were sitting comfortably together, Madeleine resting against Edgar, Edgar's hand on Madeleine's knee, when her mobile rang. It had a shocking ringtone; it rang like an old house phone but at full volume, shrill and startling. Edgar had asked Madeleine if she might turn it down or maybe choose something a little easier on the ear but she had given him a look and said that she had chosen that ringtone for professional reasons.

It was her daughter, Desiree. She sounded dreadfully upset about something or other, she kept Madeleine on the phone for ages. But when Madeleine finally rang off after repeating lovingly, "Good night sweetheart, good night," Edgar was surprised to hear the problem was only a lower than expected mark on a piece of university coursework. Silly girl, she should have worked harder. Still, he knew better than to criticise Madeleine's children. Her patients were one thing, her children were out of bounds.

They were just settling down again when the phone rang a second time: Desiree again. This time, the call was shorter: a lost hair care product.

Madeleine sighed when she finished the call. "My baby's jealous," she commented, "doesn't like her Mum going out and having fun."

Edgar swallowed his indignation. He tried to smile.

Madeleine seemed unsettled. She got up and went into the kitchen to finish clearing up. Edgar followed her but was shooed out. Joan used to do that too.

While he waited for Madeleine to come back, his eye fell on the recorder, still waiting. Suddenly, his life struck him as rather threadbare: just he and Joan and all those years spent in a stuffy department store. Madeleine's life was jam-packed full.

"I think *you* should be telling your life story, you know," he said when she returned. "Not me."

Madeleine laughed, a deep, rueful laugh. "There's not enough room in that recorder. Anyways, I doubt anyone would want to listen."

She sat back down beside him. "Come on, cheer me up with one of your stories. You are such a lovely talker, Edgar." She smiled at him. "Put me in the mood."

She leant forward and fiddled with the buttons.

Edgar said, "I don't know where to start."

Madeleine tutted. "So begin at the beginning. When and where were you born?"

Winter

Dorothy

By November, with Christmas looming, the pressure on Dorothy was mounting. Iris had treated them to a long and tedious presentation about her parents, Somebody and Somebody Plumstead, accompanied by a tinful of stiff-looking black and white family photos. Enid had deeply offended Iris by asking her if she had ever considered cutting up the photos and making a collage of family body parts. That had been, frankly, the most exciting moment of Iris's presentation.

When the fireworks had died down and Dorothy had, with difficulty, regained control of the group, Renée spoke up. The way she did it, it seemed as if she was just tactfully trying to change the subject and not as if she wanted to talk about herself at all.

Dorothy was beginning to have a soft spot for Renée – and for Pearl too. They were both so appreciative and attentive. They sat politely, side by side, you could tell they had been well behaved at school and, if they didn't say much, at least they never thrust themselves forward or upset anybody else. Dorothy had supposed, until Renée spoke up, that neither of them had anything much to say.

Renée said, "I noticed the background and the furniture too in your pictures, Iris. We had a mantelpiece and a sideboard just like yours. Looking at your pictures brought back so many memories. I'm sure *your* family was every bit as proper and respectable as they looked." She added, quite unjustifiably, Dorothy thought, "Your father has such a fine, honourable face."

Iris said, "My father was a marvellous man."

"Well," Renée said, "you were very lucky. My father looked just like your father. I mean, he dressed the same and our home looked just like yours too. But appearances can be deceptive, can't they? I'm sure your father *was* a perfect gentleman. But mine, even though he looked the part and sounded the part, he wasn't a gentleman at all." She blushed and fell silent.

No one seemed to know quite what to say so Dorothy rushed them all on to a seasonal reminiscence exercise.

The week after, it was Pearl's turn to speak up. "I been thinking about what Renée said about her Dad," she began. "Well, I don't know what he did wrong. But at least he was *there*. Mine wasn't." She hesitated, already she looked as if she regretted opening her mouth. She looked around the semi-circle almost defiantly. "I never really knew my Dad."

Apart from a tutting noise from Iris, nobody said a thing. Vaguely, Esther murmured, "A parent can be there and yet *not* be there, if you see what I mean."

Pearl went on, "I mean, so far you've all talked about *two* parents. But not all of us had two parents. So," she trailed away, "I just thought I'd mention it."

"Snap," Enid Harkin said, in her grating voice. "I grew up in a one-parent family too. Except my one parent was my Dad."

At that point, quite unexpectedly, she stood up, produced a battered-looking mouth organ from her trouser pocket and played a shrill and rasping tune on it for a few uncomfortable minutes. "My father's favourite song," she announced when she had finished and she gave a spindly bow.

Enid had barely sat down when there was a loud knock at the door and Lavonda came in.

"I'm sorry to interrupt Dorothy," she said. Dorothy could see she was not sorry at all. "But we've had a complaint."

Dorothy felt herself flush. "A complaint?"

"Yes," Lavonda repeated. "A complaint. Noise. Birendra is trying to teach his yoga class next door and he's just come to me saying they can't hear themselves think."

"Oh, for God's sake," Enid burst out. "It was *music*." She brandished the mouth organ in Lavonda's direction. "Music! Why can't they tie themselves in knots to the tune of 'The Minstrel Boy'?"

Dorothy said faintly, "Enid, please."

Lavonda drew herself up and turned her glare on Enid. Her arched eyebrows were now half way to her hairline. "At the Second Chance Centre," she said, "we want to give *everyone* a chance. Try and think of others. It's not all about *you*."

She turned to Dorothy. "Please make sure it doesn't happen again."

She made to leave but turned back in the doorway. "I've got my eye on you Enid Harkin," she said. "Don't think I've forgotten what you got up to last term in aromatherapy." And to Dorothy she added, "There was no mention of music in your course outline Dorothy. We've never had a complaint about noise from a writing class before."

That little interlude naturally distracted everyone from what Pearl had said and her words were more or less forgotten. Recovering from the shock of Lavonda's rebuke and its renewed threat took Dorothy the rest of the class.

Her only consolation came from Edgar who stopped on his

way out at the end and said to her, "Don't pay too much attention to that manager. My late wife used to come here a lot and she told me all about her. Her bark is worse than her bite."

The truth was Dorothy's worry about Lavonda took second place. By the end of November, the only person who had still not contributed anything was Dorothy herself. Sabine and Esther were prolific; almost every week they came along with yet another chapter and read it out to the group. Whenever there was a lull, Edgar could always be relied upon to tell one of his amusing anecdotes about his years working in the menswear department. Even Enid's peculiar drawings were, Dorothy supposed, a contribution of sorts.

Three weeks before the end of term, with all of them breathing down her neck, Dorothy panicked. She knew she had to come up with something. But how were you supposed to tell your life story when you had not had that much of a life? Dorothy thought that she could probably write down every single memorable thing which had happened to her between being born and being forced to leave the library on a couple of sides of A4. At Mercy House, she had witnessed some strange things, true, but what had she actually *experienced*?

She supposed she could try and tell them the bare facts. But how uninteresting her story would seem, especially compared to the goings-on at the bottom of the garden in Sabine's Belgian childhood or Edgar's saucy revelations from the fitting room. Above all she feared being exposed; someone who had been appointed to run a life stories group yet lacked any dramatic life experiences.

Experimentally, one dark weekend, she tried jotting down a few notes. It was hopeless. She decided to pay a visit to Gerald's library. She had taken to dropping in there from time to time, partly for the company and partly for the uncharitable pleasure of seeing what a shambles it had become. One of Gerald's inter-faith volunteers hadn't shown up so Dorothy helped him to reshelve his returned books. They chatted, Gerald explaining to Dorothy how difficult it was to have to take so many different religious festivals into account when drawing up his roster, Dorothy telling him about the life stories group. She enjoyed the old familiarity of her gestures, the feeling of the faintly sticky laminated volumes in her hands.

She was reshelving biographies, always popular, when her attention was distracted by the title of one of them: *The Story of a Russian Princess*. She considered the tawdry cover disdainfully. It showed a plump woman in a tiara against a black and white photomontage of onion domes, silver birch trees and horse-drawn sleighs. Dorothy thought, "Probably a total fabrication. I dare say she's no more a princess than I am." In that instant, she thought of a solution to her predicament. She put the book to one side, flushing, as if Gerald – or anyone else for that matter – could read her thoughts. She knew that her idea was not a good one, that in the months to come she would no doubt regret it no end. But, at the same time, she felt terribly excited and she knew that she was going to go ahead with it anyway.

Classes ended at the Second Chance Centre a week before Christmas. Dorothy settled down for a period of solitude, preparing new material for the spring term. She knew she had a lot of work to do to prepare her own contribution.

She was woken in the middle of the night before Christmas by what she would later describe to everyone as a battering on the door. Shocked awake, her heart racing, she saw it was half past one. The battering went on, she was petrified. As she sat in bed, quaking, she heard that whoever was battering on her door was also calling out her name.

"Dorothy, Dorothy, wake up. Are you there? DOROTHY!"

She didn't recognise the voice, she had no idea who it was but the fact they knew her name made it ever so slightly less terrifying. She got out of bed and fumbled her way, shaking, into her dressing gown.

"DOROTHY!"

"Who is it?" She quavered. "What's the matter?"

"Dorothy," the voice panted. "It's Martin, Christopher's friend. Please open the door, please, it's really urgent."

Dorothy hesitated behind the door. Martin, one of Christopher's lonely lexicographer friends: she did remember him. Of course, it could just be somebody impersonating Martin and if she opened the door, he might rush in and batter her to death.

She asked, "Are you sure?" That wasn't quite what she meant to say of course but it was the middle of the night.

"Oh for god's SAKE! Of course I'm sure. Open the door PLEASE. It's an emergency!"

"How," Dorothy wavered, "how do I know you're really Martin?"

"You met me at Christopher's last Christmas. You're a librarian, a – a *head* librarian. Please, this is DESPERATE."

Keeping the chain on, Dorothy opened the door a crack. It was Martin. He looked frantic.

Through the narrow crack he gabbled at her, "I, I understand it's late and I'm sorry and everything but do you have the key to Christopher's flat? He's not answering the door

84

and he's not picking up his phone and I'm really worried something awful's happened. He, he was expecting me to come over earlier but I – er – got delayed and when I rang him to tell him I might not make it, he sounded really strange. Please, I'm so scared. Have you?"

"Yes," Dorothy said. "I have. Wait there." She added patronisingly, "Calm down."

As she went to fetch the key, she began to shake uncontrollably. Had something awful really happened to poor dear Christopher? What was she about to walk into?

She went downstairs together with Martin, even though he didn't ask her to. Martin let himself in, Dorothy followed. Although it was the middle of the night, all the lights were on. Nothing looked amiss though in the ramshackle untidiness of Christopher's flat, it was hard to tell. Martin rushed straight into the bedroom and let out a scream.

"Oh God! Call an ambulance."

Dorothy came fearfully to the bedroom door. She could make out Christopher lying on the bed, fully dressed, either unconscious or dead.

Martin became what she would later describe as a gibbering wreck, crying and moaning and flapping over Christopher. To her surprise, Dorothy stayed calm and in control. She knew Christopher didn't have a landline, there was no time to go hunting around his messy flat for his mobile so she said briskly, "I'll go upstairs and call for one."

Martin wailed, "No!" From his pocket, he virtually thrust his phone at Dorothy. "Go on. Quickly! Oh GOD."

In all her life, Dorothy had never dialled 999. She would never have expected that it would feel so empowering.

The ambulance arrived pretty quickly, despite everything you heard about delays on the news. The paramedics lumbered down the stairs. They pronounced Christopher unconscious but still breathing and bundled him up into the ambulance – together with a whole lot of little bottles from off his bedside chest which Dorothy had not noticed. They told Martin, who was distraught, that he couldn't come with them in the ambulance but they were taking Christopher to St Mary's.

Martin and Dorothy followed in a minicab which, it being Christmas Eve, took forever to come. Martin hadn't actually asked Dorothy to come too but there was no way she was missing out. Besides, Martin was in no fit state.

When they arrived at A&E, they couldn't see Christopher for a while because he was having his stomach pumped. When Martin heard this, he had to run to the toilet. Dorothy watched the other people waiting with fascination. It was after two o'clock in the morning but the waiting room was full. Plenty of people, Dorothy observed, were not having a Merry Christmas either.

She and Martin waited for more than an hour, saying very little, only Martin crying on and off and repeating, "Oh God, I just hope he's ok. Please let him be ok."

Finally a doctor with dark circles under his eyes came out to talk to them. He asked what their relationship was to Christopher. Dorothy was about to answer virtuously, "I'm his neighbour" when Martin surprised her by saying, "I'm his partner."

Dorothy did her best not to look surprised. She felt suddenly side-lined.

Wearily but kindly, the doctor told them that Christopher would be alright but that he had to stay in hospital and be seen by a psychiatrist in the morning. They could go in to talk to him, he said, but he was rather groggy.

After a moment's hesitation, Dorothy followed Martin and he didn't stop her. In a curtained cubicle, they found Christopher, a dreadful, bloodless grey colour, his eyes barely open.

When he saw them, he opened his mouth and began to struggle, "S-s-s-s-s—"

Martin said, "No, I'm sorry, I'm sorry. Everything's my fault, I let you down, oh GOD, I'm so so sorry, promise me, promise me you won't ever do anything like this again."

Christopher mouthed, "N-n-n-n—"

Dorothy spoke up, "Don't strain yourself Christopher."

He seemed to see her for the first time. "D-d-d-d-d—"

Dorothy couldn't bear to watch him struggling. She cut him short with the first thing that came into her head, "Merry Christmas!"

Martin and Christopher looked at her in amazement. She supposed it was rather a tactless thing to say. In the midst of everything, they must have totally forgotten that it was now Christmas morning. Martin began to laugh and cry simultaneously. He clutched at Christopher's grey hand.

Dorothy looked at them both, Christopher attempting the slightest suggestion of a smile. Suddenly, she felt exhausted. "I'm going to leave you two now," she said faintly. "I'll get a minicab back."

Martin leapt at her and enfolded her in a sweaty hug. "Thank you so much, Dorothy. Really, thank you. I couldn't have coped without you."

In the minicab, Dorothy felt acutely alone. But she also felt strangely elated; tonight she knew she had lived life to the full and she would always remember this Christmas.

Pearl

KAI WAS HAVING a strop. He didn't often, in fact, to be fair, strops were more Pearl's thing. And Tracy's. But from time to time, when everything got too much for him, he would yank up that bloody hood of his, go into his room and bang the door shut after him and Pearl wouldn't hear a word out of him all day long.

She knew it didn't make much sense but she liked Kai's strops; a sign of something of her in the boy, like when he used to angrily refuse cooked vegetables as a small child. You couldn't say it was a good thing but, no two ways about it, it was *yours*.

Kai's strop had started after they went to see Mr Robinson. It had taken three phone calls and quite a few weeks to fix their appointment and then, when finally they got to see him, he said term was too far gone for Kai to join the sixth form and catch up. Pearl protested that the delay was Prithi's fault, (Prithi whose precious son was well on his way at Manchester University). But Mr Robinson said, quite reasonably, that if Kai had started at the beginning of term along with everyone else, they wouldn't be in this situation in the first place.

"You see?" Pearl said furiously to Kai. "I *told* you. I've been telling you *since* September."

Mr Robinson intervened. "I think at this point," he said, "we need to look forward and not back."

He turned to Kai who was looking miserable. "Have you thought about your subjects Kai? If you *were* going to do A levels, here or elsewhere, have you thought about which ones you'd like to do?"

Kai squirmed.

Pearl was about to burst out, "Of course he hasn't. He doesn't think about *anything*."

Kai said, "Maybe music?"

"Music!" Pearl exclaimed. She was about to add something else when she caught Mr Robinson's thoughtful eye upon her and promptly shut up. Really, it was impressive how he did that discipline thing; he didn't raise his voice or give you a death stare or anything but he had you under his thumb, no doubt about it. Pearl had always kept out of trouble at school. She sat back and let Mr Robinson do the talking.

"You got your five GCSEs, didn't you Kai?" he said. "Your grades weren't all that wonderful but you did well enough to continue, if that's what you want to do. The thing is: *do* you?"

He and Pearl both looked at Kai and waited.

After a moment, Kai answered, "I dunno."

Pearl smacked her knees in frustration. "Kai!"

"Well, some days I do," Kai said defensively, "and some days I don't. I can't help it."

"You're wasting Mr Robinson's time," Pearl hissed at him. "Why did we even *come* up here?"

"He's not wasting my time Mrs Barter," Mr Robinson said. "But Kai, you do need to make up your mind, you know. You've missed the boat here but you haven't missed it at Larkvale, you know, the college. I believe they have a January intake in some subjects for late arrivals and you can take your exams the following January instead of in the summer. It's doable. But you mustn't hang around, you need to make your choices and you need to enrol. Maybe it's not A levels you want but a BTEC."

Pearl didn't dare ask what that was. Kai said nothing. He just stared wretchedly at the floor.

Mr Robinson looked at his watch. "I tell you what," he said, as if he'd only just thought of it, although Pearl was pretty sure this had been his plan all along. "This is the website address of Larkvale College. Take a look at it, see what appeals to you and then come back and see me at half past four on Friday and we'll take it from there. Look at the A levels *and* the BTECs. They might be more up your street. If you decide you want to go there, I'll process your application, I'll make it happen."

Pearl thanked him gratefully. Kai didn't say anything, he just squirmed.

He didn't say anything all the way home either although, to be fair, Pearl scarcely gave him a chance.

"What was the point Kai?" she raged. "What was the *point* of our going up to see Mr Robinson and wasting his time, he's a busy man, he's got *hundreds* of other kids to deal with, not just you, you know. And my going to all that trouble and making those phone calls? Believe me, it wasn't easy and dealing with that snooty cow Prithi, what was the *point*? If you were just going to say you didn't actually *know* if you wanted to do A levels or not? Why did you *do* that Kai? What does that make *me* look like? Did you think about that? No, I dare say you didn't. Did you think about it at all? Why we were going up there, what you were going to say? I thought you were going to come out with 'History and English Mr Robinson'. Or 'Maths and Science Mr Robinson'. Or *anything*. But not 'I dunno'. '*I dunno!*' What's going on in your *head* Kai? Sometimes I wonder if anything at *all's* going on in your head, really I do.

"And *music*! What's all that about? You can't *just* do music, you know. And anyway, don't you have to be able to play an instrument? I'm sure it's not just a case of sitting around listening to your usual music with your earphones in like you do all the time at home.

"Though what would I know? I never *had* your chances. I left school at sixteen and went straight to work, that was how it was. Early shifts at the Co-op bakery – that was how I started off. I never got to *choose subjects*.

"I saw your Mum blow her chances Kai. I'm not letting you go down the same road. Don't think I am. When we get back, you're going on that website and finding out about this college and you're making up your mind what you're going to do. And if you don't, I'll decide for you. I mean it Kai, I really do."

Pearl was so wrapped up in her furious tirade that she did not notice a woman in front of the block of flats they were passing. She nearly jumped out of her skin at the sudden loud cry: "Pearl! Pearl! Kai!"

It was Enid Harkin, coming back to Meadowcroft, wearing a weird umbrella-shaped hat. She seemed beside herself with excitement.

"I had no idea you were Kai's grandmother!" she cried. "Hi Kai! Kai was one of my brightest and best. Such a shame he dropped Art."

Pearl looked from Enid to Kai in bewilderment. What was all *this* about? Kai one of her "brightest and best"? What was the woman on about? Pearl had gone to all of Kai's parent evenings but she and Enid had never spoken. Kai had said Miss Harkin taught him in years 7 and 8, hadn't he, but he never mentioned that he was any good. It had never crossed Pearl's mind to speak to the funny art teacher at those difficult evenings. Maths and English were important, not art. But if Kai was so good, why on earth had he dropped it? Why had Enid let him?

"Well, this is news to me," Pearl said. "Kai keeps his talents hidden from me."

Enid grinned, apparently oblivious to Pearl's put-down. "I never forget a pupil," she said. "Especially not a talented one. What are you up to now then Kai?"

Kai looked as if he wanted the ground to swallow him up. He mumbled, "I might be going to college."

Enid gave a thumbs up sign with a gnarled discoloured thumb. "Great," she said. "College is great. I hope you'll be doing something creative." She turned to Pearl. "It must run in the family. I remember Tracy was very creative too, poor dear."

Pearl turned to stone. No-one mentioned Tracy.

But Enid carried on, apparently impervious to the effect she was having. "Well, I wish you luck Kai. I'm sure you'll do well. Follow your star."

She added to Pearl, almost as an afterthought, "You weren't at our group this afternoon?"

Pearl said, "We had an appointment."

She had been sorry to miss the life story group, now everyone was starting to spill the beans. But of course Kai came first.

"You didn't miss much," Enid said. "Lady Iris treated us to another of her family sagas. Boring snoring. Your buddy Renée was much more interesting. She told us some more about her Dad. What a rotter. She wouldn't even tell us his name, she was that ashamed. Still –" she raised her eyebrows extravagantly, "we're not meant to talk about it all outside the group, are we?" She cackled. "Top secret. See you next week people."

Pearl and Kai walked the rest of the short way home in silence. Pearl had half a mind to give Kai a hard time about dropping art too but she felt her anger running out. She had no energy to carry on. Kai plodded along wordlessly beside her, deep inside his hood, his face to the pavement.

When they got back, he went straight to his room and slammed the door behind him.

Pearl yelled half-heartedly, "Don't slam the door" but she was spent. She was too old to be dealing with a teenager. She rarely let herself feel sorry for herself because there would be no end to it. But now, in the kitchen, too tired even to put the kettle on, she allowed herself a weep. Then she made tea. It was a shame she had missed the group too, just when Renée had come out with something interesting. What was it she had said before about her Dad? "Mine looked the part and sounded the part but he wasn't a gentleman at all." Well, Pearl could keep her company there. Her own father certainly wasn't a gentleman either.

She sat for a bit and thought about starting her story. That was where she would start; with the father who had led her young mum up the garden path and then run away when she fell pregnant, back to the wife and child he had never mentioned.

After a while, it had got completely dark outside and the lights had come on in the buildings opposite, Pearl stirred herself. She went to the kitchen door and called, "Well, are you looking at that college website Kai?"

He shouted, "That's what I'm doing right *now*."

"Good," Pearl called back. "Well, when you're done, come out please. I missed my group this afternoon because of going to see Mr Robinson. I've got some catching up to do and I'm going to need your help with it."

Esther

ESTHER FELT SHE didn't really belong in the life story class. She told her gym buddy Samson she was the odd one out.

He considered. "What's the others like?"

"Old," Esther said. "Or at least much older than me." She was about to say more but stopped herself. It occurred to her that Samson was one of only two black people working at the gym but you never heard him complain about that. "It's that funny place on the estate," she said. "You know." People at the gym made fun of the Second Chance Centre where they still had Keep Fit classes and had never even heard of kickboxing or spinning. Esther added, "I think your kids go there for holiday courses sometimes, don't they?"

Samson assumed the vague expression he always wore when his children were mentioned, like – how come? It annoyed Esther no end.

"Samson," she said, "you must *know* where your kids go, stop pretending you don't."

Samson laughed to himself and went on looking vague. It had taken Esther the best part of a year to establish that Samson had three young children by two different women but didn't live with either of them. If Esther tried to probe, Samson withdrew into hazy generalities like "Some things aren't meant to be." Because she loved to hang out with Samson, Esther didn't push it. She supposed there was a lot about Samson which she didn't properly understand, the same way Samson didn't remotely understand her. But Esther liked that, it was refreshing and she especially loved it when Samson came out with something totally incongruous like, "So this therapist of yours – does he do massage?"

Esther knew she was only one of any number of women at the gym who Samson was friends with. And that was all it was: friends. But there was something incredibly liberating about talking to Samson because he just didn't seem to operate by the same norms as other people. If you were upset about something, half the time you would have to explain to Samson why it was even upsetting in the first place and by the time you had done that, it usually seemed a lot less serious.

"Don't sweat the small stuff," Samson liked to say. Or, "Isn't there a herb for that, me darling?"

If anyone else had tried to downplay Esther's issues, she would most probably have taken offence but somehow when Samson did it, it was ok. And it was true, it was hard to explain to anyone how something which had happened to her mother so long ago had managed to affect Esther's whole life.

Who am I? That is the burning question I will never be able to properly answer. Up to the age of eleven when I first began to suspect, I honestly had no idea why I felt such a misfit. I thought I must just be another kind of oddball. In our community there was no shortage of those: there was poor old Mrs Rabinowicz who talked to herself all the time in the street in either Polish or

Yiddish because of the War and Cyril Levine who we all thought was crazy because he had married a non-Jewish Irish woman, stopped coming to shul (the synagogue) and everybody said he ate bacon sandwiches.

Yes, you may find it hard to believe but in the world in which I grew up, eating a bacon sandwich meant you were completely crazy. In fact it meant you were even crazier than somebody who took off all their clothes in the street because you could do that and still go on being Jewish (never mind the funny looks) but if you stopped coming to shul and went around eating bacon sandwiches and pork scratchings then you weren't really Jewish anymore and that aparently was a fate worse than death.

"How come," said Esther, "I have even got this far without saying the word Jewish? The trouble is now I have got started, everything is just pouring out randomly and it is so hard to make sense of it all."

She looked around for reassurance but didn't get any. Everyone just looked politely puzzled apart from Iris who looked disapproving.

"Anyway. Remember now," Esther said, "this is my Mum Rita speaking." She drew breath and read on as confidently as she could.

My parents were Morris Solomon and Rachel Marcus. They were both born in Hackney and they moved to Hendon not long after they got married. They were on the way up but they weren't quite up there yet. My father worked in the garment industry like so many others. My mother worked as an assistant in a nice dress shop before she got married but after she got married she was supposed to give that up and stay at home and keep house and have babies. I don't think she was very happy about that because she went on talking about the dress shop for the rest of her life as if it had been some sort of idilic period.

Their marriage was far from idilic. My father Morris was a good man, he worked hard to support his family, as far as I know he didn't have any secret vices. But he wasn't much fun. He worked hard all week and when Friday night came, he liked to put his feet up and after Friday night dinner just have a snooze. He went to shul on Saturday morning but that was about it, he never really did anything else. Also he was a bit of a domestic tyrant. He liked everything to be just so and he would get all cross and shouty if it wasn't.

My mother Rachel was more of a free spirit. She always wanted to go out and do stuff, see people and she would cry when my father said no. Maybe she wouldn't have minded so much if she had had children right away. At least she would have been kept busy. But they had to wait ten years before I came along and I think it was the long wait which did for them. By the time I arrived, all the happiness was pretty much gone from their marriage.

As I have said, I have no memories of my early childhood. At least, when I was growing up, sometimes

I would have sort of glimpses, maybe I would see something which reminded me of something else or I would imagine I remembered something from long ago. For instance once I told my mother the patterned tiled floor in the fishmonger's was just like our old floor but she frowned and told me we had never had a floor anything like that. Another time I asked her where the square was where we used to go with the big beautiful splashy fountain. She got quite cross and told me not to make things up. We had never lived near a square with a fountain, I should stop telling tales. Worst of all was the dog incident. One day I saw a little black and white dog, nothing special, not a breed or anything, going along the other side of the street with quite a scruffy boy and, I have no idea why, I shouted out, "Look, it's just like our old dog!" That day my mother was livid: 1) shouting in the street 2) pointing and 3) making people round about think that we had ever owned such a common, scruffy-looking dog.

Well of course when you are a child, you believe grown-ups, don't you, especially your own mother. Her memory must be better than yours because she is older and so what she remembers (or doesn't remember) must be right. You are just a shameful little girl who likes to make things up.

So those glimpses which may have been bits and pieces of early memories were denied and I was left with nothing. In the blackness before my first day at school there was only a deep down disturbing feeling that something, everything was wrong.

Sabine

SABINE DECIDED SHE would just not tell Michael what she was writing. She had been surprised and thrilled by the compliments from the class after she read out her first chapter and she was sure that Michael's reaction would not be anything like as complimentary. She would keep the "Memories of my Belgian Childhood" to herself, as she had kept a number of other things to herself over the years.

2. *The Family*

Sabine's family was extremely typical of Belgium in the 1950s. Her father Alfred, the doctor, was a large authoritarian man with a full blonde moustache and beard. He had an established reputation in the neighbourhood as a good and careful doctor, reliable, rather conservative, not too fond of modern medical fads. He cared very much about his reputation which was of course essential to maintain his supply of patients and the worst thing any of the children could do would be a shameful act which would harm the reputation of Dr Mertens.

Sabine's mother was a complexed woman. To the community, she was the doctor's wife, a model of virtue and discretion. She kept house, she brought up her three young children and she never talked about patients' medical problems in the street. (The women of the neighbourhood confided in her, told her things they were too prude to tell the doctor.) But at home Bernadette was sometimes nervous and angry. Perhaps she felt frustrated by the limits of her life. In those days the wife of a professional man did not work; it would have been badly viewed. However Sabine's parents' marriage was totally happy and harmonious and Bernadette was all the time a model mother.

The first years of the marriage must have been very hard. Bernadette and Alfred married in 1937, the twins Laurent and Charles were born in 1939 and the war years must have been a nightmare for her with two small babies and everything lacking: food, medicines, heating, clothes. Their good fortune was that Alfred was not sent to fight. He served as a doctor in a military hospital in Brussels through the whole war. Most of the time, he slept at the hospital. Bernadette and the babies went to live with her parents in the small and dull town of Bouillon in the Ardennes. She and Alfred had to live apart for more than three years. But, in common with most Belgians in the post-War years, they hardly ever spoke about the War.

Certainly, compared to those black years, the Mertens' family life in the lovely house on the Avenue Parmentier was a paradise. The family led a traditional Belgian life, following the round of seasons and festivals which made of every year a long succession of pleasures and celebrations.

The year began on the first Sunday in January with Epiphany, the Festival of Kings. The family always ate the traditional pastry, the *galette des Rois* (the Kings' cake). There was a small white china figure hidden in this cake, the size of half a thumb, and the one who found the figure in their piece of cake was crowned king for the year. As the youngest child, it was Sabine's role to sit under the table – where unfortunately her brothers could kick her – and point to each person in turn to choose who would receive their piece of cake next. Sabine's mother was very clever and it was always one of the three children who found the little figure. If Laurent or Charles found it, they would choose their mother to be their queen, if Sabine found it, she would choose her Papa as her king. Never would she choose one of her brothers and of course never would they choose her.

After Epiphany came Mardi Gras and *Carnaval* in February. At Mardi Gras the children always ate as many pancakes as they could swallow, at *Carnaval* they sometimes went to watch the traditional processions of masked men with their frightening man doll faces.

Later came Easter. In those days, before the word obesity was ever spoken, Easter celebrations were very different. Today only the dentists rub their hands. When Sabine was a child, the children would have to wait impatiently until the church bells rang on Easter Sunday before they were allowed to run out into the long narrow garden to hunt for their eggs. Their father hid them very well, so well that one or two were never found until autumn. The hunt was a desperate, deadly competition. There was only a small quantity of chocolate eggs and of course whoever found them kept them. When Sabine was very small, Charles and Laurent would usually find all the eggs, Sabine would cry and her father would console her with two or three eggs he had kept intentionally in his pocket. But, as Sabine grew, she discovered she had a better memory than Laurent and Charles; she could remember where their father had hidden the eggs the year before. As the doctor had a tendency to leave the eggs in the same places every year – some of them surprising places for a doctor to choose – soon Sabine found them all. Laurent and Charles were furious, they accused Sabine of cheating and, even though their parents knew that little Sabine could not possibly have cheated, still they made her share her precious eggs with her brothers.

Those were the joyful spring festivals. Later in the year, the winter festivals were darker, sometimes with a sinister aspect. On the first of November was *La Toussaint*. In Belgium, the American Halloween had not yet been heard of. *La Toussaint* was the day when people commemorated their dead. It was already dark and cold, winter was approaching. People would go to the cemeteries, carrying big bouquets of chrysanthemums to put on the graves. In those post-War decades, there were so many dead. Even today, when I see a bouquet of chrysanthemums, I shiver – and if someone offers me one, not knowing...

On the sixth of December came the children's

favourite festival *Saint Nicola*s. On this day, Saint Nicolas comes to all Belgian children's homes, bringing chocolates and gifts. He is accompanied by a magic donkey and also by his sinister assistant Black Peter. The good children receive chocolates and presents, the naughty children are supposed to get a whipping from Black Peter. (He is also called *Le Père Fouettard* which means "the whipping father"). The night before Saint Nicolas' visit all children leave out their shoes and in the morning, if they have been good, the shoes are filled with chocolates and treats. They also leave out a bowl of water and a carrot for the donkey and a glass of something strong for Saint Nicolas. In the Mertens' home, the children's shoes were always well-filled with sweets and no one was ever whipped although secretly Sabine sometimes felt that Laurent and Charles deserved to be.

Each season of the year brought its own joys for the children. In winter, there was always snow, real, deep, pure white snow which made the parks of Woluwé Saint Pierre into a Flemish winter canvas. The children would go sledging in the big Parc de Woluwé. There was a popular slope with a little wooden cabin where the children could buy hot chocolate and the adults *vin chaud* (mulled wine). Sometimes they went ice skating too. Before Christmas, there were the traditional Christmas Markets in the main squares of many communes.

After the cold months, spring announced itself with displays of wild flowers, the sweet scent of wisteria in the streets of their suburb and quantities of frogspawn in the ponds. On the first of May, there were little bunches of lily of the valley in all the flower shops.

Summer was the best season of all because the Mertens family would go on holiday to the Belgian coast. Bernadette and the three children would leave soon after school finished at the end of June and Alfred would come and join them at weekends and during August. They always stayed in the same small *pension* in Knokke-Le Zoute. In Knokke, the children were freer than in Brussels, provided they did not drown. It was usually too cold to swim so there was not too much danger of that. They spent their days on the long beach and in the dunes, playing endless games, flying kites in the fierce wind, searching for treasure washed up by the waves or tormenting small sea creatures in the rock pools.

Bernadette seemed happier in Knokke too. She spent her days painting mystic watercolours of the sea and the sky, the magical light of the Belgian coast. She was free from the burden of preparing family meals because they ate most of their meals in the *pension*. In fact, the children preferred their mother's cooking to the meals in the *pension* which smelt of stale soups and where once, to Sabine's disgust, brains were served in a cheese sauce.

It was, from all points of view, a perfect childhood. Looking back, I see Sabine and her big brothers playing in every season. Sometimes Sabine is running after her brothers to catch up, sometimes they are running after her.

Iris

IRIS DECIDED TO bring a big ribbon-wrapped panettone and a couple of bottles of Prosecco to the last class before Christmas. Let them all enjoy some high-class Christmas fare at her expense. This meant taking a taxi since there was no way she could manage on the bus with the bottles and the box. She also brought plastic tumblers, paper plates and serviettes. Naughtily, she quite liked the thought of turning up at the Second Chance Centre in a taxi. She even timed it so she would get there five or ten minutes early and hopefully make an impression on the others as they arrived.

Unfortunately, when her taxi pulled up outside the Centre, there was no one around to see Iris get out of it. But when she got to the classroom, clanking and rustling across the front hall, Renée, Pearl and Esther were already sitting there.

Renée and Pearl exclaimed gratifyingly as Iris laid out her bounty on the single table at the side of the room.

Esther added snidely, "Very posh." (She pronounced it *pohsh*.)

That stuck in Iris's throat; to go to all that trouble and then be made fun of. She gave Esther a reproachful look and said, "Well, I thought we could do with a bit of Christmas spirit."

Esther said, "Pardon?"

Iris couldn't see what Esther was getting at. She carried on, "We've shared each other's tales of woe, haven't we? Now let's share some Christmas cheer."

"Some of us," Esther said, "don't celebrate Christmas."

Iris faltered as the penny dropped. She replied, "Oh my dear, *everyone* celebrates Christmas. Even my dear friends, Mina and Subhamoy Chatterjee, who set up this centre, celebrated Christmas and they were devout Hindus."

"Actually," Esther said, "not everyone *does* celebrate Christmas." Then, obviously feeling she had gone too far, she added, "But listen, I don't want to spoil the fun. It can be our end of term party."

Neither Renée nor Pearl said anything but it seemed to Iris they must surely be on her side. Pearl murmured, "Beautiful cake."

Just then, Sabine came in with a tin of home-made Belgian Christmas biscuits and the awkward moment passed.

Iris thought how lucky it was that Dorothy was running late today; she would have got so flustered by that exchange, poor thing. She was obviously out of her depth running this group. It was fortunate for her that she had someone like Iris there, someone with presence and poise who could help her to keep things running smoothly.

Dorothy hurried in, carrying two unimaginative boxes of Sainsbury's mince pies and then Edgar and Enid, both slightly late, both empty-handed and they exclaimed at the spread. Everyone settled down and they began with Esther's next chapter, then Sabine's and then, to everyone's surprise, Pearl said she had something for them to listen to. They all made eager, encouraging noises. Pearl had made her first recording, she said, with the help of her grandson and, if it was ok with everyone, she would like to play it to them. Hopefully she could manage her grandson's phone.

Iris did not have high hopes of Pearl's recording of course. Still she sat back and listened politely.

Pearl's voice emerged from the recorder surprisingly strongly. She sounded defiant, angry almost, as if she were telling them all off. As she listened, Iris understood that it seemed it didn't really matter where you were born or who you were. There were certain constants: men walking out on you, men dying on you, men simply not *being* there when they were needed.

Pearl's story began like this: she was born in Denmark Hill in South London on November 19, 1942. Her young (unmarried) mother was actually from Kilburn, not far away from here, but because of war-time dangers and because of the embarrassment of the pregnancy, she was sent to a home for unmarried mothers which was a bit more out of the way. It was after the Blitz but before the V1s and the V2s. Still, everyone was on edge. And Denmark Hill, in those days, was a lot more like countryside than Kilburn. Or anyway it was a good excuse for getting the shameful sight of the young woman with the swelling belly away from the neighbourhood gossips.

Pearl's mother's name was Rose Annie Jessop and, when Pearl was born, she was barely twenty years old. She had been led up the garden path by a well-spoken young man who worked in the management of the hotel where she was a chambermaid. She was very pretty, nineteen-year-old Rose

Jessop and he took a fancy to her. One thing led to another and, even though Rose came from a line of strong women, her head was turned.

What the young man, Neville Cheevers his name was, failed to mention, until it was disastrously too late, was that he was already married with a little girl of his own.

That was the gist of it. There was a lot more besides, involving a dismal description of the home for unmarried mothers and the arrangements they made to force the unmarried mothers to give their babies up for adoption. But Rose refused to give up her baby, her little Pearl. She stole away with her under cover of darkness, war or no war and made her perilous way home to Kilburn through the blackout because she had nowhere else to go. Her Mum took her in of course, she wasn't one of those who turned their own daughters away on the doorstep. She took in her daughter and her baby granddaughter and, all together, the family, who were really hard up, set about giving little Pearl the best start in life they could.

When Pearl's recording finished, Iris looked around the circle. Everyone was sitting with a solemn respectful expression on their face, everyone apart from Renée who looked, for some reason, utterly horrified.

Enid was the first to speak. "Great job Pearl," she rasped. "A picture in words. It makes me want to paint that night-time scene: the young girl fleeing with her babe in arms across the blacked-out cityscape. Incredibly powerful."

Pearl said, "Thank you."

Dorothy added, "Good on you for taking the plunge Pearl."

Iris took another look at Renée. Something was clearly very wrong; Renée had gone as white as a sheet, she was staring into the middle distance as if she had seen a ghost. Since Dorothy seemed unaware that anything was amiss, Iris took it upon herself to act.

"Are you all right Renée?" she asked loudly. Renée looked practically on the verge of unconsciousness.

Renée started. She said faintly, "I don't feel well."

Everyone spoke at once.

Sabine said, "Lie flat on the floor. I'm a first aider."

Pearl said, "I'll get you some water."

Esther flapped her hands and said, "Oh my God, oh my God."

Renée stood up unsteadily. "I need to go home. I'm sorry."

Sabine exclaimed, "Take care! You may fall."

Pearl said, "I'll come with you dear."

"No," Renée said, almost angrily. "No one come with me. I just need to —"

She grabbed her coat and walked stiffly towards the door.

Sabine pleadingly said something about low blood pressure and Dorothy gabbled about Health and Safety. But it was too late. Renée didn't look back. She opened the door wildly and then she was gone.

Iris was thoroughly put out that her Christmas tea was overshadowed by Renée's dramatic departure. Obviously, it wasn't Renée's fault if she was taken ill but still it was annoying. Instead of enjoying themselves and being grateful to Iris, everyone was preoccupied, busy fretting about Renée and speculating what the matter might be.

111

Lavonda's arrival was the last straw. She knocked and came in simultaneously. For a moment, it seemed as if she might just have come along to wish them all a Merry Christmas. But then she saw the bottles of Prosecco and she turned terribly stern.

"Dorothy," she said, "are you not aware of our no-alcohol policy?"

Dorothy, of course straightaway blushing beetroot red, answered, "We didn't have one at the library."

"Such a shame," Iris said tartly to Lavonda. "We would have offered you a glass."

Lavonda turned on her. "I understand it was *you* who brought it in, Iris. Reception told me. But when they said bottles, I assumed soft drinks. Absolutely *no* alcohol is allowed at the Second Chance Centre. I would have thought you of all people knew that. You need to stop drinking right now and put it away."

"Oh come on dear," Edgar said. "It's Christmas."

Lavonda directed her glare at him. "We don't celebrate Christmas here," she said icily. "We have diversity and inclusivity and Christmas isn't diverse *or* inclusive."

Iris said, "What a load of gobbledygook" and then looked furtively at Esther.

"Listen," Lavonda said, "it's simple: either you put the booze away or I'll go and get the caretaker to escort you off the premises. All of you."

Sabine murmured, "*Mon Dieu!*"

Edgar said, "Keep your hair on."

But Lavonda simply stood and glared until they had all reluctantly returned their plastic tumblers to the table – except for Enid who downed hers in a last, defiant noisy swig. Lavonda waited until Iris had done her best to jam the corks back into the half-drunk bottles. Then she stalked out.

Iris went home in a foul mood. All her good intentions, her generosity had been flung back in her face. Now she had nothing to look forward to, only Christmas dinner with Joanna and her partner Nat to dread. Iris had never had a "partner"; she had had boyfriends and husbands, three of them, but never a "partner". She considered the word primarily a business term. However, if anyone was ever a "partner", she supposed it was Nat Gordon, Joanna's abrasive companion for the past fifteen years and civil partner for the last three.

Iris and Nat had never got on from the word go. Nat seemed, if possible, to disapprove of Iris even more than Joanna did. And Iris simply could not abide Nat. She was a small, shrill woman, about half the size of hefty Joanna but with an incredibly ferocious temper. The strangest things could provoke her to an outburst: allegedly pretentious pronunciation, euphemistic terminology, the purchase of imported miniature vegetables, possession of a decades old fur coat. Iris refused to go in fear of Nat; if she was honest, she would have to admit that she was in fact more likely to serve baby sweetcorn and to say that she was "visiting the conveniences" or that someone had "passed away" if Nat was present. In her heart of hearts, she could not forgive Nat for finding her dreadful daughter so lovable. Iris felt it showed her up. She considered it the ultimate slap in the face that Joanna had made her Nat Gordon's mother-in-law.

For years, despite everything, Joanna had continued to

come home to her mother's for Christmas. But she came, it seemed to Iris, to criticise, to argue and to make upsetting scenes. When she started to bring Nat with her, at first things had been a little easier since she and Nat always spent quite a lot of time arguing with each other which took the pressure off Iris. But that turned out to be only part of the early passionate phase and once they had settled down into mature companionship, they always sided together against Iris. It was like being in court on trial, facing the two of them and their barrage of accusations over the turkey and the Christmas pud. Sometimes Iris thought she would rather face a firing squad than another Christmas dinner with Joanna and Nat.

Edgar

WHEN THE AUTUMN term at the Second Chance Centre came to an end, Edgar breathed a deep sigh of relief. Given half a chance, he would not go back for the next term. He had sat through the classes dutifully, doing what he was told, but he had not enjoyed them one bit. It wasn't his thing at all, all that baring your soul and, besides, in so many of the women's stories, men were the villains. As the only representative of the male species present, he felt responsible somehow, in the dock. It was uncomfortable. Even though they all tried their level best to be nice to him, he felt like a fish out of water. Worse, it seemed to him that things might actually go more easily if he wasn't there. Sometimes he sensed a reluctance, a coyness, things left unsaid and he suspected the women wanted to talk about women's business but, with Edgar in their midst, they couldn't. He would be doing them all a favour if he bowed out.

But Madeleine and Joan kept him there. Madeleine loved everything about the life story group; she loved recording Edgar's reminiscences with him and she loved hearing about the classes afterwards. She knew each person in the group by name and she had strong opinions about some of them. There was no way she would let Edgar leave.

It was true there were certain things she disapproved of: "How come there's no black people in your group?" she demanded one Thursday evening. "Or Indian people? Or Chinese people? How come everybody's *white*?"

Edgar thought this over. To be honest, he hadn't noticed before. But it was strange when you stopped to think about it; the estate and the streets round about were so mixed yet you rarely saw a black or Indian face at the Second Chance Centre, other than that fearsome manager.

"Maybe they've got better things to do with their time," he joked. "Or maybe they find the classes too pricey."

Madeleine shook her head. "It's not that," she said slowly. She thought it over. "I guess they feel their stories would fall on deaf ears," she said. "Nobody would understand where they were coming from."

Edgar said, "Could be. But there's more than one way to be the odd one out you know. Believe me, being the only man's no picnic either."

Madeleine laughed. "So now I have to feel sorry for you because you're a *man*?" The laughter rippled across her opulent body and she shook her head in disbelief.

"If I had my way," Edgar said tetchily, "I wouldn't keep on going you know."

Madeleine frowned. "No way!" she exclaimed. "No way!"

Edgar believed Joan would have been glad he was going along too. Every week, when he walked into the centre, he felt close to her. Sometimes he imagined her coming towards him out of one or other of the classrooms, very pale, how she was at the end, carefully carrying a piece of handicraft or a beautifully decorated cake. Although it made him feel weepy, it jogged his memory too: the embroidered cushion cover with their initials entwined – where had that gone? – the cake for his sixtieth with a perfectly suited little marzipan man on top, raising his hat. Joan had been here before him, he was following in her footsteps and he was sure she would be pleased.

The last day of term, on a whim, he stopped at the front desk and asked the young girl who sat there whether they had any record of a Mrs Joan Whistler coming to the centre.

The girl looked disapproving. She said, "I can't give out contact details."

Edgar gave her a long hard stare before he could bring himself to say, "She was my late wife."

The girl looked puzzled but not apologetic at all. "Well, so what are you after?" she asked.

"I want to know," Edgar said – and the question only formed in his head as he spoke – "what was the last class she came to here?"

"When would that have been?" the girl asked.

Edgar paused. "She passed away nearly six years ago so – before then. D'you still have the records?"

"Ye-es," said the girl, gesturing at her computer and rolling her eyes. Really, Edgar thought, young people nowadays had no manners.

She tapped away at her computer for a few moments, double checked the spelling of Whistler, expressed surprise and doubt that it had an "h" and then read out, "Whistler, Joan, creative writing."

"No," Edgar said, "that's not right. She never did creative writing."

The girl swivelled her screen round to show him. Edgar peered at it, his eyesight wasn't what it was but he could make out "Creative Writing Autumn Term 2006" and underneath a long list of names in little boxes, ending with "Whistler, Joan."

"Someone's made a mistake there," he said confidently. "I know for a fact she never did creative writing. It wouldn't be her sort of thing at all. Cake decorating, yes, sewing, yes, I believe she did pottery once but never ever creative writing."

The girl did a bit more busy typing at her computer. She read out, "2001 Cake Decorating Beginners, 2002 Cake Decorating Advanced, 2003 Embroidery, 2004 Pottery, just one term, 2005 Embroidery again and 2006 Creative Writing, all three terms." She looked up at Edgar triumphantly.

He wasn't a man with a temper but he could feel himself getting angry. "Show me that list again," he said. He scrutinized it as if he could somehow spot the mistake. There was Joan's name and there, he now saw, two or three names higher up the list, was Thorpe, Renée.

"I'll get to the bottom of this," he said shortly and turned away. He walked along to Dorothy's classroom, fuming. How dare they write down something which wasn't true about someone who was dead and couldn't put it right? Joan would never ever have gone to a creative writing class, she didn't have the confidence and, besides, what did she have to write about? He wondered if he might have a quiet word with Renée after the class, she seemed a good soul. Of course, she was unlikely to remember who was or wasn't in a class she had gone to six or seven years ago and, even if she had no recollection of Joan, it wouldn't be absolute proof, would it, that Joan hadn't been there? Edgar realised that a smidgeon of doubt had entered his mind.

What if he asked Renée and she said, "Oh yes, I remember Joan, poor dear. We sat next to each other, she was such a lovely lady." What then? It would mean that Joan had hidden something from him, something important and yet they had no secrets from each other. Edgar decided he would say nothing for now.

The possibility of changing his mind was whisked away from him when Renée left early because she felt unwell. He decided it was maybe for the best. If Joan had been to a creative writing class, he reflected on the way home, she must have written something. If so, where was it? And, above all, *what* was it? The answer to the conundrum might be under his own roof. No need to involve Renée or anybody else for that matter. A bit of detective work in the cupboards and drawers he hadn't dared touch since Joan's death might turn up his answer. But he wasn't going to rush into looking right away. Sufficient unto the day, that was his motto. He had had a bellyful of the whole thing anyway: life stories and writing and the Second Chance Centre. At least he would have a bit of a breather over Christmas.

Christmas Day itself was always going to be a washout because Madeleine spent it with her children. Even though Luke was twenty and Desiree eighteen, they were still entitled to a tree and presents and a Christmas dinner cooked by their mum. Madeleine had been wearing herself out the past few weeks getting everything ready. For the first time since Joan passed away, Edgar made an excuse not to go to her sister Gilly's where he had forlornly spent the five previous Christmases. Gilly and her silent husband Desmond only invited him for Joan's sake and, with Madeleine in the background, he felt he would be going along on false pretences. He came up with an inspired excuse which Gilly swallowed hook, line and sinker. He told her he had been going to a cookery class recently, to get better at making his own meals and one of his fellow students had organized a get-together for those on their own: everybody was to bring a dish. As he put the phone down, he thought, "Why, I could have gone to creative writing classes too." Christmas Day and Boxing Day would be dreary, he would most probably go up to the Pristina café which Murat kept open defiantly right through the holiday period. But no matter how miserable Christmas was, he knew he would get through it because Madeleine was coming to stay for New Year.

It was she who had suggested it. He could barely believe his ears. Luke and Desiree were both going out to New Year parties and, whatever they thought of their mother's relationship with Edgar, they could hardly expect her to sit alone at home on New Year's Eve. Edgar had reacted joyfully. He promised Madeleine a New Year's Eve to remember. He would take her out for a slap-up meal, he said, they could go dancing, if Madeleine wanted they could go somewhere fancy in the West End. He felt a sharp pang of guilt for he had never offered such a thing to Joan.

Madeleine considered. "On New Year's Eve the West End will be so crowded. And the Tube will be full of rowdy people who've been drinking. Why don't we just go to that Italian place we went the first time and then come back here and see in the New Year together?"

When he heard that, Edgar had a glorious vision. Seeing in the New Year with Madeleine conjured up such tantalizing images that, just imagining it, he could hardly contain himself.

Madeleine would arrive, beautifully dressed. He would dress up too and he would wear cologne. After dinner at Da Luigi's, they would stroll home, arm in arm and settle down together on the sofa. They would drink champagne in front of the telly at midnight and then they would go to bed and Edgar would enter Paradise.

He wondered sometimes whether it was right and proper for a man of his years to spend so much time thinking about Madeleine's body. Madeleine, Mrs Madeleine Baxter, was fifty-four years old, a mature woman of generous proportions and Edgar was in awe of her beauty.

He found each individual region of her body so mesmerizing that he found it hard to visualise her whole. Madeleine was also shy, reluctant to be seen completely naked and that habit of hers encouraged him to focus on her glimpsed parts.

Seeing Madeleine's bottom rise as she bent to tuck in

the bed, to take food out of the oven, to wipe a troubling spillage from the floor excited Edgar unbelievably. There was something so immense, imposing almost about it. While it was obviously the bottom of a woman on a grand scale, there was also a stately dignity to it, something majestic even. It made Edgar think of dimly remembered terms from an astronomy series he had once watched on the telly: the transit of Venus, the moons of Saturn. But he was always careful not to single Madeleine's bottom out for praise, to couch his compliments about her physique more generally. For he was well aware that a woman of Madeleine's proportions was likely to be sensitive about the scale of her backside.

Her legs, released from her nurse's support tights, were shapely and statuesque, like the sculpted legs of a black marble figure with all sorts of muscles and sinews and veins pulsing through them. In the evenings, when she sat with her tired feet up, Edgar would position himself, like a school boy, so he could best look up the dark alluring folds of her skirt.

Her breasts, first sighted, left him speechless. They were without a doubt the biggest breasts he had ever seen, even their nipples were the size and colour of damsons. He repressed a shameful comparison with Joan's small white ones which had in their time been so very dear. Madeleine's breasts, released from their severe bra, spread, they sprawled, they offered themselves to Edgar. When at last he laid his head between them, he felt that death could come whenever it chose; nothing would ever outdo that glorious moment.

Spring

THE SECOND CHANCE CENTRE

Spring Term 2013 Register

Course: Life Story Writing			Day: Thursday Time: 2pm			
Instructor: Dorothy Woodward			Room Number: G3			
Student Name						
Pearl Barter						
Iris Bennett						
Enid Harkin						
Sabine Moreton						
Esther Solomon						
Edgar Whistler						

Dorothy

By the time classes started again in January, Dorothy had finished the first part of her story. She was extremely proud of what she had written even though not one word of it was true. She was in fact even prouder of her work because it was all made up than she might have been if it were true; it seemed more of an achievement somehow to invent a life rather than unimaginatively to record a dull one which had actually taken place.

She had borrowed *The Story of a Russian Princess* from Gerald, along with a couple of books about Russia and she had spent hours and hours online doing her research. When Gerald queried her new interest in things Russian, she told him that lately she had felt drawn to the Eastern Orthodox Church and he looked appropriately solemn and respectful. She wondered at her growing inventiveness. She had always liked story telling but this was a new departure. She had created a richly fantastic family history for herself which bore no relation to reality and which in fact grandiosely surpassed it.

When she entered the Second Chance Centre on the first day of the new term, not especially cold but penetratingly damp, Lavonda was standing in the front hall. She was greeting people as they arrived with a false professional smile, wishing them a happy New Year and handing out Quality Street from a big tin. She gave Dorothy a slightly less friendly smile and offered her the tin.

Dorothy shook her head. She was still seething at Lavonda's rebuke over the sparkling wine at the Christmas do. She couldn't resist saying, "I see you celebrate New Year here even if you don't celebrate Christmas."

Lavonda looked at her. "Christmas," she said, "is not for everyone. New Year is."

"No actually," Dorothy surprised herself by answering back, "it isn't. Russians celebrate New Year on a completely different day from us."

Lavonda raised her eyebrows. "Really?"

"Yes," Dorothy said. "They do." She thought of Parvaneh, her sad-eyed assistant at Mercy House. "And Iranians too. *Their* New Year is in our spring."

Lavonda looked concerned but she retorted, "My, you learnt a lot in your library, didn't you? But, you know what, I don't think we've got that many Russians here."

Dorothy said, "You'd be surprised."

She went off down the corridor to G3, feeling she had scored a small victory. She found Pearl sitting all by herself looking worried.

"Hello," Dorothy greeted her brightly. "How was your Christmas?"

"Lovely thanks," Pearl said, equally brightly. "And yours?"

"Oh," Dorothy said, "lovely."

She busied herself unpacking her papers and, while she was sorting herself out, Pearl asked, "Have you heard anything from Renée? D'you know if she's ok?"

Dorothy hadn't heard anything. How would she? She hadn't had so much as a Christmas card from the Second Chance Centre. At the library, she had always given her assistant a card

126

and a small gift – chocolate or soap – on the last afternoon before the Christmas closure.

"No I haven't," she said. "But I expect she's feeling better by now, don't you?"

"I'm really worried about her," Pearl said. "I feel terrible."

Dorothy didn't understand. "Why on earth Pearl? It's not your fault she felt ill."

"Oh," Pearl said, "actually I think it might be." She hesitated. "I been thinking about it over Christmas. I think maybe she was upset about something in my recording."

"No!" Dorothy exclaimed. "How could that be? It was *your* story, it was all about *you*. It wasn't anything to do with Renée."

Pearl looked troubled. "I don't know," she said, "I just got a really bad feeling."

At that point Sabine came in, complaining that she had spent the whole of the Christmas holidays entertaining her relatives from Belgium and had had no time at all to write. After Sabine, Esther who reminded them that she had not celebrated Christmas but had written loads. By the time everyone had arrived, Pearl's curious comment had slipped Dorothy's mind. There was still no sign of Renée but Dorothy was eager to begin.

When she told the group she would start the new term with her own first instalment, there was a ripple of polite excitement. Dorothy supposed they privately anticipated dullness. They were in for a shock, if so. For an instant, she feared exposure and then she plunged in.

She had given herself a Russian emigré father and an English ballerina mother. Her father had taken the name Woodward because it ever so slightly resembled his Russian name of Vronsky. Her mother had died young in tragic circumstances which she alluded to but drew a veil over. Where her imagination ran out, she made it look like discretion. She was six when her mother died, of mysterious and not entirely natural causes; old enough to remember her, to cherish the ghostly image of her pirouetting magically in a white tutu on a spotlit stage, young enough to recover and grow up. Her poor dear father, heartbroken, never recovered. Dorothy grew up on her own with him in a rather grand old-fashioned flat in Bayswater, full of Russian memorabilia, samovars and Fabergé eggs. To say her father brought her up would be an exaggeration; he was too sunk in grief to do more than sigh and reminisce and give way to soulful Russian depressions. Dorothy had to give him a job, a source of income and, after some thought, she made him an unusually successful antiquarian book dealer – which tied in with her own profession of librarian.

She felt rather guilty, as she wrote, about her real parents whom she had written out of existence: Tilly and Late Lamented. But it was the idea of divulging the tiny horrors of her childhood, alone in that shoebox of a flat in Northolt with her half-mad widowed mother which had driven her to create a fantasy childhood in the first place so her guilt was short-lived.

Her first chapter set the scene: she briefly told the story of her paternal grandparents' flight from Russia in 1917 at the time of the Russian Revolution, her father, then little Nikolai Vladimirovich Vronsky, just a baby. She described the grand mansion they left behind in Moscow from photographs in one of Gerald's books. She learnt the word "caryatid" and used it. She skimmed over their rise from romantic penniless refugees to prosperous antique dealers. She leapfrogged forward to 1947 when her father, by now to all intents and purposes Nicholas

Woodward, a debonair bachelor, first saw her mother dancing on stage and fell immediately and dramatically in love with her.

She wrote about their whirlwind romance – which she particularly enjoyed doing – and their wedding in the Russian Orthodox church in Bayswater. She worried that she had gone into a little too much detail about the wedding ritual but it seemed a shame to waste so much good material when you had it to hand. She recounted her own birth five years later. Her mother, Giselle, had delayed having children so as to carry on dancing. She shared a few early memories: her mother buying her her first pair of little pink ballet pumps, her father telling her Russian fairytales about Baba Yaga, a witch who lived in the forest in a hut on chicken's feet. Then she came to the dreadful day of her mother's death: the discovery of her mother's lifeless body in the wings of the theatre, the curtain brought down on the performance and her distraught father raging through their apartment, crying out that he could not go on and brandishing a revolver but being restrained by relatives.

She then described the even more dreadful day a year later when she found her father hanging from a metal ring in their library ceiling which had previously supported an enormous chandelier, conveniently removed for cleaning. He had been unable to stand life without Giselle and he had taken advantage of little Dorothy and the nanny being out at a ballet lesson. Dorothy recalled the heavy leather armchair lying on its side beneath him where he had kicked it away and she and the nanny struggling to right it and put it under his feet. Whereupon his feet miraculously came to rest on one padded arm and he stood there, choking and gasping with the most fearfully bloodshot eyes. Her ballet lesson had been cancelled because the teacher had shingles and they had come home just in the nick of time. Her father lifted the noose off over his head and collapsed in the armchair. He lay there, gasping and groaning and clutching at his horribly bruised neck and that was the end of her first chapter.

When she finished reading, Iris asked – it would be Iris – "Do you have any family photos?"

For a moment, Dorothy panicked. How stupid she was not to have thought of that. But, quickly, her newly fertile imagination came to her rescue. "We lost them all in a house fire," she said promptly. "That comes much later."

"I never would have thought," Sabine said, "that you have Russian blood. You seem so very English."

"Oh there's no telling nowadays," Iris said. "Everyone's so mixed up, aren't they?" She glanced quickly around as if to check that no one had taken offence.

Enid cackled. "I 'spect you go back to the Norman Conquest, don't you, Iris?"

"Well," Iris said, "as a matter of fact —"

Enid cut her off. She said to Dorothy, "I loved all that Russian stuff. It was like watching a period drama on the telly. Great work!"

Esther added, "I loved the ghostly image of your mother twirling round on stage."

Edgar, who rarely spoke, said, "I had a Russian customer for many years, Mr Ichilov. Used to come in twice a year, spring and autumn, for years. A very smart chap, always perfectly turned out. Don't suppose you knew him?"

Dorothy shook her head. "My poor father didn't socialise much."

Pearl said, "You've not said anything about your

grandparents Dorothy. Didn't they help out after your mum passed away?"

Dorothy felt herself flushing terribly; so many things she hadn't thought of. "Well, my mother's parents didn't really approve of my father," she said quickly. "They weren't all that happy about her marrying a Russian. And my father's parents were old and frail, you know. They had been through so much already."

"Can you speak Russian?" Sabine asked.

Dorothy fought back panic. "Not a word," she said. "My father never had the energy to teach me."

"But you must understand it surely?" Sabine insisted. "I mean, I didn't properly teach my children French but they can still understand pretty much everything."

Iris, the know-all, came to Dorothy's rescue. "Russian's a much harder language than French, I believe."

Dorothy nodded. "Of course," she said recklessly, "I do know the odd word or two."

"Ooh go on, say something," said Esther.

Everyone waited.

With more authority than she could usually muster, Dorothy said firmly, "No, that's more than enough about me. I want to hear what *you've* all been up to. Who else has got something for us to listen to today?"

On her way home after the class, she patted herself on the back. They had asked her a lot of awkward questions but she was confident that no one had suspected anything. When she opened her front door, Whittington came sidling up out of nowhere, purring and winding himself around her legs, seemingly congratulating her on her performance.

Sabine

3. The Forest

COMPARED TO THE sedentary life of modern children, Sabine and her brothers were very active. It was normal for them to play outside even in bad weather. As you probably know, it rains a great deal in Belgium, we even have our own Belgian rain, the *drâche nationale*, a light continuous drizzle. Because it rains so much, rain is absolutely not considered a reason to stay inside. Belgians judge a woman who leaves her house without an umbrella even on a sunny day to be a frivolous person. So Sabine's parents saw nothing bad in the children playing outside for long periods in every weather.

From the age of eight, many Belgian children join the young scouts, *les louveteaux* which means the wolf cubs. Laurent and Charles were very enthusiastic wolf cubs and later proper scouts. They would regularly go off on camping trips with their scout troop. The philosophy of the *louveteaux* was to teach children healthy physical vigour and communal life in nature. Laurent and Charles and their scout troop would march through the forest singing their special songs, sleep outside in home-made shelters and cook their dinner over a fire. They learnt all sorts of particular outdoor skills. When Sabine was five or six, too young to be a wolf cub yet, her big brothers were sometimes allowed to take her out to play in nature and show her some of those particular outdoor skills.

They were supposed to play in the parks, there were several of them in the neighbourhood or to go to popular places at the edge of the forest but instead they sometimes took little Sabine into the deep forest. Their *scoutisme* had introduced them to the attractions of the forest and what 13-year-old boy would play in a park or a picnic place when so close there was a real forest?

The Forest of Soignes was a very old and still a little spooky place. There had been wolves in the forest right up to the 19th century and, although they had disappeared, there was still an atmosphere of wolves in the forest and many menacing stories. An adolescent boy could really frighten a little girl with some of the stories.

The Forest of Soignes is a beech forest, full of big shady trees and most beautiful in autumn when the trees all turn a deep orange and the light in the forest is incandescent. Old paths cross the forest in all different directions, some of them paved with big old flagstones. Some of the paths have very strange names which you can find on the oldest maps: *Drève des Brûlés* (Burnt People Drive), *Coin du Balai* (Broom Corner), *Drève de la Longue Queue* (Long Tail Drive) and, worst of all, *Drève des Enfants Noyés* (Drowned Children Drive). Close by was a small lake, the *Etang des Enfants Noyés*.

Laurent and Charles liked to tell Sabine a story about a boy whose dog had run out onto the ice in Woluwé Park in winter and the boy had run after the dog. The ice had cracked open and they had both fallen through.

How Sabine loved to go to the forest with her big brothers. Laurent and Charles would walk along the forest paths, both holding little Sabine by the hand. When she got too tired to walk, one or other twin would carry her on his shoulders. They always brought a rucksack full of provisions prepared by their mother and the brother who did not carry the rucksack would have to carry Sabine. The boys knew the names of all the birds which called in the forest, the squirrels and the chipmunks. They knew which plants were poisonous and which ones were medicinal. They knew which mushrooms were safe to eat.

When Sabine grew tired and hungry, which happened quickly, the boys would tease her by singing a song which went, "*Un kilomètre à pied, Ça use, ça use, ça use les souliers, Deux kilomètres, trois kilomètres*" etc etc. (One kilometer by foot, it wears, it wears, it wears down your shoes, Two kilometers, three kilometers and so on), making her believe they still had a long way to walk.

Soon they would find an isolated place, far from the path, maybe beside a small pool or under a giant old tree. They would make a fire, the scout way, and they would eat their picnic. After they had eaten, they would play games. Laurent and Charles would show Sabine how to whistle with a leaf of grass, how to make a catapult with a twig and stones and how to hide from the rain in a dark old hollow tree.

Sometimes their games were not nice. They would play hide and seek but when it was Sabine's turn to look for them, they would hide themselves so well that she could not find them and she would run around crying, all alone in the middle of the forest. Sometimes they would pretend they had seen an angry wild boar or even a wolf. They would scream, "Look out Sabine, look out – a wolf is coming," and she would run away, terrified, her heart beating and her brothers would laugh for a long time.

The Forest of Soignes was so beautiful. For the children it seemed to be a magic kingdom where the rules of the adult world did not exist, where they were free to do anything they wanted, anything at all.

Sometimes, on a Sunday, they would go to a different popular part of the forest with their parents, everyone on bicycles, they would eat *gaufres* (waffles) after a vigorous ride and then the forest seemed totally different. It seemed bright and safe and good-humoured. It was a friendly forest in a storybook. There were no shadows of creeping wolves and no unusual games.

But one time their father explained to them the origin of the strange names in the forest. He told them that the people who were burnt on *Drève des Brûlés* were probably witches. The brooms and cats and cauldrons which you could find in place names across the forest were all related to witches too. In mediaeval times, local people believed that witches gathered in the Forest of

Soignes to hold their witches' sabbaths and to make their wicked spells. Dr Mertens laughed loudly to show that he, a rational man, did not believe such nonsense and Laurent and Charles loudly copied him. But little Sabine was very frightened. Already she had to worry about wolves and boars and certain of her brothers' games, now she had to fear witches too.

But yet the beauty of nature and the children's freedom made their excursions into the forest a magical memory. When I compare this glorious forest of my childhood with the morose urban parks of London, again I realize how very special my Belgian childhood was.

Esther

WHEN ESTHER ENTERED the classroom, she always had the feeling she had interrupted a conversation which she was not meant to be part of. Not that she imagined the older ladies who got there early had anything specially interesting to talk about. But still: she had to shuffle around her clients at the spa to be free on a Thursday afternoon. It would be nice to feel welcome. When she read, everyone was perfectly polite, they praised her devotion to her Mum. But no-one came up with anything really meaningful.

Just once, Edgar said, "My Russian customer, Mr Ichilov was Jewish, I believe. Always very well dressed."

Another time, Enid said, "I would draw your family all wearing masks," which wasn't exactly helpful. But that was it.

Esther complained to Samson, "Honestly, I might as well be writing about Eskimos," which Samson naturally found hilarious.

Today is May Woodgate's birthday party. May is my best friend in primary school and she is unfortunately not Jewish. There are a couple of other little Jewish girls in my class and my mother would far rather I had picked one of them as my best friend. But I don't like either of them and they definetely don't like me. May is lovely.

137

She has beautiful blonde hair and lovely blue eyes and the kind of complexion people used to call "peaches and cream". She lives in a detached house on a nice road, quite a lot nicer than ours and she has everything you could ever wish for. She has loads of pretty dresses, all the latest toys and a sweet white poodle called Flossie. Best of all, she has Mrs Woodgate for her mother. Mrs Woodgate is my idea of perfection and I have a big crush on her. Don't get me wrong, not that I don't love my own mother, I adore her but she is not nearly as glamorous as May Woodgate's mum.

Mrs Woodgate and my Mum both find our friendship a bit embarassing. My Mum believes she ought to look down on Mrs Woodgate because she isn't Jewish but actually she looks up to her because she is better off than us. This contradiction makes her uncomfortable and because she feels uncomfortable she is always rather mean about my friendship with May. I don't know what Mrs Woodgate feels because she is more sophisticated than my Mum and she knows to always keep her feelings hidden. She is always extra specialy nice to me but this might be because the War is not long over and she knows that if Hitler had made it across the Channel, that would have been the end for me and my family.

So anyway it is May's birthday party, maybe her seventh or her eighth I don't rightly remember. All the little girls from our class are there in their best dresses and, even though there is rationing, there is an extra special afternoon tea. I don't know how they managed that. One of the special treats is little cocktail sausages on sticks. Because they're a special treat and because there aren't that many of them, they are being passed around by Mrs Plumstead (Joan Plumstead's mother who is lending a hand).

I am not meant to hear what is being whispered by Mrs Woodgate and Mrs Plumstead but somehow or other I do. I can still hear their voices today, soft and catty.

"No sausages for Rita Solomon, remember."

"Oh?"

"They don't eat pork."

"Oh I never knew. But —"

"I know, not that it actually *matters*."

I don't understand this conversation at all. Of course I know perfectly well I am not meant to eat the little sausages and if they had been offered to me, I would have said politely, "No thank you Mrs Plumstead." But what do they mean, it doesn't actually *matter*? Do they mean that there is actually nothing wrong with eating pork sausages? How could that be? Or do they mean something else? Do they mean there is some other reason — which I don't know — why it doesn't actually matter if I eat the little sausages? How could that possibly be? But they are both looking at me in a funny way and Mrs Woodgate gives me a smile which is too big and too bright, it is not real. I feel so uncomfortable, I want to be sick and I have to run away from the birthday tea table before I am.

There is something wrong with me, there is no doubt

and again and again in sneaky ways I keep being reminded of it.

Probably one of the most wrong things about me is that I love singing hymns. All my life I have carried on singing them – in the kitchen, in the shower – and, growing up, my daughter Esther told me off no end for that. But remember in those days every school day began with morning assembly and hymn singing. There was no question of the Jewish children being excused either. The words "ethnic minority" and "multi-cultural" hadn't even been invented then. In any case, who wanted to be excused? Nobody wanted to be singled out for name-calling. We wanted to fit in and just be like everyone else. The other Jewish kids had their own way of dealing with it; either they just went "La-la-la" or they sang but they left out the really bad words – "Jesus" and "Mary" or anything too Christmassy. I think I was the only one who sang along with everything. I didn't just sing along in fact, I sang with all my heart and soul. My favourites were "Immortal, invisible, God only wise", "Almighty Father strong to save" and best of all, "There is a green hill far away". Why did I like that one the best when it was actually the worst, the most Christian, the most *wrong*? The words went like this:

"There is a green hill far away,
Without a city wall
Where our dear Lord was crusified
Who died to save us all."

140

I knew I must be a terrible person to love that one the most.

One morning I was singing away – I remember funnily enough it was "All Things Bright and Beautiful" – when I noticed my form teacher Miss Piggott was watching me. She had a big grin all over her fat face as if me singing the hymn was quite the funniest thing she had seen in a long while. When she saw me looking at her, her big grin vannished and she tried to look all stern. But a few moments later I sneaked another look and she wasn't only grinning, she was descreetly elbowing her buddy Miss Matthews and signalling at me. Miss Matthews was smiling too, nastily. I felt so upset I practically stopped singing. Why *me*? Why was my singing the hymn funnier than any of the other Jewish children singing? Why was Miss Piggott laughing at *me*? There must be something else. It was that thing, that unknown awful thing which had dogged me my whole life. It was as if I had a tail – or wings – something no one else had which made me different, which made me odd.

We had a few relatives living nearby in the Hendon area and I think the only times we ever went out as a family were to visit our relatives: Auntie Beryl and Auntie Violet. Auntie Violet was Mum's sister and Auntie Beryl was Dad's. Their husbands were Uncle Ned and Uncle Reuben. At Auntie Violet's house there were two cousins, Pamela and Shirley and at Auntie Beryl's three, Simon, Ruth and Benjamin. I was the only only. I liked going to Auntie Beryl's the least because at least at Auntie

Violet's my two big girl cousins who were much older would play with me in a pretend nice, patronising kind of way. Going to Auntie Beryl's was always a torment. But I wasn't allowed to kick up a fuss about going. Auntie Beryl and Uncle Reuben were Family and Family was just about the most important thing in the whole world. Family meant that even if you didn't like Auntie Beryl (fat and bossy) and Uncle Reuben (silly jokes), you still had to love them and, as for my cousins Simon, Ruth and Benjy, who were all three stuck up and superior, apparently I was supposed to love them too.

Ruth and I were almost the same age. When this next bit happened, I think I was nine and she was ten. The family liked to say we were close and wasn't that nice when Rita didn't have a sister? But in actual fact we weren't close at all. The only time we were the least bit close was when the boys ganged up on us, played some mean trick and we were thrown together as girly victims: "The boys are being mean!"

"Look," Simon said meanly. "They blub in exactly the same way," and he imitated us blubbing and sniffing and rubbing our eyes on our sleeves.

"Shut up," Ruth sobbed. "I'll tell on you."

I don't remember anymore what the trick was or why Ruth and I were so upset that day but I remember all too clearly what came next.

The boys don't care, they are too carried away by their mean mischief. Sucking up to his big brother, Benjy adds, "Yes and they've got the same fat face and the same silly hair and the same big bums."

At this, Ruth loses it completely. She runs into the living room where the grown-ups are sitting chatting and she shouts out, "Simon and Benjy are being horrible. They're saying Rita and I both look the same: fat and ugly." (I don't believe the boys ever actually used the word "ugly" by the way.)

Auntie Beryl and my Mum both go bright red. I've followed Ruth in and I see them blush. For a second or two, no one seems sure quite what to say. Then Uncle Reuben cracks one of his silly jokes. "They must need glasses if they really said such a silly thing. Time for a visit to the optician's. Oh dear, more expense." No one laughs. Auntie Beryl says bossily, "Don't be such a sissy Ruth. You know you're neither of you the least bit fat or ugly. And as for looking the same, well, you're cousins aren't you?"

Then everyone goes red. Uncle Reuben obviously feels he has fallen short. He giggles and adds, "As alike as two peas in a pod."

The atmosphere in the room is terrible. Somehow something is terribly wrong. Suddenly I sense it coming towards me, like the tip of an iceberg. I know there is a big huge hidden secret which the grown-ups are keeping from me and I am the doomed ship sailing towards it. If you haven't worked out by now what it was, all will be revealed soon enough.

Iris

EVEN ON THE briefest days of winter, Iris always made sure she was home before dark. It made for long evenings but she no longer felt safe out and about once night fell. She moved at a snail's pace and these days the streets were full of shady people up to no good. Not that she had that many places to go: the shops mainly, the doctor's, the Second Chance Centre and, lately, the volunteer-run library in the Unitarian church hall. She had switched there when Mercy House closed down but she didn't much care for it. It was shambolic and, to be honest, its main attraction was not its rather odd selection of books but its good-looking chief librarian, Gerald Shrimsley.

Passing eighty had, to Iris's slight surprise, not made her immune to the charms of men, if anything rather the contrary. As she felt herself slipping away from the stage of life ruled by passion, she found her attraction to the lure of good-looking men growing ever more acute. Now there was no longer any risk, she supposed, of an entanglement or some frightful embarrassment like with Yusuf, she could finally let herself go. If she liked the look of a handsome man, she could smile and flirt with him freely – with no fear of the consequences.

Gerald Shrimsley was an exceptionally handsome man. He also had a lovely gentle way about him; he spoke in a soft voice, the result, Iris supposed, of a life spent working in libraries. It gave him a pastoral, almost priestly air as he moved quietly among his mainly female volunteers, all of whom visibly adored him.

Of course Iris had to borrow a book or two to conceal her real reason for visiting the library. She had little interest in the extensive shelves of spiritual and self-help books. The selection of historical romances, her favourite, was meagre. So she would just choose some random volume or other mainly to show Joanna and Nat, should they come round, that her mind was still in good working order although she had no serious intention of reading it.

On one visit, she ran into Dorothy, standing at the counter deep in conversation with Gerald and a small patient queue forming behind her. Although Iris felt slightly self-conscious, as if her motivation for visiting the library was somehow visible, she took the initiative and greeted Dorothy graciously.

Dorothy whipped round, startled. Iris supposed Dorothy came to the library because she too was sweet on Gerald and now she was embarrassed at being found out.

"Goodness," Dorothy said, "I must get a move on. I'm holding everybody up."

She scooped up a small stack of books from the counter and said busily, "You've dealt with this little lot I brought back, haven't you Gerald? I'll pop them on the returns trolley for you."

From the safety of the far side of the trolley, she asked, "All well Iris?" and Iris smiled magnanimously and answered, "As you see, Dorothy."

Dorothy seemed to dither. Then she blurted out, "Well,

sorry I can't stop. I have to dash. See you at the Centre," and she scuttled out.

"Your little crush is safe with me," Iris thought. She advanced to the counter when her turn came and beamed at Gerald. "Such a bundle of nerves," she said, "isn't she, poor Dorothy?"

"Ah," Gerald said, "um," and Iris, disappointed, wondered whether Gerald's quietness concealed the profundity she imagined.

After she had checked her books out, it occurred to her to take a quick look at the returns trolley and see what books Dorothy had just brought back. It was a bit nosy but it might be revealing; rather like snooping in someone's medicine cabinet to see what embarrassing ailments they secretly suffered from.

She was initially disappointed when she saw that the last book on the returns trolley was *Teach Yourself Russian*. Next to it was an equally dull-looking book about the Russian Orthodox Church but alongside that Iris saw *The Story of a Russian Princess* which looked more to her taste. It was a battered old volume, it had clearly been around for a good many years. She picked it up, flipped through it and added it to the books she had already checked out. It meant queueing up in front of Gerald again but she hardly minded that.

On her way home, she stopped at her local Indian shop to pass the time of day with Javed at the till. She didn't really need any shopping, she ate less and less these days but an encounter with Javed, his jokey backchat and his infinite eyelashes, always cheered her. So, after taking out the library books which she had no real intention of reading, she stepped into Fairprice Foods to buy a snack which she had no real intention of eating.

Javed greeted her. "Long time no see," and waggled his head enthusiastically.

Iris pretended to look guilty. "I'm afraid I've been unfaithful to you at Sainsbury's."

Javed reacted as if Iris had said something deeply shocking. His jaw dropped and he exclaimed, "Unfaithful? At Sainsbury's?" He looked aghast.

"I mean," Iris said laboriously, "I've been doing my shopping at Sainsbury's instead of coming in here. Naughty me."

Javed gave a shrill giggle. "I got that. Ooh, Mrs Bennett, what did you *think* I was thinking?" Mischievously, he put his forefinger to his pursed lips. He rolled his dark eyes at Iris suggestively and she felt ancient stirrings.

Coyly, she answered, "I've no idea what you were thinking Javed. At my age!"

Javed smiled ravishingly. "Age has nothing to do with it, Mrs Bennett. You're a lovely lady."

"Oh Javed," Iris scoffed but of course she was thrilled. For the price of a few Ritz crackers, he made her feel fully human again.

But a Polish workman in paint-splashed overalls stood behind Iris with two cans of beer and he looked in no mood to wait.

Iris paid for her purchase and promised Javed, "I won't leave it so long next time."

"You better not," Javed chided her. He gave her her change and winked extravagantly.

Then he turned to the Polish workman and, with chilling

rapidity, Iris noticed, his face became a mask of stony indifference. "Two forty," he snapped.

A day or two later, it was the day of the life story group, Iris remembered *The Story of a Russian Princess*. She had not much enjoyed the first session of the new term, being upstaged by Dorothy's exotic revelations. Iris enjoyed being the doyenne of the group, the oldest and without a doubt the grandest. But even if Dorothy was now a mere ex-librarian, her family background was inescapably grander than Iris's and that Iris found hard to forgive her. The Plumsteads were from Hendon which was all very well but there was no denying that Bayswater and Moscow trounced that.

Esther had annoyed her too. Only last week out of the blue Iris's cousin Joan had disconcertingly popped up in Esther's mother's story (not a person with whom Iris imagined she had anything in common). Joan's mother, Iris's Auntie Winnie, had been accused of making a racial remark involving cocktail sausages. Iris had spoken up in defence of her aunt who, she assured Esther, would never in a million years stoop to that sort of thing. Esther had looked knowing and said nothing.

Iris found *The Story of a Russian Princess* in the downstairs lavatory. She usually left her library books there so that Joanna and Nat couldn't fail to spot them. But she retrieved it and took it into the sitting room. She sat in her usual armchair and flipped through it half-heartedly, distracted by thoughts of the afternoon's session and the need to make another contribution soon herself. She wondered idly what had become of Renée and whether she had in fact died. She lingered over the book's black and white photographs with objects just like those in Dorothy's story – samovars and Fabergé eggs – along with tall, well-built people who looked nothing at all like mousy little Dorothy Woodward. She was especially drawn to one portrait photo of a handsome, somewhat fleshy man, with heavy lidded eyes and a full dark beard. Iris had always had a weakness for facial hair. She wondered if she might not dip into the book after all.

She turned back to the beginning and settled to read the opening lines: "I was born in a splendid mansion on the Sofiyskaya Embankment in Moscow. Our family home for many generations, it was an imposing three-storey stone building with an elegant front entrance and a façade adorned by tall windows supported by voluptuous caryatids."

Pearl

KAI CAME IN from college droning away to himself. From his earphones, Pearl could hear a dense battery of bass.

"You'll damage your hearing," she said loudly but Kai didn't hear.

He headed for the fridge and began to rummage around inside.

Pearl said louder, "You'll spoil your tea."

Obviously, Kai couldn't hear her.

She yelled, *"KAI!"* and he jumped, poor boy. He pulled out his earphones and asked, "What Nan?" As an afterthought, he flipped his hood off.

"I said you'll spoil your tea," Pearl said more quietly. "I'm making a nice casserole."

Kai said, "Sorry, I won't be here for tea, I'm going right out again."

He helped himself to the cheese and shut the fridge with theatrical care.

"You might have told me," Pearl said limply.

"Sorry," Kai said again. He set about making a baggy cheese and pickle sandwich directly on the kitchen table. Pearl considered saying, "Get a plate" but she couldn't be bothered.

Kai hadn't turned off his music which continued to thud

away from the earphones slung around his neck. To Pearl's ear, it barely sounded like music at all.

She gestured at the earphones. "What *is* that you're listening to?"

Kai suppressed a smile. "Nothing you'd have heard of."

"Yes but what *is* it?" Pearl persisted. "It sounds like someone digging up the road."

Kai grinned. "It's a weird American band. Death metal."

"Death metal?" Pearl repeated in horror. "What does that even mean?"

"It's kind of like heavy metal," Kai explained, "but more extreme."

Looking pleased with himself, he set about eating his enormous sandwich. The barrage of bass from the earphones still hanging round his neck suddenly stopped and gave way to a shrill squawking.

Pearl raised her eyebrows.

Kai laughed. Through a mouthful, he said, "It's a parrot."

"A *parrot*?"

"Yes, it's their thing. Their singer's a parrot. They're called Hatebeak."

Pearl felt the nasty knot of tension, which kept her shoulders permanently ratcheted up to the base of her neck, suddenly relax. The name of a band; why hadn't she thought of that? All those nights she had spent worrying what Kai was up to on the computer, what sort of trouble he might be getting himself into – it was all just *music*. Since the night, two or three months back, she had heard him ask somebody, "So d'you like Hatebeak then?" a range of nightmare possibilities had tormented her. Crime was the first thing you thought of if you were bringing up a boy on the estates. But she had also imagined a cult, some sort of nasty underground group or other which, while not exactly criminal, was not anything you would want any boy of yours mixed up in. Of course, above all, she dreaded drugs, drugs which had destroyed Tracy and which had threatened to destroy Kai before he was even born. She was so glad that Hatebeak was just a daft band that she laughed out loud.

Kai grinned back. She could tell he was pleased he had made her laugh. He took advantage of her good mood to stand up and swig directly from the milk carton in the fridge instead of pouring himself a glass.

Pearl murmured, "Kai," but she let it go.

Since he had started at the college, Kai had been so much happier and easier to get along with, she tried to turn a blind eye to the small stuff. He was always in and out now, no more lying around in bed, he seemed to have made new friends there too, he was always texting someone or other. At night, he slept. Pearl supposed that her own loneliness was a small price to pay for Kai's future.

Still, she could not resist asking, "Will you be home one night this week, d'you suppose? I really ought to do another recording for the group."

"Should be," Kai said, swallowing the last of his sandwich and standing up. "What's it gonna be about this time?"

Pearl thought. "My first memories, I suppose, the end of the War, VE Day, what little I remember of it, then just London after the War, us kids playing on the bomb sites, rationing, the winter of '47, chilblains, junior school, whooping cough, family stuff."

152

Kai paused. "It's not fair," he said, to her astonishment. "People your age got all the best stories. People my age, our life stories will be just rubbish." Before Pearl could come up with a decent answer, tell him just how grim her early years had been, he had left.

Since Renée had stopped coming, Pearl wasn't much enjoying the life story class. Somehow or other, Renée had felt like a friend. Without her, the group was just a bunch of odds and sods where Pearl felt hopelessly out of place. But she had paid for all three terms in one go because it was cheaper that way – whatever had got into her? – and now she was stuck. She kept hoping that Renée might come back although privately she thought it unlikely. She was convinced it was something in her recording which had made poor Renée go as white as a sheet and then run away – although what it might have been she hadn't a clue.

No one else agreed with her when she suggested this to the group. Sabine still thought it was low blood pressure, Esther thought maybe it was something she had eaten. But then none of them seemed to care what had become of Renée the way Pearl did. Dorothy worried aloud about her numbers; with Renée's departure, the group was down to six and the rule at the Second Chance Centre was that a class with fewer than six members got closed. Dorothy kept reminding them of this as January wore on and Renée didn't come back. Pearl thought that was quite wrong; pressuring people to stay on for Dorothy's sake. She did think about jacking it in – in spite of the money which she knew she wouldn't get back – but she had always set store by doing the right thing and staying on was obviously the right thing.

Besides there was always the faint hope that Renée might come back.

A few weeks into the new term, she stopped at the reception desk on her way out after class and asked for Renée Thorpe's phone number.

The girl told her, "Can't give out contact details I'm afraid. Data protection."

Pearl felt stupid for not having swapped numbers with Renée when she had the chance. Most probably she would never find her now.

When she and Kai finished their second recording, he seemed all fired up and wanted to ask her loads more questions. Pearl had given him the money to buy a better recorder. His phone wasn't really up to the job and besides, now he was at college, he needed it every minute of the day. He couldn't lend it to Pearl for a Thursday afternoon. He made a great fuss of positioning both Pearl and the recorder in the best possible place. He started the session by switching on the device and loudly going, "Testing, testing, testing one, two, three." Before she began, he announced, "The life story of Pearl Barter, part two. Sound recordist, Kai Barter."

Pearl didn't think she had said anything out of the ordinary. What she had talked about were any London child's memories of the late Forties. She was too young to remember the actual war, she could just about recall the celebrations on VE day but, apart from that, what she mainly remembered was hardship but that hardship seemed, somehow or other, thrilling to Kai.

"You got all the best stories," he repeated rancorously. "You had a war and stuff. All we got is shit."

"But Kai," Pearl protested, "you've got *opportunities*. We didn't have any opportunities. We just left school at sixteen and we had to do whatever rubbish jobs we could find. People like us didn't go to college back then. Things are *much* better for young people now. You just don't realize."

Kai frowned with the effort of formulating something extremely complex. "I'm not talking about food and stuff," he said. "Like I know it's better to have McDonald's and pizza and everything than rationing. But nothing *means* anything anymore, like there's no point? When you were my age, Nan, people didn't know yet the world was fucked, did they?"

Pearl said, "Pardon?" Although she swore a fair bit herself, she didn't like to hear Kai do it.

Kai said, "Like we're all going to die?"

Pearl considered her grandson. For the life of her, she couldn't see what he was on about. The idea that anyone should envy her childhood, let alone Kai, studying for his music practitioner diploma and saving for a holiday in Ibiza with his mates, made no sense at all to her. She shook her head. "I think you'll find that people live much better lives now Kai."

He said gloomily, "You don't get it."

"No," Pearl said, "I don't."

They glowered at each other. Then Pearl said something she regretted right away. "Well, next time you'll hear all about my stepdad," she said bitterly. "Just be thankful you never had to live with anyone like that."

It seemed they both winced. For neither one of them was allowed to mention Tracy but Pearl had just come perilously close.

155

Edgar

MADELEINE TOLD EDGAR she wanted him to meet her children. His heart plummeted; this would be the beginning of the end.

It was New Year's morning. 2013. They were lying in bed, enjoying their idleness and the unaccustomed fact that Madeleine did not have to rush off anywhere. They had both made an extra effort for this special night spent together; Edgar was wearing his best going-to hospital pyjamas and he had splashed on a quantity of cologne. Madeleine emerged from the bathroom in a deep blueygreen silky nightie Edgar had never seen before and she was wearing a particularly powerful scent. Edgar loved the smell of Madeleine without scent too but he would not have dreamt of saying anything. The quantity of mingled perfume in the small bedroom had been almost overwhelming the night before; it had made Edgar's head spin. But by morning it had worn off and everything smelt as it should. Lying there, Edgar knew he had never been happier – until Madeleine's simple sentence made icicles form in the room.

He knew that Madeleine's children, Luke and Desiree, did not approve of him. They weren't that happy about their mother having a sweetheart in the first place.

Selfish creatures. The fact that Edgar was old, white and not even well off had all been negatively commented on. How did Edgar know this? Madeleine had joked about it, reported snippets back to him as if they were innocently amusing. But, even though he didn't have children himself, Edgar well understood their destructive potential – perhaps *because* he didn't have children. He could just see how they might undermine your better judgement and make you do things which were wrong.

He took Madeleine's nearby hand in his and caressed it.

"Is that a good idea?" he asked.

Madeleine raised her eyebrows. "Whyever not?"

Edgar hesitated. Whatever he said, wherever he trod, something would give way. "Well," he ventured, "by the sound of it, I'm not all that popular with your children, am I?"

Madeleine tutted. Her tut was a powerful one she used to good effect. "Pay no attention," she chided him. "They just need reassuring, that's all. They need to see for themselves what sort of a man you really are."

Edgar wondered what sort of a man he really was.

"Maybe," he said cautiously, "they won't like what they see."

"Oh," Madeleine answered, "I doubt that very much. Their idea of you is way off."

"What's their idea of me?"

Madeleine looked uncomfortable. She looked as if she might say something but seemed to think better of it and decided to say something else instead. "It's to do with

157

their Dad leaving when they were so young," she explained. "They're mistrustful."

Edgar looked out of the window. So early on New Year's Day, the estate looked dead, with no one about. In the block across the way, almost all the curtains were still drawn. He wondered who else was having their life dismantled on New Year's morning.

"Well," he said and he suddenly felt sick, "if it matters to you Madeleine, of course I'll do it. But I'm really not sure it's wise, you know."

Madeleine looked at him. "I see where you're coming from," she said slowly, "but that road leads nowhere."

Edgar wondered what she meant. If not meeting Madeleine's children led nowhere, where would meeting them lead? As far as he was concerned, it would surely lead, in short order, to confrontation, unpleasantness and, down the line, disaster. He could not let that happen. Let him and Madeleine stay safe in their bubble – which he envisaged that New Year's morning as a small perspex snowdome – and not let anyone else inside.

It occurred to him that, as far as Madeleine was concerned, her children were already inside. He was thankful that he and Joan had had no children. He realised that, in Madeleine's case, having children sprang from her warm, generous, caring nature. But it was still a weakness; her children were her Achilles heel which would let her down.

Battling queasiness, he found he had agreed to come to Sunday lunch at Madeleine's the very next weekend. It overshadowed all the rest of the day and even though

Madeleine seemed very happy about this new development and sang full blast in the shower, Edgar's mood did not recover.

Since 1 January fell on a Tuesday that year, there were only four days before the dreaded lunch, four days Edgar spent in a state of fretful suspense. He missed Joan a good deal more than usual; nonsensical as it seemed, he would have welcomed her advice. All along, he had felt that his relationship with Madeleine had Joan's posthumous blessing. But now he was going to Madeleine's home, meeting her children – children Joan had never had – he was no longer so sure.

Wondering how Joan might have felt about things led his thoughts back to the mystery of the creative writing class, the class Joan was supposed to have attended throughout the last year of her life. He had tried to put it out of his mind over the holidays. Now the mystery came creeping back. He was fairly certain it was all just a mistake but if he assumed it was a mistake and did nothing more about it, then the mystery and uncertainty would continue to niggle him. He had no choice really but to admit the possibility that Joan might have hidden something from him in order to get to the bottom of it and put his mind at rest.

He had a sudden recollection of Joan's handwriting: small, neat and purposeful, advancing across the page in tidy lines. What on earth could Joan possibly have written in a creative writing class? He had only ever seen her handwriting in shopping lists, birthday cards or in her regular letters of complaint to Tesco, London Transport and Brent Council. The idea that Joan might have written something invented was absurd. She wouldn't have wasted her time on it.

He put off looking for a manuscript but by Friday, with only two days to go before the big lunch, he was in such a state he couldn't settle to anything and so he decided to have a look round.

Joan's sister Gilly had come and helped him with the miserable task of clearing out Joan's clothes and shoes a few months afterwards. He had offered Gilly to help herself to some of the nicer things but Gilly had asked him crossly if he had not noticed that she had a much fuller figure than Joan. The small cupboard in the front room where Joan kept her bits and pieces he had not touched.

Now, feeling as guilty as if he was accusing Joan of a transgression, Edgar opened the doors of the small cupboard. It had a key but it was unlocked. Everything inside was very tidy, as he would have expected and, sitting right at the top of the top pile, was a dark red exercise book. Edgar stared at it. Joan had left it there for him to find and he felt absolutely mortified that he had waited for six long years to look inside.

He couldn't bring himself to pick the notebook up. He felt so ashamed. This was what Joan must have meant when she used to accuse him of taking her for granted. It was not that he was not interested in what Joan got up to; he had simply assumed she didn't get up to anything. On the front cover of the exercise book she had written, in her careful writing, "Creative Writing, Autumn 2006" and underneath she had drawn a completely uncharacteristic fancy curlicue. Edgar sat and looked at the book. As well as feeling ashamed, he felt frightened. What secrets were in that little book? He surprised himself by shutting the cupboard. He locked it and took the key out too. There was only so much trouble he could handle in the one week.

Of course, when he wasn't thinking about the lunch, he thought about the exercise book and when he wasn't thinking about the exercise book, he thought about the lunch. Not for the first time, he had the feeling that Madeleine and Joan were ganging up on him. Drat the Second Chance Centre which had caused him nothing but trouble.

By Sunday morning, of course the lunch had the upper hand. He was up by six, washed and dressed by seven and he still had five hours before it was time to set out to Madeleine's. At eleven, he got out the exercise book. At least, he thought, it would take his mind off the lunch. He sat and held it for a while, thinking that Joan's hands had been the last to touch it. He imagined her putting it away in the cupboard, thinking Edgar would find it not long after she was gone. The exercise book – and whatever was in it – was like a message, maybe a gift but maybe not. He had let Joan down; he hadn't bothered to look in her cupboard. Now he had forsaken her, yes forsaken her for Madeleine Baxter. He felt so unworthy, he could barely bring himself to open the book. But, after a while, curiosity got the better of him and he decided to read just the beginning – of whatever it was.

The title, written out tidily on the first page and

161

underlined with a ruler, was "A Description of My Favourite Place". Edgar supposed it was homework. He read the first few lines apprehensively and his eyes filled with tears; Joan had written about Eastbourne where they had gone on their honeymoon. He didn't know whether or not it was well written but he liked her turns of phrase: "three miles of sea front, three miles of happiness" and, later on, "floral displays all the way along which looked like they had been put there just for us".

At the end of "My Favourite Place", which was a little over two pages long, Edgar stopped. He mustn't read any more. It was going to get him all worked up and he couldn't risk being late for Madeleine. Besides, there was clearly nothing to worry about here: no revelations, no dark secrets. He put the book tenderly back in the cupboard and locked it. A last little freshen-up in the bathroom and it would be time to leave for Madeleine's.

All the way on the bus – Madeleine lived up towards Neasden – he battled with his nerves. He told himself that he was 72 and Desiree and Luke only 18 and 20. Youngsters. He could surely get the better of them. But he imagined their stern young faces passing judgement on him and he knew he was bound to fall short. Madeleine had of course shown him pictures of her children. Even in their pictures, they seemed to look stern. Desiree was pretty but stern, Luke was just stern.

Edgar listened out carefully for the right stop and got down in the midst of grey tower blocks. Madeleine had warned him that where she lived was not nearly as nice as the Larkrise Estate. Edgar made his way between the grey blocks, following Madeleine's directions. He felt self-conscious with his big bouquet and his big box of chocolates. He had been unable to choose between chocolates and flowers so in the end he had splashed out on both. He hoped no one would try to relieve him of them.

Madeleine's block looked no different from any of the others. He cricked his neck, looking up to count to the tenth floor where her flat was. Her windows – if they were her windows – looked no different from anyone else's. He had somehow expected that they would. The entryphone was not working – as she had warned him. But while he was fumbling for his phone, which Madeleine made him always carry in case of emergencies, a woman wearing a big black headscarf came out and, after giving him a deeply suspicious look, let him in.

The lift smelt bad and it was a long way up to the tenth floor. Edgar didn't like the thought of Madeleine – *his* Madeleine, the light of his life – riding up and down every day in this nasty lift. When he got out at the tenth floor, he found four identical blank grey doors facing him which looked more like cupboard doors than front doors. He had to walk around and peer at the numbers on each one before he found Madeleine's. For a moment, he stood there and tried to compose himself. Then, with a shaking hand, he rang the bell.

As soon as he saw Madeleine's delighted face, he felt much better. They gave each other a restrained peck on the cheek and Madeleine drew him in. He handed over the flowers and the box of chocolates and she exclaimed, "Oh Edgar, you shouldn't have."

They stood close together in the narrow hallway, struggling with the flowers and the chocolates and hanging up Edgar's coat and hat. He could smell Madeleine's scent and something delicious cooking somewhere. It was only after a minute or two that, getting over the first excitement of seeing her, he became aware, through a doorway, of two figures standing watching them. He wondered if he had done wrong already by standing too close to Madeleine, by giving her a kiss. She sensed his hesitation and turned towards the doorway.

"Luke and Desiree," she instructed, "meet Edgar."

The two figures came forward, looking not stern but polite and both shook Edgar's hand. He noted that they had nice manners.

After that, they just stood there, a very tall, thin young man in sportswear and a pretty young woman with an eye-catching hairdo. Edgar realised that he had to say something, anything to prevent an awkward silence developing. He cleared his throat where a large lump seemed to be sitting and, desperately, he began, "Very pleased to meet you. Your mum's told me a lot about you both. She's very proud of you – as I'm sure you know."

In a surprisingly deep voice, Luke replied, "She's told us a lot about you too."

Desiree giggled.

Behind Edgar, Madeleine said, "Now Luke —"

"What?" Luke protested. "What did I say? You *have* told us a lot about him."

With an entirely false jollity, Edgar said, "Nothing too bad, I hope?"

Desiree said, "No, nothing bad, chill."

Madeleine joked, "I believe I may have mentioned that you don't always follow my healthy eating plan. And that you try to cut your classes at the centre."

Desiree chipped in, "Mum, you're so *bossy*."

"In a good cause," Edgar said hastily, "in a good cause. Who knows where I might be if your Mum hadn't given me a good talking to one day?"

"It's nice someone appreciates my good advice," Madeleine said pointedly to her children. "Edgar likes a home-cooked meal you know. He doesn't live off Subway and McDonald's."

Desiree rolled her eyes.

Luke said, "Talking of food —"

"Ok," Madeleine said, "ok. We all know you're starving and you've got football later. Take care of Edgar while I finish the lunch."

"I'll help," Desiree said eagerly.

Madeleine gave her a hard look. "For once you offer, I'll say no," she said. "Please stay and be with Edgar."

Desiree muttered something Edgar didn't catch. She tossed her extravagant hairdo. Edgar wondered if it was all her own hair. But she drew out a chair from the table which was beautifully laid for four and said politely, "Here, have a seat."

Edgar sat down gladly, his legs were shaking and Luke sat down to one side of him. Desiree still hung around in the kitchen doorway as if she might yet make her escape.

"So," Edgar said heavily to Luke, "you are studying business management, I gather? How's that going?"

Luke said, "Ok."

Maybe he saw the despair in Edgar's eyes. He added, "I liked the first year best when I lived in halls. Now I'm back living at home, it's not that great to be honest."

None of that made much sense to Edgar but he nodded sagely as if it did. "How far d'you have to go for your classes?"

Luke smiled. "That's not really the problem."

Desiree began, "It's his —" but was silenced by a roar from her brother. She retreated into the kitchen.

Edgar and Luke sat together in silence, fidgetting.

Madeleine emerged from the kitchen in the nick of time, bearing an enormous pan, followed by Desiree carrying a smaller one.

"Chicken with rice and beans," she announced, depositing her pan on the table. She turned back to the kitchen, adding cheerfully, "with some lovely greens of course."

Once they were all four sitting around the table eating, with Madeleine comfortably in charge, things started to feel a little easier. It dawned on Edgar that Luke and Desiree were, in their own way, probably just as nervous as he was. Meeting your Mum's new boyfriend was a big deal. Of course Edgar was far too old to be called a boyfriend but still the idea that Luke and Desiree might think of him as Madeleine's boyfriend cheered him no end. He smiled expansively at them and said, "Your mother is a wonderful cook."

Madeleine said, "Desiree doesn't think so." She pouted.

Edgar turned to Desiree in astonishment. "Whyever not?"

Madeleine said, "She only likes junk food, that one: burger, pizza, chips."

Crossly, Desiree said, "That's not junk food."

Edgar looked from one to the other. Loyally, he said, "Give me Madeleine's cooking over a burger any day."

Luke, in his surprisingly deep voice, added, "Me too." He had, astonishingly, already cleared his plate and was waiting, hungrily but politely, for seconds.

Desiree glowered at her brother. "You go McDonald's and KFC too. You know you do."

"Not when I'm training," Luke said smugly.

"Yeah but when you're *not*. I seen you and your mates with Bargain Buckets and Krush'ems."

"That was ages ago," Luke said. "Now I'm eating healthy and drinking energy drinks."

"*Not* ages ago —" Desiree began but Madeleine silenced her.

"Edgar did not come over to listen to you two fighting."

Desiree and Luke looked sheepish, Edgar took in the view.

Madeleine said to Edgar, "I been telling them about your time in menswear and all your stories."

Edgar wondered whether Luke and Desiree would enjoy his stories. For their generation, everything was so open, what was that expression they used, "in your face". Would they even find Edgar's stories about what went on in the fitting room funny?

"Oh, I don't want to bore them," he said.

Madeleine looked disappointed. "Your stories aren't boring, Edgar." She looked at him expectantly.

Edgar cleared his throat. "Well," he said apologetically to Luke and Desiree, "if your mother insists —"

He embarked on one of his familiar repertoire: the short little chap who came in, tried on every overcoat in the store and then complained to Edgar that he didn't look tall enough in any of them. His girlfriend was six foot, he said and he needed a coat which would make him tall.

As he told the familiar tale, he began to feel a little more confident. Luke and Desiree were definitely listening to him and they didn't look bored. At the punchline, they both smiled.

"Tell us another," Madeleine said, fondly.

"Only short please," Luke said, "cos I've got to go to football."

Edgar took a drink of water. Against all the odds, he could feel himself getting into his stride. "Set your stopwatch," he said to Luke, "this one takes all of three minutes."

As he embarked on the story of the good-looking young man who had come in one day to buy a three-piece suit but, glimpsed through the fitting room curtains, had turned out to be a young woman, he felt an entirely unexpected sensation; he was happy. Madeleine and her children were looking at him and listening to him. Maybe Luke and Desiree hadn't warmed to him yet but they hadn't rejected him outright either. Maybe he was in with a chance here after all? If he played his cards right, if he didn't put a foot wrong, maybe, just maybe Luke and Desiree might take to him? They laughed when he came to the final twist of his story and Desiree asked, "Did stuff like that happen a lot?"

Edgar sat back in his chair. He glanced at Madeleine and she was smiling at him affectionately. She leant forward and took advantage of the fact he was starting a new story to put a large dollop of greens on his plate. Luke and Desiree had stopped looking polite. In fact, glancing around the table, it seemed to Edgar, for a brief glad moment, that everyone was enjoying themselves.

On the bus on the way home, he knew it had gone well. He had stayed until after dark, Luke had long left for his football and Desiree had melted away. He and Madeleine sat comfortably on the sofa and talked about this and that. It felt as if he had already spent many Sunday afternoons there. As he sat on the slow bus carrying him back to Brondesbury, he thought how very fortunate it was that he had not taken the road which led nowhere.

Esther

IT IS HARD to remember now how drab and horrible and depressing London was in those post-War years. There had been the Blitz, all over the place there were bomb sites, people were tired and worn out and fed up. Soon I would start senior school but no one cared about young people having fun and making the most of their youth the way they all do now. Everyone just wanted you to grow up as quickly as possible and bring home a pay packet. It seemed to us school was just something to be got through. There was no sense that learning could be fun or worthwhile in its own right. You just sat in the classroom and waited to be sixteen for it to be over. For girls like me there was no question of staying on at school, let alone university. It was straight into the first job you could find and then marriage, hopefully to someone your parents aproved of. We didn't have the choices our daughters had and, truth to tell, when their time came we were jealous of them.

Now visions of horror rise up and overwhelm me. I am sitting in the cinema but I am choking, suffocating. What I see on the screen takes my breath away. It is too terrible to be believed except it is true. I am sitting in the cinema with my Mum and Dad and we are watching the Pathé newsreel about the concentration camps. There are piles and piles of dead people, all stacked higeldy-pigeldy together like dry sticks for a bonfire but the dry sticks are skeleton arms and legs. The camera waits long enough for the audience to take in this horror before it moves on to something even worse. Not far away there is a crowd of skeletons with the same dry sticks for arms and legs and skulls for faces but these skeletons are *alive*. They are standing behind a barbed wire fence looking out and they have no expression on their faces. Perhaps this is the scariest thing of all. They are still (just) alive but in a way they are already dead inside. Their eyes look out at us, sitting in the Odeon cinema in Hendon on those prickly dark red plush seats, grumbling about rationing and chilblains and we feel terrible. We feel terrible and at the same time we feel sick. The commentator's voice is telling us these living dead people are Jewish, this is what the Nazis did to them – and also to Gypsies and other people they wanted to get rid of – and we understand that, if things had turned out differently, that would have been us.

That would have been *us*. We go home silently, not a word of comfort for me from Mum and Dad, they are as shocked and horrified as I am. Mum unlocks our solid, safe front door, we hang up our warm coats, still no one says anything. Finally Mum says, "Tea anyone?" And Dad barks at her. "Tea? Tea Rachel? Is that the best you can come out with?"

I say goodnight to my parents and I go to bed without tea. But I can't sleep. After a long time, I get up

171

and tiptoe downstairs. I am a big girl now, I think ten or eleven and I have no business getting up at night because I'm scared. My parents are still sitting in the lounge, talking in quiet voices. I creep to the door, not really intending to eavesdrop but ashamed of being up in the night like a baby.

I hear my father say, "I suppose they wouldn't have taken Rita."

"Don't," my Mum says. "Don't."

I can hear her voice is shaky. I wait, not understanding what I am hearing. Who wouldn't have taken me? Are they still talking about the Pathé News? Do they mean the Nazis? Why wouldn't they have taken me? They took everyone, it said so in the film, even babies and small children. There was no earthly reason why they would spare a ten-year-old girl. Unless – I start to feel faint – unless she wasn't actually Jewish? Unless she *wasn't actually her parents' child*? I step into the lounge and drop down in a dead faint.

When I come round, my parents are kneeling over me. They are beside themselves which takes them both differently. My father is furious, scolding me even as I'm laying flat on the floor for creeping around eavesdropping on people and my Mum looks ready to keel over herself from the upset. I realise I can't do this to her. Even though I'm desprate to ask my question, I know I can't do it. Mum is terrified that if I find out the truth, I will stop loving her the way I do, I will want to go off searching for my "real" mother. She clutches at me, she is crying, "Rita, Rita, come back to me."

172

Gradually I come round. Dad brings me a glass of water and tells me off some more. Mum is white and shaking and doesn't say anything at all. No one says anything about what I overheard which made me faint. My parents carry on doing what they are aparently very good at – pretending.

But for me life is never going to be the same again. Even though part of me still believes it is a story I have made up, I start to imagine that I am adopted. There, I've said it now – adopted, the word my parents didn't dare say. I was at the age when you begin to think that your parents are strange anyway so this new idea that I was maybe adopted made perfect sense to me.

To start off with, I kept it to myself. I thought about it a lot, especially at night, going over and over my past and guessing at all the pointers and signs I might have missed. But eventually the story was too good to keep to myself.

My memories of secondary school are a mixed bag. I had lost my darling May because she went to private school and of course I went to state. She soon forgot all about me for her posh new friends and doubtless both our mothers breathed a sigh of relief. I became part of a tight little threesome with Shirley Palmer and Valerie Pratt. Two of us were always ganging up on the third. It went on right through our teens. I'm not saying I was always the odd one out but when it was me, the teasing took a particular nasty turn.

One day when Shirley and Valerie were ganging up on me, talking about what they wanted for Christmas or some such and Valerie said to me in a spiteful way, "Rita, you wouldn't understand," I said to her mysteriously, "Well actually *you're* the one who doesn't understand."

"Oh yes?" Valerie huffed. "What don't I understand then?"

For just one tiny second I hesitated and then I lept. "Actually I'm just pretend Jewish, you know. I'm adopted."

Both of them gaped at me.

"You've just made that up," Shirley said, "because you want Christmas presents too."

"That's not true!" I protested. "I won't get Christmas presents anyway because my Mum and Dad don't believe in it – even though really by rights I *should* get them."

Shirley and Valerie looked at me pityingly. Then Shirley said, "Well we could give you *secret* Christmas presents couldn't we? Your Mum and Dad need never know."

So that was what we did. From then on, I got secret Christmas presents, secret Easter eggs and even, I'm sorry to say, secret ham sandwiches. Even though I felt ever so guilty, I loved it too. But the strange thing was that all the while, deep down, I never completely believed it. I still thought it was most probably a story I had made up. Because after all I so didn't want it to be true. Even if it meant I would have been taken too. I would far rather have been taken, along with Mum and Dad, than spared all by myself.

Dorothy

DOROTHY SUPPOSED THAT her nightmares were a small price to pay for the delight of creating a totally new past for herself. They had started straight after she read her first chapter to the group and they continued to plague her. It was as if her real parents, banished from the record, were trying to reclaim their unfaithful daughter in her sleep.

Car headlights spun across the ceiling of the shoebox flat. Outside on the A312, which even fifty years ago had been a busy road, other people were driving away. Perhaps they were fleeing their horrible homes in Northolt at dead of night. Perhaps they were heading down to Heathrow to catch early flights, to escape. Only Dorothy was stuck in her tiny bedroom between her crazy mother and her late lamented father. Every night she would lie there and watch the headlights freewheeling past, she would listen to the never ending traffic noise which muted her mother's cries and hate her entire life.

In the nightmares, her mother's frightened voice called out, "Be careful, watch out, don't Dorothy, don't." Their windows had grilles, their front door had two chains. The flat was a prison, a prison created by her mother to keep them safe. But of course they could never really be safe because the world was such a constantly dangerous place. Wherever you went, whoever you spoke to, people were out to get you, trick you, trap you and the only way you could keep one step ahead of them was round the clock vigilance. Now Tilly came wailing back into Dorothy's nightmares: the bus conductor was a pervert, sit by the window, not the aisle, you couldn't trust the greengrocer who was a cheat and worst, worst of all, their landlord was having deadly dangerous air vents installed. He said they were for ventilation but she knew, Tilly knew they were in actual fact to secretly pump sleeping gas into the flat and, while they were unconscious, rape and murder them both.

Dorothy would wake with Tilly's cries of doom still ringing in her ears after all these years. It took her a good while to recover. For of course she blamed Tilly. It was Tilly's fault that Dorothy had led such a limited life. She consoled herself with her magnificent make-believe childhood. Tilly and Late Lamented couldn't get their hands on that.

Dorothy had to wait two or three weeks before reading her next instalment; it was only fair. At the beginning of the January term, Enid had come up with one of her ideas.

"I want to talk about the long lost stationery of my childhood," she had announced one Thursday afternoon. It was after Sabine but before Esther. Without further ado, she had launched into a long lament for all the vanished items of stationery she apparently so sorely missed.

"Who remembers fountain pens?" She began. She produced an old marbled blue one from her pocket and passed it round. "Osmiroid 65," she declared. "Open it. Listen to the noise as you unscrew it, uncorking the power of the pen. See that once golden nib? Remember the way it scratched the paper, literally gouging out your words? And when you opened up the pen to fill it, remember the squeezy rubber bladder inside which filled

176

up with ink? See the little lever in the side which never quite did the job? Remember that sucking noise as the pen drew up the ink? Remember the ink! Quink in handsome dark blue bottles. Handle with care! Remember your worst ever ink stains?"

When Enid's pen reached Dorothy, she saw it was extremely chewed. She passed it quickly on.

"Blotting paper!" Enid continued, waving a folded piece of something very stained. "Kids nowadays don't even know what blotting paper *is*. But blotting paper taught us so much, didn't it? Forget the nasty pink colour, I dare say no such colour exists in nature. Remember all the stuff you found out from blotting paper? The answers to sums, test questions, those supposedly secret messages blotted for all to read. I learnt that my mother, who I thought was dead, was actually alive from a sheet of blotting paper. Of which more later. And what about glue? They think glue sniffing is a modern thing. Well, let me tell you, I was sniffing glue before there was even a name for it. And rubbers – where do I start? An unfortunate name," she cackled, "but what a delight for schoolkids; you could squeeze them, chew them, deface them, demolish them."

It had gone on and on. Even though Dorothy had been put out at first, felt her group had been hijacked, the fact of the matter was everyone had loved it. Esther had said, "Ooh can I do sweets next?" and Sabine had clasped her hands and exclaimed to everyone's surprise, "Lingerie!" The ode to long lost things had become a regular feature and, while Dorothy didn't object to it on principle – she thought she might have talked about her favourite patent medicines – it did take up a fair bit of every session.

Of course the life story group did not by any means fill the huge hole left in Dorothy's life by the library. One especially grey January day, she decided to take the bus along to Mercy House just to have a look at it. She knew it would upset her but she missed the place so much she couldn't resist it. The ugly Second Chance Centre, with its bossy notices and its smells, was no match for the elegance and atmosphere of Mercy House.

She regretted her decision as soon as she got on the bus where everyone seemed to be suffering from heavy colds. The bus resounded with coughing and sneezing and Dorothy feared she was bound to catch something.

When she got to the entrance to the grounds, she was taken aback to see a big shiny hoarding had gone up there. "Mercy House," it read, above a lot of pictures of ultra-modern kitchens and bathrooms, "country living in NW6." Dorothy hurried forward. They were converting Mercy House into flats; she couldn't believe it. Philistines with ultra-modern kitchens and bathrooms, who probably never ever read a *book*, were going to take possession of Mercy House. Her palpitations were so strong she thought she might not make it up the drive.

As she rounded the bend, the dear, familiar old bend she had rounded so many times before, she stopped dead. For an instant, she simply couldn't take in what she was seeing; it must be some sort of optical illusion, a hallucination. Mercy House wasn't there. It had gone and in its' place there was only vacant sky and mud.

Dorothy cried out. She stood frozen in shock in the driveway and stared at the ghastly scene. Mercy House had not only been demolished, its remains had apparently been carted away too. In front of her, there was just a great gaping muddy hole in the middle of the ruined gardens.

Dorothy could not understand how this could have

happened without her knowing anything about it. Why hadn't Gerald or one of the other librarians told her? Why hadn't it been in the papers? How could something like this just happen incidentally – *as if it didn't matter?*

Sobbing, she stumbled back down the gravel drive, now deeply rutted by all the lorries and caught another bus to Gerald's library. She was crying uncontrollably, she didn't care who coughed or sneezed on her now, she may as well catch pneumonia and be done with it.

Gerald looked alarmed at Dorothy's sudden distraught appearance. But when he heard what she was so upset about, he raised his eyebrows. "Didn't you know?" he asked. "How come you didn't know?"

"How was I supposed to know?" Dorothy said indignantly. "No one told me anything."

"Well, *we* all knew," Gerald said. Dorothy thought he sounded distinctly smug. "We've known about it for *months*. We've talked about it a lot."

"Well, how come you didn't tell me?" Dorothy demanded.

Gerald opened his pastoral hands in a gesture of helplessness. "I assumed you knew," he answered. "I didn't want to upset you by mentioning it. It's been common knowledge round here for a long time. You have been rather out of the loop you know."

Dorothy gave him a hard look. Was that a reproach for not having joined his team of inter-faith do-gooders?

"I've been busy Gerald," she said. "I have new responsibilities now. I do think you might have told me."

Gerald said, "Well I had no idea you didn't know. Of course if I'd known —" He hesitated but seemed to find enlightenment.

"We're having a prayer meeting later. Would you like to join us?"

Dorothy coldly turned down the offer of the prayer meeting. She went straight home. Her shock and grief were turning to rage. How dare they, how *dare* they demolish her past? Not only hers of course: poor Pam and Parvaneh (a refugee from tyranny and oppression) had found solace during their long peaceful years at Mercy House. What about all her library users: the faithful few and then the homeless men who came in from the rain? How could they just destroy a building which meant so much and sweep the whole thing away? As she waited at the bus stop, she wondered at what point she and everyone like her had become left-over people.

Nothing could restore Mercy House of course. The shocking, barbarian act of destruction would stay with her forever. But, she resolved, it would not go unpunished. Giving Christopher, who accosted her in the front hall, the brush-off, she hurried into her flat. Without even stopping for a cup of tea, she shrugged off her coat and went to get the notebook in which she had been writing her Russian childhood memoir.

Why stop at childhood? There were only a couple of chapters more she could manage before she ran out of material. But why not carry on? Not a made-up life this time but the *truth*. On the surface, twenty-seven years working as a librarian at Mercy House might seem unexciting. But she knew things which no one else did. There had been all sorts of goings-on at Mercy House over the years which had been hushed up: things left for collection in the letter box, the building secretly used as a company address by all sorts of shady characters, rooms used at night for dirty deeds. Dorothy had turned a blind eye, not wanted to get herself into trouble. But now she found she didn't care anymore. The same high-ups who had let Mercy House be used for all sorts of illicit activities while it still stood had let it be demolished without turning a hair. They had doubtless profited from the deal in some way too and they thought they had got away with it. Well, Dorothy would see to it that they didn't. Despite Tilly's frantic cries of warning in the background, Dorothy decided she would write the secret history of Mercy House. When word got out, heads would roll. People who callously demolished other people's pasts did not deserve a happy ending.

Sabine

4. The Art Class

WHEN SHE WAS six years old, Sabine started school. She went to a local primary school, the charmingly named Ecole du Bois Joli which was at the edge of the forest, an energetic walk away in every weather. What she experienced at school was not so charming. She was not an enthusiastic student and while she certainly did not dare disgrace the doctor with bad marks, she was never top of the class in any subject either. That was Laurent and Charles's role – competing for top place in maths and science and physical education. Sabine preferred to draw and paint and make lovely objects with her hands. There was no opportunity to do that at school in Belgium in the 1950s. The education was very traditional: reading, writing, spelling, maths and in the higher classes the plague of obligatory Flemish lessons which all the children hated. The Flemish teacher, Mr Dierckx, was particularly mean. He had a small straight moustache like a toothbrush – or like a hated leader whose name one did not then like to mention. He did not shout when he grew angry, like certain teachers, he governed the children with a cold cruelty. He knew these snobbish French-speaking brats of Woluwé Saint Pierre scorned his mother tongue and he would take his revenge on them with constant tests and punishments.

One other thing Sabine did not like at school was the lunches. It was considered very important for all children to have a proper hot meal at lunchtime with two or three courses. This was so different from London now when children may freely go to school with a lunch box full of jam sandwiches, crisps, chocolate and the revolting cheese strings. The meal had to be nutritious and it had to be Belgian but I do not think it was written anywhere that it had to be delicious. How Sabine hated those school lunches. The school cooks served unappetising pots of lumpy *stoemp*, a stew of mashed potatoes and mashed vegetables garnished with a little meat, bitter boiled endives, the Belgians' favourite vegetable, wrapped in slices of pink ham and vol-au-vents filled with a gluey sauce in which were found certain soft objects unidentifiable even when chewed. Some days Sabine would eat so little of her lunch, the lunchtime supervisor would tell her off and she would have to pretend she had a stomach ache. Then she would be so very hungry in her class for all the afternoon.

Sabine liked really only three things at school: the company of her friends Annick, Josette and Geneviève, the absence of her brothers who, being eight years older, were already in secondary school and, best of all, Wednesday afternoons.

On Wednesday afternoons there is no school in Belgium. The children were supposed to spend their free time doing activities like swimming or music which they did not study in school. For the first year or so, Sabine attended swimming lessons at a local pool. The instructor, who was called Monsieur Cedric, was eighty years old. Although small and thin with bowed legs, Monsieur Cedric was very fit and healthy, which he attributed to the fact that he swam in the River Meuse every day summer and winter and regularly rode up to Brussels by bicycle to give his swimming lessons.

Once she had finally learnt to swim to Monsieur Cedric's satisfaction, Sabine asked if she could go to an art class on Wednesday afternoons instead. Her friend Josette already went there and told her wonderful tales about the class. Dr Mertens preferred Sabine to persevere with sport but her mother contradicted him, a very rare occurrence, and insisted that Sabine must go to the art class. Unusually she triumphed and Sabine was allowed to go.

From then on, Sabine spent all her Wednesday afternoons at the house of an artistic neighbour, Madame Hortense d'Hennezel. Madame d'Hennezel lived in one of the oldest, most curious houses in the neighbourhood. It looked like a romantic castle although it had actually been built around 1900 and was a complete fake. The children naturally did not realize this, they believed that Madame d'Hennezel's house really was an old castle and this was one of the many reasons they loved to go there. The house looked older than it really was also because it was so neglected. It had two high gates which gave onto the street, they were always open and one of them hung at a perilous angle. Like the house, the big gates were overgrown with vegetation.

The castle was built sideways on the land so that through the gates you saw only the end with a tall ornamental turret and practically no windows. You had to walk along a short driveway which turned around the house to stand before the elegant front door. It had two staircases going up to it, one to each side, what we call in French a *perron*.

The children did of course not go in through the elegant front door. They walked along the path to the other end of the house where Madame d'Hennezel greeted them at the kitchen door.

It was only many years after these art classes that we learnt the true story of Madame d'Hennezel. She had inherited the house from her grandfather but no fortune to maintain it. Her husband had been killed right at the beginning of the War in the German offensive, leaving her with two school-age children to raise in that extravagant house. She did not abandon the house, she took in paying guests which apparently provoked much gossip in the neighbourhood. People were scandalized that someone with an aristocratic name who lived in such a big house should take paying guests. You would have thought that during the War they had more important things to talk about. But it was only many years later when Madame d'Hennezel died and she was written about in the newspaper that people discovered the truth. Madame d'Hennezel was in the Resistance, a real heroine, her tenants were all kinds of brave people too but they were only a distraction. Unknown to everyone, for two years, Madame d'Hennezel had hidden a number of Jews in a secret part of the cellar of her fantastic castle. In the post-War decades, people did not talk about those things, perhaps because so many of them were ashamed of what they had done – or maybe not done. Today of course each one is a hero.

Madame d'Hennezel would greet the children enthusiastically every Wednesday afternoon, *"Bonjour les artistes!"* She was a tall woman with wild, auburn hair unsuccessfully maintained in a chignon with combs which fell all the time. She was very thin and she gesticulated continually with her long fine hands. To the children, her clothes and shoes looked as if they came out of a museum. Probably she had not had enough money to buy new clothes for decades. In that epoch, bourgeois Belgian women all dressed very conventionally, certainly all the children's mothers did and Madame d'Hennezel's strange appearance was also something they loved.

But the most powerful attraction of Sabine's Wednesday afternoons was of course the art class itself. I do not think that Madame d'Hennezel was a professional artist but she had studied at art school and she possessed a passionate love of art which inspired the children. She treated them like real artists: when they were ready to paint with oils, they had easels and proper canvases stretched tight on wooden frames. To start with, they would draw sketches on sugar paper with sticks of real charcoal. Everything was authentic, you could almost say professional. She had nicknames for all of them according to their different styles and influences: Josette was *Mademoiselle Picasso*, Sabine was *Mademoiselle Monet*. So, as well as teaching the children to draw and paint, she educated them also about the great artists.

The classes took place in her kitchen, an immense, old-fashioned, very untidy space. The floor was of big old stone tiles so it did not matter what paints or oils the children spilled there. To add to the chaos, Madame d'Hennezel's old dog who was half blind would walk about, bumping into things, knocking things over and occasionally annoying her temperamental cat who would leap up offended, hissing angrily and take refuge on a windowsill or next to the sink where the children washed their brushes.

The children all felt comfortable in Madame d'Hennezel's chaotic kitchen because they knew, so long as they worked seriously, they would never get into trouble there. They might spill something, mess something up, they might hate their drawing and crumple it up and throw it on the floor, Madame d'Hennezel would never tell them off.

She talked to the children constantly, walking about the kitchen, commenting and instructing them about their work. She would explain to them about the colour spectrum, about light and darkness. She would tell them stories about famous artists and how they created their great works. Sometimes, as time passed and the children grew more confident, they might talk about other things too. A boy might volunteer that his father was brutal, a girl might say that she believed her mother preferred her prettier younger sister or another girl might confide that she was frightened of her big brothers' nasty games. Madame d'Hennezel listened gravely to each one, consoled and offered wise words. Of course, in most cases, she could do nothing but the children knew at least that they were listened to, that Madame d'Hennezel knew and cared about their troubles.

Every week Madame d'Hennezel would provide a new attraction for them. One week there was a special brown ink she prepared with crushed walnuts from the tree in her garden. The children learnt to draw nature in her own colours. Another time they arrived to discover a tray of three-day-old chickens in the middle of the kitchen floor. (That day, the cat and the dog were shut outside.) They had to try and quickly draw the little balls of yellow fluff, always moving, never still. One magic Wednesday afternoon, they discovered that the temperamental cat had had kittens. She was lying proudly on her side in a big comfortable basket, which actually belonged to the dog, with six minuscule kittens suckling at her abdomen. The children, thrilled, were allowed to choose names for them and then they had to sit in a semicircle and draw the proud cat and her kittens.

At the end of each school year, Madame d'Hennezel held an exhibition of the children's best work. This took place in one of the grand rooms of the castle where normally the children were not allowed to go. Their works were displayed on special big boards all around the room. It looked like a real professional show. On the first evening, the children's parents were invited to the *vernissage* (opening party). Sabine's mother always came and admired her work. Unfortunately, her father had his consultations at that hour. Laurent and Charles never came. Do I need to add that the final pleasure of Sabine's Wednesday afternoons was that Laurent and Charles would never dream of coming to an art class?

Pearl

PEARL COULD HEAR Mavis coughing inside before she opened the front door. Mavis's smoker's cough had been an old friend nearly as long as Mavis. Pearl nagged her about giving up, year in, year out and got nowhere. Mavis without her fags would not be Mavis.

She opened the door, coughing and beckoned Pearl in while she got her breath back.

"So you've still not tried the e-cigs then?" Pearl said tartly, shutting the door behind her.

Mavis grimaced. She spluttered, "Don't start."

Pearl followed her into the kitchen. The smoky fug in Mavis's little flat seemed worse than ever. Without asking, Pearl opened the kitchen window a fraction and, behind her, Mavis laughed throatily. "You don't let up, do you?"

She made the tea and they sat as usual at the kitchen table. On the radio there was a talk show, a posh plummy voice saying that what the people of London really needed was a more imaginative range of transport options. Mavis said, "Fuck off Boris" and switched the radio off. She took a swig of her tea and said to Pearl, "So tell me."

Pearl and Mavis had met at the school gates: Tracy and Matt's first day, nearly thirty years ago now. Their kids were the ones who didn't want to start school, young for their year and shy. That had been a bond. They had got chatting and soon enough they had worked out that they could manage their lives much better if they took turns to mind both the children. Tracy and Matt didn't get on particularly well but that was tough luck. They had kept it up the whole way through the junior school, sometimes with another Mum, Cheryl, joining in too. Whatever had happened to Cheryl? They joked that they were like a married couple; taking it in turns to mind the kids while the other one went out to work. That was of course another bond; they neither of them had a husband. Or rather, they had both had husbands originally – and weddings and everything. After all, it was the Sixties, people still got married back then. But by the time Tracy and Matt were old enough to start school, they had both parted company from theirs. They made a joke of it even though it wasn't funny really. It wasn't funny at all.

Matt's Dad had gone back to Jamaica to visit his family there when Matt was no more than a year old and he had never returned. Pearl had thrown Tracy's Dad out when she discovered he was carrying on with a girl at work, had been the whole way through and she never mentioned him ever again. But she and Mavis had both been raised in the school of hard knocks, they were tough and they had just got on with things.

When Tracy and Matt went to secondary school, of course they could come home on their own. They didn't need minding anymore. But Mavis and Pearl stayed good friends. As the years went by, they shared new bonds; neither of their children gave them an easy time of it. That early reluctance to go to school turned into the worst of teenage troubles. Tracy went off the rails completely, dropped out of school, started messing with drugs, had Kai when she was eighteen. Through it all, Mavis was Pearl's shoulder to cry on. Not that Pearl cried much; she felt she had run out of tears early on.

Mavis had her own sorrows too. You could only ask for so much sympathy from someone who had Matt as a son. He had always been a bit strange, Matt. You couldn't quite put your finger on it but there was definitely something not quite right about him. Still, he had finished school, started an apprenticeship, he might have done well for himself. But, God knows why, he had fallen in with some funny people who had maybe taken advantage of him. He started hanging around the mosque and converted to Islam. First, he grew a big beard, then he started going round in robes. Then, because Mavis wasn't having any of it, he wouldn't have anything more to do with Mavis. He changed his name and disappeared. He dropped out of her life. Mavis repeated bitterly he might as well be dead although, after Tracy, of course she stopped saying that. So that was another bond.

Nowadays, living so close by on the Larkrise Estate, they saw each other most weeks and they had conversations which ran on from one week to the next.

"So tell me," Mavis said to Pearl. "How did it go?"

Pearl shrugged. "Everyone's got *something* in their life you know. So when I told them my stepdad took a strap to me, they weren't that shocked. I mean, they haven't all of them come out with it yet. But that Belgian woman, I bet you something nasty happened to her. And Esther, the Jewish one, she's damaged goods. And the art teacher, talking about body parts and drawing her parents without heads – well, heaven help us."

Mavis laughed and it turned into another fit of coughing. She loved hearing about the life story group even though she firmly resisted Pearl's attempts to get her to come along and take Renée's place.

"Of course," Pearl said, "some of them pretend nothing bad's ever happened to them, they've had these perfect lives, tra-la-la but there's no way that could possibly be true, could it?"

"No," Mavis agreed.

They drank their tea in silence for a minute.

Mavis asked, "How's Kai doing?"

Pearl smiled. Quickly, she tried not to look too pleased with herself. "So far, so good," she said but couldn't resist adding, "he did well in his exam."

Mavis looked impressed; a child doing well in an exam was a novelty for both of them. "What's he planning to do when he finishes college?" she asked. "Does he have any idea?"

Pearl shook her head. "Just let him get through it," she said.

As that thought led directly to Tracy who hadn't even finished school and to Matt who had given up on his apprenticeship, she changed the subject quickly. "I still keep thinking all the time about that Renée," she said. "It really bugs me; *why* did she run off like that? And how do I go about finding her?"

Mavis looked at her intently through the smoke of another newly lit cigarette. "What's it to you?" she asked sourly. "Why d'you *want* to find her? She's just some posh woman you met at a club."

Pearl corrected her, "A class, not a club."

She supposed Mavis was jealous, didn't like the thought of Pearl having a new friend. Really, the pair of them were just like an old married couple.

She thought. "In one way, you're right of course but she didn't *feel* like just some posh woman. I mean, I know I barely know her but she felt like a friend."

Mavis raised her eyebrows. Pearl expected her to come out with something sharp but she didn't. "The day she did a runner," she asked, "what was it you told them?"

Pearl said, "It was just the beginning: about my Mum and Dad and how he ran off and left her with a baby in the middle of the war."

Mavis thought for a bit, inhaling as if she might get inspiration from the smoke. "Perhaps she had the same thing happen to her?" she suggested.

"Could be," Pearl said slowly. "But why would that make you run away? Wouldn't you want to stick around and tell everyone your story too?"

"Oh I don't know," Mavis said impatiently. "Maybe she had the runs."

Pearl knew when to shut up. The truth was in the end she had come up with an idea why Renée Thorpe might have vanished. But it was a crazy idea, she knew it, so unlikely, so fanciful that she didn't dare mention it to Mavis – or to anyone else. She didn't dare mention it and she scarcely even dared think about it either. What had occurred to her in the middle of the night a few days back was just a dream. For all she knew, Mavis was right; Renée had felt poorly, now she was busy with something or other and in a week or two she would most probably come back.

Iris

IRIS DID NOT expect to enjoy *The Story of a Russian Princess* as much as she did. She had always liked the grand sweep of a historical romance. She did not expect to share Dorothy's tastes which she imagined tended more towards the fuddy-duddy. So she was surprised to find herself lapping up the "Russian Princess" which turned out not to be fuddy-duddy at all but jam-packed with drama: revolution, civil war, flight across snowy steppes, exile in a succession of European capitals and, right from the start, passionate love affairs, duels and violent death.

There was obviously more to little Dorothy Woodward than met the eye. Not only was she harbouring a secret passion for Gerald Shrimsley, her taste in reading matter was a lot meatier than Iris had given her credit for.

As Iris read, she began to be bothered by a nagging feeling that her memory had let her down. It wasn't the first time something like this had happened. Hadn't she read this book before? She couldn't place it but, a chapter or two in, after a lavish description of the family's palatial home in Moscow and the introduction of a large and colourful family with unpronounceable names, *The Story of a Russian Princess* began to seem somehow strangely familiar.

After a brief but dramatic period in Paris where the young

princess (her name was Tatiana) decided to battle poverty by training to become a dancer, the family moved to London. They suffered nobly in various hovels before graduating to a rather grand, old-fashioned flat in Bayswater. The princess's mother revived a burgeoning career as an opera singer which she had abandoned some years previously to marry the princess's father. The princess continued with her ballet lessons. Her father sank into a soulful Russian depression.

Iris supposed she must have taken this old book out once before a long time ago and forgotten all about it.

She was distracted from the Russian princess by a totally unexpected announcement from Joanna and Nat early in February: Nat was expecting a baby. At first Iris was dumbfounded, couldn't understand how such a thing could possibly have happened. Even once Joanna had patronisingly explained the mechanics to her, it still shocked her, required a huge readjustment.

Joanna and Nat could talk of nothing else. Apparently they had been planning this for ages. Well, Joanna was not far off fifty, wasn't she, and Nat herself already forty-two (surely far too old for a baby)?

But they had it all worked out.

"Nat's going to take the full maternity leave," Joanna explained, "and then she's going to go back to work part-time. I'll be the main earner."

Iris said, "You'll be the Daddy."

Joanna shot her a filthy look. "No, I'll be Mama-Jo and Nat will be Mama-Nat."

Iris refrained from comment. She reflected that all the people to whom she had pretended for years that Nat Gordon was just Joanna's friend were going to see through that now.

"When the baby reaches school age," Joanna went on, "maybe we'll have a rethink. Maybe Nat'll go back to work full-time and I'll scale back. We'll see. We both intend to be really hands-on parents."

Iris wondered, was that a reproach too?

Nat's pregnancy had made her even more abrasive. "Pregnancy is not an illness!" she retorted angrily when Iris suggested that she slow down, take things easy. She scolded Iris for offering her wine and blue cheese.

They had an answer for everything, even the birth itself.

"A birthing pool," Nat pronounced. "Jo will be my birthing partner and she'll cut the cord."

Iris had a hundred and one questions of course but she didn't dare ask them. Who actually was the sperm donor, the *father*, and was he going to be in the picture? If not – as seemed to be the case – who would be a father figure to the little girl? Yes, the baby – due in August – was a girl. They knew that too. How would she turn out if she grew up with no men at all in her life? Iris could hear Joanna's answers: Iris had seen off three husbands, Joanna had no little brother, it was hardly her fault if there were no men in the family. On Nat's side, apparently things weren't much better: two sisters, her father long dead and only a strange uncle whom you wouldn't want anywhere near your baby.

Iris had never thought she would be a grandmother (for obvious reasons). Now she found she rather warmed to the idea. Better late than never. She thought she might rather enjoy it, once the mewling and puling stage was over; she would teach the little girl to read – stories about handsome princes –

and take her to the pantomime, that sort of thing. The child would call her Grandma Iris, as opposed to Nat's mother, forbidding Grandma Rox.

It was a good couple of weeks before Iris felt inclined to pick up the Russian princess again. It felt rather remote compared with this major new drama in her own life. But the evenings were so long at this time of year and you could only watch so much television. It was important to keep her mind active, especially with a grandchild on the way.

Tatiana's father was still sunk in a soulful Russian depression. One winter afternoon, while ten-year-old Tatiana was out at her ballet lesson, he decided to follow the example of Tatiana's uncle Boris who had attempted suicide at the outbreak of the Russian Revolution in chapter two. (His pistol had jammed.) Tatiana came home early from her ballet lesson – her teacher had the flu – and found her father hanging from a metal ring in their dining room ceiling which had previously supported an enormous chandelier, conveniently removed for cleaning.

Alone in her sitting room, Iris gave a great gasp. Of course. She realised now where she had read all this before: Dorothy Woodward had stolen her life story from the Russian princess. Iris was beside herself – with incredulity and with delight. She could barely believe what she had discovered. What a scandal *this* would be! Her own life, so lamentably uneventful in recent years, was suddenly hotting up tremendously.

She made her scandalous discovery at the weekend so she had to wait until Thursday to denounce Dorothy. She had plenty of time to plan exactly how she would drop her bombshell. Obviously, she would bring the "Russian Princess" with her. Let Dorothy see her take the book out of her bag. Iris would observe how she reacted. Then she would ask Dorothy a few probing questions, turning the pages, slowly, thrillingly bringing her to the point where she would have to confess. The thought of it made Iris shiver with excitement.

She thought too how grateful poor Mina and Subhamoy Chatterjee would be if they knew Iris had uncovered an impostor working at the Centre. Their deaths had affected Iris deeply; killed when the small private plane taking them somewhere especially exotic and secluded in the Seychelles had crashed en route. It seemed to Iris horribly cruel that Mina and Subhamoy had died while enjoying an expensive holiday. They were such modest people, usually preferring to use their wealth to help others less fortunate than themselves. And yet, if Iris looked into the darkest corner of her heart, she had to admit there was something shamefully satisfying about it too.

Thursday was a dismally foggy day. When Iris opened her curtains, the street looked so dark and sinisterly clouded, she thought she would not dare to go out to the Second Chance Centre later. She rose early, the streetlights were still on and they lit up the low-lying masses of fog with a nasty yellow colour. The air looked simply solid, the headlights of the few cars passing along the street seemed to emerge from a wall of fog, surrounded by fuzzy shimmering haloes. Hopefully, by lunchtime, it would have lifted.

Iris waited impatiently, beside herself at the prospect of confronting Dorothy. Dorothy had it coming to her of course; posing as a life story teacher when really she was nothing but a jumped-up librarian – and a fraud into the bargain. Yet Iris couldn't help feeling a little sorry for her too; she would be disgraced, she would surely be sacked. Who would run the group then?

Despite the fog and her fear, the anticipation of the drama ahead got Iris out of her front door and onto the bus. The fog had lifted a little but she still couldn't see nearly as well as she would have liked. When she got down at the Second Chance Centre, she hesitated to cross the road. It was a challenge at the best of times; now she felt she was taking her life into her hands.

Out of the fog, an attractive young man loomed up next to her. Like many of the young fellows nowadays, he was wearing a foolish woolly hat but his features were handsome, his complexion smooth and he had intent dark eyes. Afterwards, when the police asked Iris what colour he was, oddly she couldn't give an answer. She said he was the same colour as the fog and they put down "mixed race".

Iris faltered for he seemed to be blocking her way. "What is it?" she asked, concerned but not yet understanding. His look was so intense, she wondered whether he was in some sort of trouble.

He said, "Your bag."

Iris clutched her bag to her chest. Still she could barely believe what was happening to her. She said, "No. How dare you?"

The young man said, quietly but urgently, "Gimme your bag."

Iris opened her mouth to scream, the young man reached out and grabbed her bag, her dear old bag, Iris held on as tight as she could so when the young man pulled it away from her, she went flying and sprawled full-length on the pavement which was not only stony hard but slimy from the fog.

201

Esther

My FIRST BOYFRIEND was Peter Robinson. Of course my parents disapproved of him. They were bound to because they disapproved of boyfriends full stop. They said I was too young – sixteen, in my last year at school – and Peter Robinson wasn't Jewish so he couldn't be taken seriously anyway. But he was a sweet boy. He was a couple of years younger than me but very tall. He had floppy brown hair the colour of fudge and he loved to read, especialy poetry. He always smelt a bit of Vicks Vapour Rub. I was surprised he liked me actually as I was that bit older. But I was so thrilled to have a boyfriend (Shirley and Valerie both did already and they acted really patronising to me) that I didn't really stop to think. When he asked me out, I quickly said yes. Even though Mum and Dad were dead against it, funnily enough they didn't actually stop me going out with him. They just acted disapproving and Dad gave poor Peter a hard stare when he came to pick me up.

Because we started going out together in the winter, we usually went to the cinema or to a Lyons Corner House if Peter was feeling flush, at any rate places indoors with lots of other people around. Not that Peter was the sort to try anything on. We mainly just talked about school and what we were both planning to do afterwards. In the cinema there was sometimes a bit of hand-holding but never anything more. Peter wouldn't have dared. Truth to tell, once the thrill of having a boyfriend wore off I found Peter a teeny bit boring. He was a bookish boy, he was planning to stay on at school and then hopefully go to university. I was going to secretarial college. We didn't really have a whole lot in common and I did wonder sometimes what he saw in me.

I found out soon enough. When the weather warmed up, April, May-time, Peter started suggesting the park instead of the cinema or Lyons. Naturally I suspected what he might be after. Not that my mother had spelt things out to me, I was still ever so innocent. But I knew in a fuzzy way the sort of things boys liked to do. But it turned out Peter just wanted to talk. And talk and talk and talk. We would go to Hendon Park and freeze on a bench while he explained his poetry to me or sometimes catch the bus as far as Hampstead Heath. Talk, talk, talk, talk. Even on the Heath, with plenty of spots to get up to no good in, far away from Hendon tell-tales, Peter never went further with me than a peck on the cheek. But he got carried away with words.

One day he announced, "What I really like about you Rita is that you're *different*."

I didn't like that of course, I didn't want to be different, I wanted to be the same as everybody else.

It got worse. "You're not like all the others," he went on. "You're different – exotic."

I was amazed. "Am I?"

"Yes," Peter insisted. "You are. You're *Jewish*. I like it."

Well of course my heart sank like a stone. If that was the only thing Peter really liked about me, I was in trouble. Of course he didn't know anything about my double life, being pretend Jewish and getting Christmas presents. That was a girls' secret between me and Shirley and Valerie. But it had been going on for such a long time now, maybe four or five years, that it had become sort of a habit. I almost didn't know anymore which was pretend: school or home. Even if, in the beginning, Shirley and Valerie suspected it was a sneaky way of getting Christmas presents and forbidden stuff to eat, when I kept it up, when I stuck to my story, they ended up believing me. All teenage girls love a secret and mine was such a big one.

So when Peter Robinson, who was a lovely boy — even if he was younger than me, even if he talked way too much about poetry — told me that he liked me *because* I was Jewish, I pretty much panicked. I realised I was in trouble whichever way I turned. If Peter found out I wasn't really, truly Jewish, probably he would drop me. If Shirley and Valerie found out I was actually really Jewish, they would think they had been had and they would probably drop me too. Worst of all, if my parents found out about the stories I had been telling (I didn't like to call them lies) what might *they* do?

It was obvious by that stage that the only thing to do was to confront my parents and ask them straight out: was it true, was I adopted? But of course I couldn't bring myself to do that, who could? I mean, what if I was wrong? What if I had made the whole thing up? What if the fact that I was the only one in the whole family with freckles was just a coinncidence?

I felt so unhappy. I wanted to run away but even at sixteen I knew it was too late to begin all over again at the beginning. I dropped poor Peter. Of course he never properly understood where he had gone wrong. He went on writing me poems for ages though eventually they stopped. I do sometimes wonder what became of him.

"I don't get it," Enid said when Esther finished her chapter. "Why not just spill the beans?"

Esther said, "Sorry?"

"Why not come out with it?" Enid asked. "Get to the bottom of it?"

Esther gave her a hurt look. "My poor Mum was *petrified*," she said. "She didn't have any identity of her own, did she? She was lost."

"But if she'd only spoken up —" Enid began.

"Maybe," Esther said shrilly, "you've never known anything like that. I can see it might be hard to understand. But you shouldn't judge what you don't know. I don't judge your creepy drawings."

Enid beamed.

Dorothy said, "Now Esther —"

But it was of all people Pearl who made peace. "I'm sure all families have got secrets," she said, "don't they?"

Edgar

AFTER THE SUNDAY lunch, Edgar began to allow himself to think about the future. Up until that point, he had been careful only to live in the here and now. He had cautioned himself repeatedly that Madeleine Baxter's presence in his life could only be a very temporary blessing. He imagined the two of them in their brief private bubble as a moment in time, the happiest of interludes, rather like one of the few foreign holidays which he and Joan had ventured on. It wasn't real life, was it – the nice hotel and the palm trees – but it was lovely while it lasted.

But now, tentatively, as February smudged into March and the prospect of another Easter and another summer appeared on the still murky horizon, Edgar let himself begin to speculate how things might develop. There could be no question, of course, of Madeleine moving in with him. Her tenth floor flat was her children's home; no way would she give that up. His own place was too small for all four of them – thank God. For now at least, they had to make do with the status quo. But, in other ways, things could still move along, couldn't they? If Luke and Desiree accepted him, well then wasn't the sky the limit?

In this flush of happiness, Edgar felt he should pay

more attention to Joan, show her – if she could see, where she was, what was afoot – that she was gone but not forgotten. He went around the house, looking out things that were Joan's. He wasn't sure, to be honest, if he was seeking them out to placate Joan or identifying them to put them away at a later date to please Madeleine. In this uneasy confusion, he noticed that a couple of things he remembered seemed to have gone missing; before Christmas he had spotted the disappearance of the cushion embroidered with a big entwined E and J. Now he realised a wobbly little box Joan had made him in pottery for his cufflinks had vanished too. He supposed somewhere along the line it must have got broken. But what on earth had become of that cushion? Had it got dirty, fallen victim long ago to one of Joan's regular tidy ups and he had never noticed?

Thinking of Joan fussing about the place, putting everything to rights made him feel miserable. Madeleine had a jam-packed week this week too; he would not be seeing her till Friday. He decided to sit down again with Joan's creative writing book to cheer himself up. After Eastbourne, what other happy times had she written about?

But when he opened the book and saw her dear no-nonsense handwriting proceeding tidily across the page, he felt abruptly too upset to carry on. He put the book to one side for later and decided to go down to the Pristina café for a sandwich and a cup of tea.

Murat sat opposite him to keep him company while he ate. He always paid a lot of attention to his regulars and the café wasn't busy; it wasn't, strictly speaking, a meal time.

"How's the sandwich?" he asked proudly as if, Edgar thought, it was a three-course meal.

"Tasty," Edgar said briefly, chewing and taking a swallow of tea. It was cheese and chutney; not much else to be said.

"And your Madeleine?" Murat asked, smiling a little too much, "how is she?"

Edgar felt that moving on like that smoothly from discussing a sandwich to Madeleine was not entirely respectful but he supposed Murat meant no harm. "She's very well thank you," he said crisply, "hard at work."

Sometimes Edgar regretted having mentioned Madeleine; Murat showed such a keen interest in her. Once, Murat had been standing outside the café smoking when Edgar and Madeleine came past. Fortunately, Murat had also been talking non-stop on his mobile otherwise Edgar would have had to stop and introduce her. As it was, he saw Murat's eyes widen and the next time Edgar dropped in at the café, Murat's enthusiasm knew no bounds.

"Such a lovely lady," he had gushed, "boom-boom."

Edgar was not sure what Murat meant by "boom-boom" but he knew he didn't like the sound of it.

He had said sternly, "She's a nurse, you know."

Murat grinned, "Lovely."

Edgar said firmly, "A *district* nurse."

Murat didn't know what a district nurse was. Edgar took some time explaining to him but Murat lost interest.

Sometimes Edgar thought about switching to another café – there was no shortage – but he knew that despite Murat's excessive interest in Madeleine, he would miss him. Murat always took the time to talk to his customers and, on a bad day, Edgar appreciated that.

Now he enquired a bit pointedly after Murat's wife. She had gone home to Kosovo to see her parents but seemed to be taking her time coming back.

Murat grimaced. "Three months she gone."

Edgar asked, "Are her parents not well?" and Murat answered gloomily, "No, parents fine. Her, she is the problem."

He stood up and cleared Edgar's cup and plate. He offered him a sticky pastry "to give you strength" but Edgar declined.

He went back home where Joan's notebook was still lying on the sofa where he had left it. Even with the days lengthening, it still seemed to get dark far too early. The clocks hadn't yet gone forward. He switched on the standard lamp next to the sofa and sat down in its circle of warm light. "Buck up," he thought to himself. "Take a look and see what she left you to read."

Joan's second piece of writing was called "Introduction of a Familiar Character". She had written another neat couple of pages, no mistakes, no crossings out. Edgar supposed she must have done it in rough first and then copied it out. That would have been typical of Joan; she wouldn't have wanted a mess in her exercise book. She had written about a man named Edward but Edgar realised, after a couple of lines, that it must be him.

Edward is a short man – why start with that? – but he makes up for it with personality. He is the funny, jokey type, always cracking jokes and telling stories to make you laugh. Most of the time I like that, he can always be relied on to cheer you up if you're feeling down though sometimes I would rather he didn't.

Edward left school at sixteen, he did not have the opportunity to get much education but he learnt a lot in what they call the school of life. He has lovely manners which are always appreciated everywhere. They make him seem posher than he really is.

He always dresses very smartly too. He worked his way up from humble beginnings to a good job in menswear. Consequently he is always well turned out. One of my favourite things is the way he raises his hat which went out of fashion a long time ago. But he still likes to do it as a sign of respect and it is like his trademark.

So much for appearances. Describing Edward's private side is more difficult. He does not have any hobbies or interests to speak of. When he retired, he was at a loose end. He always lived for his work. He kept up his smart appearance but it was like the saying "all dressed up and nowhere to go". It is a shame because he could benefit himself by going to classes or help others by doing voluntary work. Instead he just sits in a café nowadays drinking tea and reading the paper and chatting. Sometimes I wonder if he likes to look out for pretty girls going by.

Edgar shut the book in annoyance. She was getting at him from beyond the grave. Had she read this out to her class? Had she shared his flaws with all of them and had they guessed it was her husband she was writing about? He flipped forward to read the titles of the rest of her essays. They didn't give much away: "A Journey", "One of Life's Turning Points", "A Memorable Meal" and so forth. Still it was clear already that reading Joan's work was not going to be the straightforward pleasure he had imagined. Short, uneducated and with no hobbies; why had she chosen to dwell on that? He felt quite put out especially as he *had* started going to classes – although of course it was too late to tell Joan that now.

He put the exercise book down and looked around the familiar front room: pictures of him and Joan here and there which Madeleine, with her near saintly tolerance, had never wanted moved. He picked up the nearest photo and gave it a long hard stare. It was taken on one of those few foreign holidays: blue sky, palm trees, Joan in a straw sun hat, he in a navy blue yachting cap. He stared intently at Joan's familiar face, her eyes screwed up disapprovingly against the sun. For all their long years of marriage, how much had he ever really known Joan? He would have said, if asked, that she was devoted to him. Well, she *was* devoted to him and he to her. Everyone had their grouses of course. It was no fun being tidied up after all the time. But they had shared thirty-seven years of happy marriage, hadn't they? She had no business going along secretly to a writing class and writing down all sorts of complaints and then leaving them as a ticking off from beyond the grave. What else had she written about? Like in any marriage, Edgar supposed, they had had a couple of bad patches. He did not come out of one of them too well. He hoped she hadn't written about that although he realised with a sinking heart that she most probably would have.

He wondered what he would say if he were to write about Joan. Well, he wouldn't be writing of course, he would be recording. With Madeleine operating the recorder, he had tactfully refrained from even mentioning Joan. But if he *did*, what would he actually say?

He hadn't drawn the curtains. He watched the lights coming on across the way as people came home from work. Thirty-seven years as man and wife and he couldn't think where to begin. With a feeling close to panic, he wondered how well he had really known Joan at all.

Sabine

5. The Trip to the Ardennes

IN THE LAST two years of primary school, the children would go on a class trip in the summer either to the Belgian coast or to the Ardennes. The Belgian Ardennes are the most beautiful place in the world. Well, I have not travelled as much as I would have liked but in my experience they are the most lovely place I have ever seen. Deep green valleys covered with dense woodland where deer and wild boar are still profuse. At the bottom of the valleys, small rivers flow, clear water splashes over big grey stones. Still today it is an unspoilt region (despite the summer invasion of Flemish motorbikers). When Sabine was a child, it was a pure paradise.

When she was ten, her class went to stay in a little village called Frahan far in the Ardennes. It was their first class trip, so terribly exciting. They would leave in a coach on a Monday morning in June, all the children singing and cheering, with backpacks and sleeping bags, they would spend four thrilling nights in a youth hostel in Frahan and they would return home to Woluwé Saint Pierre, exhausted and sunburnt, on Friday evening. It was the climax of the school year.

It was also Sabine's first school trip so although she was excited – what child would not be excited about kayaking, picnicking and hiking through savage woods? – she was a little nervous too. She hoped she would sleep in the same dormitory as Annick, Josette and Geneviève, she hoped she would not cry from homesickness.

When their teacher Mademoiselle Henrard was preparing them for the trip Sabine discovered something terrible. Every year, three or four teenage assistants would accompany the class trip, they were called *moniteurs* and their task was to help the teachers to supervise fifty excited young children. This year, when Mademoiselle Henrard read out the names of the *moniteurs*, two of them were Sabine's big brothers. All the other children in the class turned round to look at her and Sabine went red to her ears. Of course all the other children were jealous, they thought Sabine was so lucky, her big brothers would take special care of her and protect her. Only Sabine knew this was not true.

At home, she tried to tell her mother why she didn't want to go on the class trip anymore but her mother thought she was being a baby. (It is true, what mother could possibly imagine her daughter's real fears?) Sabine made such a fuss, she was sick. Then of course her father became involved too. He was very angry. He did not want any of his children not to participate in their class trip, to create a scandal. He told Sabine how very lucky she was, luckier than all the other children, to have her big brothers there to look after her. It was not the first time that Sabine's parents had not understood something she was trying to tell them, attributing her tears to her artistic temperament and to hysteria.

Frahan is such a heavenly place. It is situated at the bottom of a deep valley beside a beautiful turn of the river Semois. A picturesque old stone village, it is sheltered on every side by protector hills. You feel that nothing can harm you there and probably that is why it was chosen for the class trip.

Of course finally Sabine had to go. Although she did not sleep the night before the departure, although in the morning she could not eat her breakfast, she could not refuse her father. She had to put on her heavy backpack with her sleeping bag rolled up below and walk with it all the way to school. When she arrived, all the other children were jumping and screaming with excitement. Sabine had to pretend to be excited too. Already Charles and Laurent were cross with her because they suspected of course why she did not want to go.

Those five magic days in Frahan stay as clear as yesterday. As soon as the children arrived, they ran down to the river. They were allowed to paddle in the shallow water. The water was cold but so clean. You could see the fish swimming past. The children screamed and threw water on one another, they had never felt themselves so happy. They ate their picnic lunch by the river. The simple sandwiches had never tasted so good. Sabine allowed herself to feel optimistic. Charles and Laurent were in charge of the boys' dormitory.

In the afternoon, the children went on the river in kayaks. Sitting two together, they paddled along the turning Semois, shallow in summer, as far as the next tiny village. Paddling down the river, the children felt the current carry their small kayaks, it was thrilling, they became a part of nature, companions with the fishes and the birds. On the two sides, the woods were so beautiful and so quiet. All you could hear through the valley were the children's happy cries. As they got tired with the paddling, they grew quiet too. Before the next village, Sabine saw a grey heron still like a statue on the bank.

In the evening, they cooked their supper over a fire. They sang songs under the stars. At night the girls planned to tell their secret stories and eat sweets but instead they slept at once like dormice.

Those were perfect days: in the mornings, hiking and playing team games, in the afternoons kayaking on the beautiful Semois. Laurent and Charles were occupied with the naughty boys, Sabine hardly saw them.

On the Thursday, a special activity was planned: a treasure hunt in the woods. For the treasure hunt, the children were divided into teams and Sabine was very upset to discover that she was in Charles and Laurent's team. Of course there was no point protesting: it was obvious Charles and Laurent had organised it on purpose. As well, everyone would think it was very strange if Sabine did not want to be in her brothers' team. She set off into the woods feeling very nervous.

It was such a beautiful morning. The sunlight flowed down through the trees in little streams of liquid light. The air smelt so fresh. As the children walked, sometimes they could hear the small noises of small creatures hurrying away through the bushes.

The treasure hunt worked like this: Charles and Laurent had composed a series of riddles in verse. Each riddle formed a clue which led you to the place where the next clue was hidden. Because Sabine knew rather well the way Charles and Laurent's minds worked, she could understand their riddles very quickly and she led the team very quickly to the next clue. The third time she did this, Charles and Laurent became annoyed. The treasure hunt was supposed to last all the morning and here was naughty little Sabine racing through it at top speed. They told her not to hunt with the other children, instead to stay behind with them.

The rest of the team ran away through the woods, in the wrong direction Sabine already knew, but when she tried to call and tell them, Laurent put his hand over her mouth.

They sat in silence on the ground, Laurent and Charles on each side of Sabine. The noise of the excited children searching in the wrong direction grew quiet and all you could hear were the sounds of the wood living, breathing around them like a giant animal.

Laurent said to Charles, "This is our last summer, you know. In September we will go to university and everything will be different. *Adieu* the pleasures of childhood."

Charles said, "I know."

After a pause, Laurent said, "Maybe we could play our favourite game together one last time?"

217

I said, "No, no, please no!"

But they were two and I was one and already it was too late.

That evening there was a party to celebrate the children's last night in Frahan. One of the other *moniteurs* played his guitar, a kind boy with a gentle face who Sabine wished was her big brother instead. His name was Antoine Devreux and all the girls were in love with him. There was singing and clapping, fun and games and a real feast for supper. How many of the boys and girls experienced their first childish kiss that night in the darkness outside the light from the campfire? That night Sabine, Josette, Annick and Geneviève were finally too excited to sleep. They ate up all their sweets and told each other their secret stories some of which were no doubt invented.

On Friday evening, the coach took them home to Woluwé Saint Pierre. It had been a wonderful week. Of course Sabine only told her parents about the official activities, not about the game in the woods. In fact she repressed that memory so deeply that in the future years she sometimes wondered if those games with her brothers had really happened. Her Belgian childhood had been in every way so perfect, was it really possible that something like that had actually happened? Maybe she had invented it, one reads nowadays so much about false memories. But the lovely village of Frahan was real and the beautiful river Semois and the small kayaks floating down the river in the summer sun.

Dorothy

WHEN IRIS FAILED to show up one Thursday afternoon towards the end of February, Dorothy panicked. First Renée, now Iris; if Iris didn't come back, like Renée, the class would be down to five. With what relish Lavonda would close it.

Dorothy tried to hide her anxiety and said, "I suppose Iris isn't well this week? There's a lot of bugs going round."

"Maybe she didn't want to come out in the fog?" Esther suggested.

Enid laughed her rasping laugh. "She's past eighty. She'll have been in much worse fogs than this."

"The old pea soupers," Edgar agreed.

Several of them coughed and then laughed.

Sabine said, clearing her throat, "It must be psychosomatic."

Pearl passed round some lozenges.

Dorothy asked Sabine to read first. Dwelling on Iris's absence only made it worse and it wasn't as if she was the most popular member of the group anyway. Dorothy suspected nobody much liked Iris with her airs and graces and her important friends. Everyone had been much more worried when Renée vanished. "We're all looking forward to hearing about your school trip to the Ardennes," she said enthusiastically.

But when Sabine finished reading, there was a long silence.

Dorothy exclaimed, "Such beautiful descriptions of nature Sabine!" Privately, of course, she was aghast. Had she properly understood? Was the game in the woods really what she thought it was? What on earth should one say? For a moment, she missed Iris. Iris would have known what to say; Iris was never short of an opinion on any given topic. Dorothy looked around at the others. Esther clearly hadn't got it; she was saying something or other to Sabine about the soothing properties of nature. Dorothy had to remind herself that, at only forty, Esther didn't have their life experience. The game in the woods seemed to have passed Edgar by too; he was sitting looking genially vacant, as he often did. But Pearl and Enid had clearly understood; they both looked horrified.

Enid spoke up – and Dorothy didn't know whether to be glad that someone else had taken the initiative or concerned that it was Enid.

"Those brothers of yours," Enid said to Sabine, "they sound a nasty piece of work."

Sabine blushed. Hesitantly, she answered, "They were not nice to me."

"I'll say they weren't," Enid snapped. "Did you ever tell anyone? I hope you didn't let them get away with it?"

"Who could I tell?" Sabine cried, "Many times, I tried to tell my parents but they did not want to know. I was a little girl, I did not know what words to use."

"Bastards," said Enid. "Bloody bastards."

Sabine flinched. "Sometimes I wonder, did I make it up? Did it really happen? Or was it just a bad dream I had?"

"If it was a bad dream," Pearl said, "you had it an awful lot of times."

Sabine looked at Pearl and her eyes brimmed with tears. "True," she said slowly, "true," and she began to cry.

"There are places you can go, you know," Pearl said, "people you can talk to."

Pearl swapped seats and put her arm around Sabine. It seemed to Dorothy that Pearl shot her a dirty look; why am *I* doing this again instead of *you*?

Dorothy blurted out, "A lovely chapter, Sabine, thank you."

At home afterwards, she worried terribly. If the nasty game which Sabine's brothers had played with her on the school trip – and in the forest and next to the railway line and God knows where else besides – if it was what Pearl and Enid clearly believed it was, then it was a crime: a crime revealed in *her* life story group. Whatever was she meant to do? She had no idea. She had no idea and she was beside herself. Poor Sabine. Thinking back over Sabine's story, there were so many clues Dorothy had missed: Sabine's brothers chasing her over the sand dunes, Sabine's secret conviction that her brothers deserved to be whipped and then, right at the end, the way one brother had clamped his hand over her mouth to silence her. Dorothy herself felt smothered and panicky. But what was she to do? She couldn't go to the police – could she? About a crime maybe – or maybe not – committed somewhere in Belgium fifty years ago? But if she did nothing, was she any better than the wicked people at Mercy House? Was she colluding in hushing it up? Was she becoming part of the conspiracy of silence which let nasty men get away with doing unmentionable things to little children?

That wasn't all. What upset Dorothy even more was the realisation that Sabine's awful revelation was most likely only the first. They all of them had something up their sleeves; she had sensed it for some time now. A tidal wave of nasty, unspeakable revelations was rearing up over the group, ready to crash down first and foremost on her. If you listened carefully, they all had something nasty hidden in their life stories, didn't they, a piece of really bad news withheld. What other crimes would the coming months reveal? Why had she not thought of this before?

It had never occurred to Dorothy that life story writing could be so dangerous. Why, she herself had already fraudulently plagiarised a life story. That was in itself a crime – although of course an extremely minor one with no real victims. The chapter she was writing about the goings-on at Mercy House would reveal a whole catalogue of crimes. She was no different from any of the others. She thought her way around the semi-circle and tried to guess what each one's revelation might be. She felt scared stiff.

The following week, Iris was back. She had a huge purple bruise down one side of her face and she was limping worse than ever. She smiled graciously at all the exclamations of concern and staggered to her seat. Once she was settled, enjoying the attention, she told them the story of her mugging and the theft of her handbag.

Everyone was horrified. They all knew such things happened all the time of course, everyone knew someone who had been mugged. But the way it had happened, virtually on the doorstep of the Second Chance Centre, when Iris was on her way to the class, made it particularly upsetting.

Iris basked in their collective concern. "The doctor said it was a miracle I didn't break anything," she bragged. "He said I must be made of strong stuff. Which I am of course. But still, coming down on the pavement like that, I could have been terribly badly hurt. The ambulance men were worried about a head injury."

Everyone was impressed that Iris had been taken to hospital by ambulance. She told them about the police questioning too. "Of course," she said, "I had to spell Longchamp."

Enid asked, "Whyever?" and Iris gave her a withering look. "My bag," she explained condescendingly, "it was a Longchamp bag. I suppose I've seen the back of it now. Such a shame. It was a beautiful bag."

"What was in it?" Dorothy asked.

Iris seemed to give her a strange look. "Well, all the usual stuff you'd expect to have in a bag," she answered. "Plus one or two other things. An awful headache to deal with it all."

Pearl asked, "Did you have much cash on you?"

"Fortunately not," Iris said. "At least that. Less than a hundred pounds."

Dorothy could see everyone struggling to contain themselves at the idea that anything less than a hundred pounds was not much money.

Enid didn't contain herself. "So when you hung onto that bag like grim death, you weren't hanging on for the money but for the *bag*?"

"Yes," Iris answered. "I was. And for something else that was in the bag too. A book."

"A book?" Esther exclaimed. "You let yourself be dragged down for a *book*?"

"Well," Iris said, "it was a very significant book. A library book too."

"I'm sure," Dorothy said, "the library would have used their discretion. They wouldn't possibly have expected someone who lost a library book as a result of violent crime to pay for it."

Iris gave Dorothy another very odd look. This time, it seemed tinged with frank hostility. "Let's not take up any more of everyone's time with my little mishap," she said. "I'd like to have a private word with you after class Dorothy, if I may."

Pearl

IN THE END it was Kai who got her to do something, Kai with his new energy and his understanding of the mysteries of IT.

"It's really easy to find someone, you know," he told Pearl. "You just look online. I can find anyone."

But Pearl, she didn't know why, kept putting it off.

They had just finished recording her last instalment of the spring term and they were talking over how it came about that Kai had so few relatives.

"Well," Pearl said, "your grandad wasn't in the picture and your dad wasn't in the picture so that's half the relatives you might have had gone. And I was an only child and your Mum was an only child —" she faltered.

Kai took up the litany, "And I'm an only." He grinned. "We're doomed."

Pearl said, "Rubbish, of course we're not doomed." She paused. "Sitting in that group, I honestly don't think we've had more bad stuff happen to us than anyone else, you know Kai. Everyone's got something."

Kai said, "Shit happens."

Pearl frowned but didn't say anything.

Kai carried on, "All that stuff you just recorded Nan – what your stepdad done to you and how you left home and that – how come you never told me about it before?"

Pearl thought. "Well, for a start, you were too young, Kai. And then I suppose I didn't want you bothered with all the bad stuff. I didn't want you to think your family history was just one thing after another. I guess I thought you had enough to be getting on with."

They both paused for now they were dangerously near the topic they never talked about.

Pearl said, "I'll get the tea on."

While they were eating – sometimes it seemed to Pearl that even Kai's table manners had got a bit better since he started college – he said to her, as if he had only just remembered it, "I got an email from school."

"From school?" Pearl asked. "What do *they* want?"

She knew that a communication from school could only mean trouble: in the past it had meant detentions, head lice, lost books to be paid for.

Kai said, "Mr Robinson's retiring. They're having a party."

Pearl said, "Why've they sent it to *us*? You're not even *at* the school anymore. Are they asking for money?"

Kai said, "We're invited."

"Invited?" Pearl repeated. She didn't mean to sound as full of misgiving as she did. "Show me the email."

Kai fumbled in his pocket.

"No, not on your phone," Pearl said, "I can't read it."

Kai scooped up an extra large forkful of beans and went to his bedroom, chewing. He came back with his laptop, fiddled around with it and thrust it at Pearl. "There, have a look."

Pearl read the email and exploded. "Kai, when did you get this? It says 'RSVP by 15 February'."

"What does that even mean?" Kai asked.

Pearl said, "It means you need to reply by 15 February. Do you know what date it is today?"

Kai shrugged.

"Well, take a look at your phone," Pearl snapped, "and tell me."

Kai looked and said flatly, "21 February."

"So," Pearl said triumphantly, "it's too late."

Kai said, "But I want to go."

"Well, why didn't you think to show it to me before then? It's too late now." Pearl was glad it was too late of course; the last thing she wanted was to have to go up to that school with all its bad memories and stand around smiling when she just wanted to sit down and cry.

Kai said, "Why's it too late? The party's on 15 March, look."

"I know the party's on 15 March," Pearl said crossly. "I can read. But we haven't answered in time so we can't go. That's what RSVP *means*."

"Well, I don't see why," Kai said. "That's just stupid. Why do they need to know so long before?"

"Catering," Pearl said, "chairs, glasses, that sort of thing."

Kai said, "Well, if I say yes we're coming right now, like today, wouldn't that be ok? That's only a few days late."

"Kai," Pearl said, "you know what that Prithi's like."

"You just don't want to go," Kai said. "You're trying to get out of it and you're using the RSVP thing as an excuse."

Pearl thought, not for the first time, that Kai was sometimes wise beyond his years. She played for time. "Show me the invite again."

She read it slowly: "Larkrise School invites Kai Barter and parent(s) to a party to mark the retirement of our head teacher Mr Peter Robinson."

"Funny he's retiring now," she said, "and not at the end of the school year." She added, "I never knew his name was Peter."

Kai said, "What's that got to do with anything?"

Pearl asked, "Why are you so keen to go Kai? You never used to want to have anything to do with school stuff."

"That was *ages* ago," Kai said. "It's different now. Like – Mr Robinson helped me, didn't he? He got me to go to college. Like – I want him to know I'm doing well."

Of course Pearl had no choice then; she had to agree – even though it was the last thing she wanted. "So tell them yes," she said reluctantly "and we'll see what they say."

With frightening speed, Kai sent off a reply and there was nothing more to be done other than privately hope that Prithi would tell them it was too late.

They almost didn't make it to the party because, on the night, Kai forgot about it – for all that it mattered so much to him – and he came in way too late. Pearl screamed at him. She had been ready, dressed and waiting since five. She had even had her hair done. But Kai changed one shapeless hoodie for another slightly cleaner one, did something that had no visible effect to his hair and they set out.

"We'll miss the main bit, you'll see," Pearl said, "the speeches and that."

The party had been going for forty-five minutes already.

Kai said, "Chill Nan."

He turned out to be right because, when they got there, there were still loads of people walking up, all smartly dressed and looking self-conscious about going back to school.

Inside, the gym hall was packed. Pearl wasn't surprised that Mr Robinson was so popular but it was hard to breathe. They had decorated the hall really nicely but they hadn't managed to get rid of the smell of sweaty trainers. Pearl stood for a while in the crowd and the fug, feeling uncomfortable and at a loose end. Kai had slipped away to talk to some kids he had spotted from his year. Pearl couldn't see anyone she knew.

She thought of the people she knew who ought to have been there: Mavis, who knew about the party but, since Matt had gone missing, couldn't face setting foot in the school, and of course Tracy. Tracy had been in this gym hall in her day, she had scrambled up and down those wall bars, she had been good at PE.

Pearl needed to step outside for some air. She made her way through the crowd to the nearest door, saying, "'Scuse me, 'scuse me" but almost shoving people by the time she got to the door. She stood outside in the playground for a while, breathing and shaking. It wasn't cold but she could feel herself shivering. Really, she shouldn't have come along; this was too much for her.

She wondered whether Mr Robinson could possibly be Esther Solomon's mother's long-lost boyfriend. Peter Robinson was a common enough name. And wouldn't he be a bit too young? The chances were he wasn't and, anyway, she didn't think she would dare ask him such a thing. She thought about what Esther had read out: a sweet boy, she had written, with floppy brown hair the colour of fudge. Mr Robinson's hair – what little there was of it – was grey. He didn't smell of Vicks Vapour Rub or, if he did, Pearl had never been close enough to notice. But a bookish boy who had gone on to university; that *could* be Mr Robinson.

Behind Pearl, the noise of the party stopped. She supposed the presentations and the speeches were beginning. She ought to go back in. Plus the drizzle wasn't doing anything for her hair. She took another deep breath or two and forced herself to go back inside.

Just as she pushed open one of the swing doors to the gym, there was a great outburst of clapping. So she had missed the first speech already. Up on a small stage at the far end of the hall, she could just make out Mr Robinson. He was saying, "Thank you for your kind words, Desmond. And thank you to everyone at Larkrise School who has made my years here such happy ones. Thank you to the school governors for your vote of confidence in letting me stay on for nearly five years past the conventional retirement age." ("Pushing seventy," Pearl thought. "Not too young after all.") "Thank you to every one of the fantastic staff here, to the Larkrise School families and, above all, to you young people, our students." There was a ragged cheer. "For nearly 15 years, since I came here as head, you have been the reason I get up in the mornings. You are sometimes a pleasure, sometimes a challenge and," he paused, "always an inspiration. I wish every one of you good luck in your futures. It has been a privilege to lead your school." He bowed his head. He seemed to have finished and there was another deafening round of applause.

Kai popped up at Pearl's side. He looked thrilled. "Ok to stay for a bit longer?" he asked urgently. "Please Nan?"

"Half an hour," Pearl answered. "No more."

Kai fist bumped her jokily and vanished.

Pearl thought she might as well go and take a look at the refreshments. Not that she was all that hungry but they had paid their contribution to Mr Robinson's present.

As she made her way across to the refreshment tables, she was aware of Mr Robinson in the distance, moving round the hall like a VIP, shaking hands and exchanging a few words with everyone.

Pearl didn't know if she wanted him to stop and talk to her or not. She poured herself some sticky sweet apple juice from a carton and stood sipping it so as to look a bit busy. She wondered what Kai was up to. She did hope he wouldn't take ages to come back.

From a little way away, Mr Robinson spotted her and made a beeline through the crowd.

"Mrs Barter," he said. He took her hand in both of his. His hands were very warm and his face was quite red. Pearl wondered if he hadn't had a bit to drink. "How wonderful to see you here. How's Kai getting on?"

"He's doing really well," Pearl said gladly. "He's loving his course. Thank you for pushing him."

"Did I push him?" Mr Robinson asked. "Or did I just open the door? You know the Chinese proverb? 'Teachers open the doors but you must enter by yourself.'"

Already he was looking on to the next person.

231

Pearl blurted out, "Does the name Solomon mean anything to you?"

Mr Robinson paused. He said, "We have a Salman in year 9 who's quite a handful."

"No," Pearl said, "not at school. Someone from outside school. From way back. Rita Solomon."

"Good God!" Mr Robinson said. He stared at her. He seemed extremely embarrassed. "Wherever did you come across Rita Solomon?"

"I go to a class," Pearl said, pleased to tell Mr Robinson that she was getting some education too. "It's a life story class, kind of thing. There's a woman in our group, Esther Solomon and she's been writing about her mother, Rita. Your name came up."

"Good God," Mr Robinson said again. He laughed. "Well, Mrs Barter, all I can say is I hope you don't think too badly of me. Rita Solomon led me astray. She was a very troubled young woman, I remember, and she was a few years older than me." He laughed again. "Rita Solomon took it upon herself to jump start my sex education."

Pearl didn't know where to put herself. But, before she could come out with anything, Mr Robinson added, "Well, do tell Rita's daughter to remember me to her mother." He laughed again and moved on before Pearl could recover and tell him that Rita was, in actual fact, dead.

Pearl helped herself to a few little sandwiches on a paper plate. She felt quite weak. It wasn't just the embarrassment although that was bad enough. It was the realisation that Esther Solomon's life story must be a pack of lies. Either Esther wasn't telling the truth or, more likely, the story her mother had told her hadn't been true in the first place. Who knows, maybe the whole thing was made up? Maybe Esther's Mum hadn't even been adopted at all?

Pearl's head was spinning. Why stop at Esther actually? If Esther's life story wasn't true, what was to say anyone else's was either? If Sabine's tales about what her brothers did to her were true – and Pearl was pretty sure they must be – then how come she always made out her childhood had been so perfect? It didn't make any sense. It dawned on Pearl that every word which every one of them had written – or recorded – could be made up and no one would be any the wiser. Pearl felt stupid for having told the truth although, at the same time, she knew she was incapable of doing anything else.

After she had waited an age, Kai came back. He looked really pleased with himself. "Good times Nan?" he asked jauntily.

Pearl said. "You took your time."

Kai said, "I was busy."

He whistled most of the way home. Pearl didn't tell him about her talk with Mr Robinson; it was way too embarrassing. She just mentioned that he had come over and asked after Kai.

Kai said, "Uh-huh," completely casually. "He talked to me too."

Pearl felt a familiar surge of resentment. Did Kai have any *idea* what it had cost her, doing what she had done: calling school and meeting Mr Robinson and coming along to the bloody party? And if he realised, did he even *care*?

"Kai," she said on the spur of the moment, "I done you

233

a favour, I came to the party. Now I'd like you to do something for me. When we get in, I'd like you to look up that Renée I told you about and see if you can find her online like you promised."

Kai said again, "Uh-huh" and carried on jigging to a private melody.

Edgar

THIRTY-SEVEN YEARS of marriage but of course not all of them to the same woman; Joan had changed over time, so had he. He had been married to a succession of Joans. There had been the Joan of the early years when they were courting and first married: a shy, very quiet blonde girl. She didn't scream out on the fairground rides like some of them or kick up her legs so you could see up her skirt. She went white and pressed a nicely laundered hanky to her lips, she didn't scream, she held her skirt down. She kept her thoughts and feelings so private that when Edgar proposed, he had no idea if she would say yes. In the wedding photos she looked serious. He was laughing and smiling and full of the joys of spring, she looked solemn.

Then there was the Joan who found out she couldn't have children, Joan in her thirties, sad but brave, with her hair cut short and her job at the doctor's. She would get weepy sometimes talking about the mothers coming in with their newborn babies. But she seemed to get over it fairly quickly, maybe deep down she wasn't that much of the maternal type. In fact, sometimes Edgar wondered whether he didn't care about it more than she did. On and off, he thought he would have quite liked to have children.

But when he mentioned adoption, Joan would hear none of it. She said you never knew where the child came from.

Then there was Joan in middle age. She didn't seem to gain an ounce of weight, while her sister and her women friends were all filling out comfortably. She kept everything perfectly shipshape, herself included. Those were the years when her tidiness came to the fore; she was always fretting and fussing about keeping the house nice. But she wasn't just a housewife. She had her job at the new health centre and her classes. She did a lot of voluntary work too. She was always out and about. When Edgar came in from work, he liked to put his feet up, after standing on the shop floor all day. Sometimes he wished Joan would stay at home in the evenings a bit more but he couldn't complain really because she always left his dinner. He supposed it was just as well she had all her activities to fill the gap left by children.

Lastly, there was Joan at the end when her illness had taken hold: pale and thin, in certain lights almost see-through. Of course that was when he had loved her the most; when he knew she was on her way out. He supposed it must always be the way; you lived alongside someone, got used to them being there like a bit of the furniture and you only properly appreciated them when they were gone.

After his last dip into Joan's creative writing book, Edgar was in no hurry to read on. If the message Joan had left for him wasn't a fond farewell but a ticking off, why trouble himself? He half wanted to talk to Madeleine about it but until he knew what lay in store, he didn't dare. Not reading it was the same as turning a deaf ear when Joan was nagging.

Madeleine moved a few of her things into the bedroom cupboards. It was awkward, when she stayed over, not having her bits and pieces there. Edgar could breathe in her heavenly smell when he missed her presence. He could peep into her underwear drawer. He did not believe he had ever peeped into Joan's underwear drawer. But he had seen her plain white knickers often enough over the years to realise that Madeleine's ample panties were three times bigger.

One evening, in spite of himself, he got out Joan's exercise book again. He flipped through the first two chapters he had read and came to the beginning of the third one, "A Journey". It was a little longer than the first two.

"I have not travelled that much in my life," the chapter began, in Joan's small, neat handwriting,

but in recent years we have been on a few foreign holidays. My favourite was a tour one Easter time to the Bay of Naples. It wasn't too hot yet, I don't like the heat and the scenery was beautiful. In fact, I think it was the most beautiful scenery I have ever seen. When I close my eyes, I can still see it now: steep hillsides covered in blossoming trees going straight down to the bluest sea ever. We stayed at a nice hotel in Sorrento and we went on day trips to Pompeii and to Naples. Naples was very dirty and messy and I did not like it at all but everywhere else was lovely.

Something strange happened on that holiday. We were in a tour group with about thirty others, mainly older couples but a few single people too who complained that they had to pay a single supplement for their rooms and they joked that if they had known what fun the other singles were, they could have doubled up. That was the sort of jokey atmosphere on the coach. Plus we were all in holiday clothes – strap tops and shorts and the like – which made everyone feel more free and easy I suppose.

One afternoon there was time off for shopping in Sorrento. But Edward said he spent all his working days in a shop, he didn't want to spend any of his holiday traipsing round shops into the bargain. I suppose he had a fair point but it meant I had to go off by myself which felt a bit sad while Edward stayed behind to play mini-golf. Anyway, I made the most of it, I did enjoy going round all the shops and I bought a few pretty things as gifts.

In a leather shop on the main street, I ran into one of the singles from our group. He was a quiet fellow, not jokey at all, tall and thin and serious-looking and I had wondered if he didn't disapprove of all the joking on the coach.

I was really surprised when he invited me to sit down and have a cold drink with him but it was getting a bit warm so I said yes. He told me his name was Trevor. He let me order first and I had a Pepsi and he had a fresh lemonade with crushed ice and I wished I had gone for that instead.

As we had our drinks, Trevor told me his wife had passed away two years before. This was the first holiday he had felt up to since and he was finding it difficult. I felt ever so sorry for him. I asked what his wife's name was and he said, "Bianca", she was Italian and he had come to Italy in her memory.

I thought that was so sad and so romantic, I don't know what got into me, I reached out across the table and took his hand. Trevor looked surprised but he didn't take his hand away.

I said, "That's such a beautiful thing to do," and I felt myself welling up suddenly.

Trevor said, "Well, I thought it was a nice idea but it's making me feel very low."

Then he smiled and he took his hand away and said, "I mustn't rain on your holiday."

I said, "Oh you're not," but he said, "Please, at least let me buy you your drink" and he asked for the bill in fluent Italian.

We walked back to our hotel together, not saying a great deal, just commenting on the various things we saw along the way. Trevor knew a lot about Italy of course, he was very knowledgeable and he explained a good few things to me.

I noticed he was carrying a plastic bag from the leather shop and I asked him what he had bought. He told me he had bought a handbag for his grown-up daughter and he got it out and showed it to me and asked what I thought. I said truthfully that I thought it was a lovely choice and he looked pleased.

I said, "Well at least you've got your daughter," and he smiled and said yes, she was what kept him going.

He asked me, "Do you have children?"

I said, "Sadly not." I could tell he understood then that I had a sadness of my own too but as we walked the last stretch up to the hotel together, it did not feel sad. It was as if both of us having our own sadness made us somehow happy.

What was strange was that neither of us said anything about it afterwards. I didn't tell Edward, not that I'd done anything wrong of course but when we got back he was all full of beans from his mini-golf and what I had just been through felt special and serious, I didn't want him cracking jokes about it.

At the end of the holiday, everyone said their goodbyes at the airport. I hadn't spoken to Trevor again but we smiled and nodded when we saw each other. At the last minute, I wondered whether I ought to introduce him to Edward. But I didn't want Edward making jokes about swinging singles or getting the wrong idea. So, in the end, when Trevor waved goodbye to me, I just waved back. Ever after, I have wondered what became of him.

Edgar strained to remember anything out of the ordinary on that holiday. He had no recollection of Joan going off on her own shopping or of playing mini-golf. He wasn't even that keen on mini-golf anyway, whatever Joan said.

As for Joan going off and having a drink with some fellow – and a walk too – and not telling him about it afterwards, he could barely believe it. Maybe she had made the whole thing up? It was creative writing, wasn't it? Maybe it was all just a story she had invented. He put the book away and wondered whether he might not leave it at that. He couldn't help thinking that Joan, who had always been so prim and proper in life, was turning out to be quite a tease from beyond the grave.

Esther

ESTHER CLEARED HER throat and looked around the semi-circle defiantly. Now she was coming to the climax of her mother's story, surely she could expect some understanding? Yet the group did not look promising: Dorothy seemed as usual anxious and the others looked as blank as ever. Edgar was gazing out of the window.

I met my future husband Sidney Solomon on Monday, 7 July 1952. I know the date because it was the same day I started work. I finished at secretarial college on the Friday and on the Monday week I started work. That was how it was back then. There were no gap years for us, no hanging about finding yourself. Truth to tell, I don't think I ever found myself my whole life.

Anyway, my first job was at a solicitor's, Evans and Elias. There was Mr Evans, Mr Elias and two young trainee solicitors who were Colin Clarke and Sidney Solomon. There were three secretaries, Dot, Eileen – who also did the book keeping – and me and we all fancied Sidney Solomon.

I would like to say it was love at first sight but the truth is there was not much in the way of competition. Mr Evans and Mr Elias were old and grey and boring and Colin was not the sort of person you would want to get involved with. Girls would regularly ring up in tears asking for him and he wouldn't even speak to them. In contrast, Sidney was gentle and well mannered. He kept his hands to himself. He always said "Please" and "Thank you" when he asked us secretaries to do things, not like Colin who flicked papers onto your desk and acted flirty with everyone (he even acted flirty with Mr Evans and Mr Elias!)

Sidney was not a tall man and at twenty-five his hair was already reseeding. But he had a kind face and lovely soft brown eyes. Unlike Colin he was rather quiet and you couldn't tell at first if it was from shyness or because he was being clever and biding his time. The clients liked him, you could tell they thought he was a safe pair of hands and we all thought he would go far.

So I liked the look of him, yes but I can't say it was mad passion or anything like that.

I had been working there for two or three months, glad to be earning but not thinking much of it otherwise when to my surprise Sidney asked me to have lunch with him. He did it very discretely when none of the others were around. The way he asked me didn't sound that romantic actually. He said he had noticed I brought sandwiches in every day. Now the weather was getting colder, wouldn't I rather have a hot meal at lunch time for a change? I blushed. I was quite embarassed actually because the reason I brought sandwiches in was so as not to spend any of my small salary in the cafés round about and because my Mum didn't want

243

me eating forbidden foods. Now I was independent, making my lunch was one of the few things she could still do for me. But I did find her sandwiches really repetetive and so I eagerly said yes.

This may sound silly but it didn't dawn on me for a long time that Sidney was interested in me romantically. I genuinely believed he was a kind man who cared about my health and wellfare and wanted me to have a nurishing hot lunch.

For about a year that was all we did anyway: have lunch – once, maybe twice a week. I didn't tell Mum. Wastefully, I binned my sandwiches. As I said, Sidney was a slow and careful, considarate man not the least the sort for rushing in. We got to know each other. I thought he was lovely, I was madly keen on him by then but I never dared hope he felt the same way about me. He was almost seven years older for a start and much better educated – I seemed to attract the brainy boys – and I was convinced he was just being nice to me because he had a good heart.

Then I had a shock. One lunchtime he told me he was leaving Evans and Elias and before I could stop myself I burst into tears. I remember he reached his hand out across the table – we were eating cod and chips – and he took hold of one of mine. "Don't cry," he said gently. "This is good news. For both of us."

He had said "us"! He explained to me that he had been offered a promotion at another solicitor's, a much bigger smarter firm. It was good news for his career and it was also good news because now we wouldn't be working together in the same office any more – if I was agreeable – we could put our relationship on a more serious footing. Those were his actual words. I was utterly and completely beside myself. My smile must have said it all.

Well then I had to tell my parents about Sidney of course because we started going out in the evenings so I had to tell them where I was going. Remember I wasn't yet quite nineteen. Because Sidney was Jewish, there were no objections this time. In fact my Mum got quite weepy and emotional. She gave me a really close hug which went on too long. I suppose it had just dawned on her that her little Rita was growing up, that one day she would leave home.

But when Sidney came to take me out for the first time, Mum was all smiles and asked him in for a cup of tea. Naturally he made a good impression on them. He ticked all the boxes: he had a serious profession, bright prospects and he came from a good family (a bit better than us in actual fact but that my parents could live with).

Sidney's reaction to my parents was typically perseptive. He said he thought my Mum was a dear and he looked forward to getting to know my Dad. Then he added sort of jokingly, "You don't look anything like either of them."

A shiver ran down my spine. Oh no, what now? Should I tell Sidney about my suspicions or should I keep my mouth shut? I decided that for now I wouldn't say anything. But of course the worry started to eat away at me. What would Sidney think if he found out I was adopted and not properly Jewish? What would he do?

Would he walk away? It was unbearable. All my life I felt other people were on solid ground but I was on shifting sands.

It must have been two months later, Sidney invited me on a riverboat trip to Greenwich on a Sunday. It might sound ridiculous but I had never been on a boat on the Thames. It wasn't the sort of thing my parents did and when I was growing up, there weren't all the wonderful school trips they have now. So I was really excited.

We caught the boat from Charing Cross pier. It was a beautiful mild spring day. We sat out on the open deck upstairs and we enjoyed watching all the famous buildings sail past. We were perfectly content, we held hands and didn't say very much.

Then out of nowhere I felt a sudden urge to tell Sidney everything. I don't know why I chose that moment. I just wanted us to go on sailing down the river like that, holding hands, forever. I wanted us to be together forever. If my secret was going to ruin everything then better it happened now, right away.

When I finished telling Sidney everything, I sat there, all trembly, dabbing away at my tears and waiting for everything to come to an end. Sidney's response amazed me. He said calmly and seriously, "Rita it's usually pretty straightforward to find out that sort of information, you know. There are records."

I looked at him dumbstruck. I supposed he thought I was a silly goose never to have thought of that myself. Did he mean I could have spared myself all these years of torment just by going to some office and *asking*?

Sidney said no, it was a bit more complicated than that. He cleared his throat and went all lawyerly. He said that if I really seriously believed I was adopted – and he agreed it did sound quite likely – then if I wanted he would make the necessary enquiries for me.

I said, "Yes please" just like that – as if he was offering me a lift somewhere.

Sidney asked, "Are you quite sure? Maybe you should think it over first? Speak to your parents?"

"I can't do that," I said. "I can't," because the truth was I loved my parents, I loved them dearly and the last thing I wanted to do was to hurt them.

Sidney looked thoughtful. He said, "I understand you want to know Rita. But you might be opening Pandora's box."

Well firstly I had no idea what Pandora's box was and secondly I couldn't bear all this a moment longer.

I burst out, "I *need* to know. If I'm adopted, then I'm not really properly Jewish, am I and for all I know you won't want anything more to do with me."

Sidney looked horrified. "Rita!" he cried out. I still remember how he looked and his words. "How can you say such a thing? Don't you realise I love you?"

I looked at him. He loved me. He didn't care *what* I was.

In a heartfelt whisper, so the other passengers on the boat couldn't hear what he was saying, he said, "We need to move with the times Rita."

I don't know who leant in first but we kissed. It was the best moment of my life up till then, us two sailing down the river, moving with the times.

Iris

IRIS WAS KEPT in hospital for two days, for observation and she had a whale of a time. She loved all the care and attention, a succession of young nurses and doctors fussing over her, some of them not bad-looking at all. They asked her loads of questions which gave her the opportunity to keep them at her bedside with long, detailed answers. She was wheeled about for X-rays and tests and, because she had been the victim of crime, she was visited by both a policeman and a victim support person neither of whom much impressed her.

The young policeman was a lowly constable with bad skin and Iris found both his spelling and his general knowledge abysmal. He fell at the first hurdle of the number of "ns" and "ts" in Bennett and, from then on, Iris was merciless.

He asked her for a brief description of her bag and its contents and said there was no way they could go looking for a book.

Iris said, "It is an immensely important book."

"Like an antique?" the policeman asked.

Iris frowned. "Antiquarian," she corrected him, "that's what you say for books. Antique is for furniture, that sort of thing. No, it's not antiquarian but it matters a great deal to *me. And* it belongs to the library."

"If you take your crime reference number to the library," the policeman said, "I'm sure they'll let you off paying a fine."

Iris looked at him. "I'm not worried about having to pay a fine," she said. "I *need* the book back. You don't seem to understand. I dare say you're not a great reader? Some books mean a lot to people and this one means a lot to *me*."

The policeman fidgetted. He said, "You can probably claim a lot of what you've lost back on your insurance, you know. If you've got insurance?"

"Of course I've got insurance," Iris snapped although, actually, she wasn't at all sure she did.

"Well, so you can buy another book," the policeman said, putting away his notepad.

Exasperated, Iris exclaimed, "You can't just replace a book like a pair of socks you know. This one was quite old, not actually antiquarian but almost certainly out of print. There's no way I'd be able to find another copy." She lay back on her pillows theatrically. Raising her voice made her head hurt.

When she opened her eyes, after a dramatically long pause, the policeman had gone. Iris was outraged. He hadn't taken her loss seriously at all. All that tedious advice about stopping her bank cards and changing the locks on her front door but the one thing that really *mattered* – *The Story of a Russian Princess* – he couldn't be bothered with.

The young woman from Victim Support was no better. She introduced herself, "Hi there Iris, I'm Zahreen." She settled on Iris's visitor's chair. Besides a perfunctory visit from Joanna, Iris had not had any visitors. Zahreen leant forward and took Iris's hand – as if they were going to be bosom buddies.

"How *are* you?" she began. "Are you ok to talk about what happened?"

Iris considered Zahreen through narrowed lids. She was wearing a voluminous headscarf and tight jeans. Her flirtatious manner suggested that she was a very attractive woman but, in actual fact, she was nothing of the sort. She was certainly curvaceous but she had a beaky face.

"I'm perfectly capable of talking about what happened," Iris answered, "but I prefer to be called Mrs Bennett."

She saw Zahreen flinch. She let go of Iris's hand and sat back in her chair. She looked as if she had just heard that what Iris had was catching. "That's fine Mrs Bennett," she said coldly. "So just tell me what happened in your own words."

Although Zahreen was a fat lot of use, when her visit was over, Iris was actually sorry to see her go since even busybody Zahreen was preferable to no visitors at all.

The truth was there was not much wrong with Iris. Apart from the shock and a few bumps and bruises, she was totally unharmed. She was disappointed when they told her she could go home. Joanna and Nat, who came to collect her on the Saturday morning, seemed disappointed too. Preoccupied by the baby's arrival, they must have hoped that Iris's hospital stay would be a fair bit longer. They didn't want to be burdened with taking care of Iris on top of everything else. But Iris was a tough old bird and, by Thursday, she was well enough to go back to the class.

She enjoyed her entrance: everyone exclaiming over her awful bruises and being shocked and concerned. But, as they settled down, Iris sensed that in her absence something had changed. She had missed something but she couldn't for the

250

life of her work out what it was. There seemed to be a new caution in the group, everyone treading extra carefully. But when Iris asked Sabine, *sotto voce*, if anyone had read anything out of the ordinary the week before, Sabine shook her head.

Iris was of course preoccupied by the coming confrontation with Dorothy. She had thought about it a lot; she had imagined being triumphant, she had imagined being magnanimous. But, whichever way she imagined it, she found it very hard to predict Dorothy's reaction.

Without the book, Iris was of course at a serious disadvantage. She couldn't simply show Dorothy the offending pages where her life story and the Russian princess's so flagrantly coincided. She had to rely on her own memory and she supposed it was just possible that Dorothy might simply deny all knowledge of it. "Prove it," she might say. "Bring the book along and show me Iris, if you're so sure," and of course Iris couldn't do that.

At the start of the class, she said to Dorothy, "I'd like to have a private word with you after class, if I may," and watched her reaction like a hawk but there was none. Dorothy couldn't be innocent, could she? It was impossible. She must be a much more accomplished fraudster than you would think. Was there actually more to the little librarian than met the eye? For the first time, Iris considered Dorothy with a touch of grudging admiration.

Staying to have a showdown in the classroom turned out not to be an option because the minute their time was up, the caretaker barged in and announced he had work to do in there. Even before they all had their coats on, he had started dragging in his trolley with cleaning materials and a metal step ladder which made a frightful din.

He taunted Dorothy, "'Ow's the life stories comin' along then? I'm tellin' yer – you should 'ear mine." He gave a filthy laugh. "Though might be a bit strong for you lot. I'm X-rated, I am."

In the passage outside, Iris rolled her eyes and sighed, "Dreadful man."

Dorothy looked, as usual, long-suffering.

"So," Iris said, "do you have an office here we could go to?" She knew perfectly well that Dorothy didn't.

Dorothy shook her head.

"Oh dear," Iris said.

To her surprise, Dorothy said impatiently, "What is it Iris? Can't we just talk here?"

"No," Iris answered. "We can't. It's something which needs to be discussed in private."

For the first time, she saw a tremor of concern cross Dorothy's face. Good.

"I could ask Gemma on the reception if there's somewhere free we could sit for five minutes?" Dorothy suggested.

Iris said, "No." She knew the young woman on the front desk would refuse any favour if she knew it was for Iris. "I tell you what. Let's go and have a quick cup of tea somewhere. There must be some half decent places round here."

Dorothy looked both alarmed and suspicious. "I haven't got long."

Iris said, "It won't *take* long," and, for the first time, she allowed herself to give Dorothy a really filthy look.

They sat in the first place they came to since Iris couldn't walk far and Dorothy insisted she didn't have long. It was a scruffy-looking café close to where Larkrise Road joined the High Road. Iris ordered a pot of tea for two and, even though the owner pushed his cakes, they both said no.

Iris had been intending to play a cat-and-mouse game with Dorothy, to draw out the malicious pleasure of the moment by playing with her victim. But once they were sitting opposite each other, her excitement got the better of her and she blurted out, "I borrowed a fascinating book from the library, *The Story of a Russian Princess*."

Dorothy didn't bat an eyelid. She asked coolly, "Who is it by?" and of course Iris couldn't remember.

She hesitated. "Some Russian name." Then she moved in for the kill. "The thing is Dorothy, parts of it were exactly the same as *your* life story."

"That's hardly surprising," Dorothy said, shrugging. "The experiences of those Russian emigré families were often sadly similar. The same suffering, the same difficulties of adjustment."

"Yes," Iris said, "but the story about your father trying to hang himself, it was in *her* book too."

Dorothy said, "Well, of course, there were a lot of suicide attempts – some of them successful alas." She looked down. "It's still very painful for me to talk about it Iris."

To her amazement, Iris felt her triumph slipping away from her. She insisted, "But Dorothy, it was identical in almost every detail. I think you copied it. I know you borrowed it from the library just before me. I picked it up off the trolley."

Dorothy looked her straight in the eye. She didn't falter. She said, "I *beg* your pardon Iris?"

Iris could scarcely believe what was happening. "It's just not possible," she said, "for two people's stories to be so absolutely identical. Unless —"

Dorothy interrupted her. "I find you very presumptuous Iris. And not for the first time. I did help Gerald reshelve some books that day. I often do. But they weren't all mine. Anyway, why don't you show me this book? Let me see what you're talking about."

Iris said, "I can't. I don't have it anymore. That was the book that was stolen."

"So how do you know," Dorothy exclaimed, "that *she* didn't copy *me*? I mean the story of my poor father's attempted suicide was well known in Russian circles. How do you know this so-called princess didn't decide to include it in hers to pep things up a bit?"

"Well," Iris said, "that seems highly unlikely to me."

"Does it?" Dorothy said shrilly. "Does it? Haven't you noticed *everyone* embroiders their life story?" She glared at Iris, she did appear to be genuinely offended. "Surely you must have noticed everyone's at it?" she demanded. "All of them – making things out to be oh so much better than they really were: Sabine with her storybook Belgian childhood and Esther pretending her mother was such a poor innocent victim when she was obviously a manipulative minx. No-one's telling the truth."

"What about you?" Iris asked. "Were *you* telling the truth, Dorothy?"

"Yes," Dorothy said. "I was." She blinked. "And if you've come across a book which tells a similar story, I can only suppose my own dreadful experience wasn't unique. In fact

I'm wondering if this princess isn't actually a distant relative of ours because we were connected to Russian royalty, you know."

It was beyond belief. Of course, Iris didn't believe a word Dorothy said but, without the book, she was at a loss.

As she fixed Dorothy with a steely stare, Dorothy changed the subject abruptly.

"Actually I'm glad you asked me to have a word, Iris," she said, "because there's something I'd like to discuss with *you*. Do you remember Mercy House?"

Iris stiffened. The library book she had never returned; surely Dorothy wasn't going to bring that up now?

"Yes," she said, after a moment. "I do. Ramshackle place."

"I thought I remembered you coming to the library," Dorothy said. She paused while Iris swallowed a lot of tea. "The thing is this Iris: I've written a new chapter – about my time at Mercy House. There were a lot of things which went on there behind the scenes, you know. Involving high-ups. Things were covered up which shouldn't have been. And now the building's been sold and knocked down without a by your leave and there's a block of flats going up and I can't keep quiet anymore. I've written a chapter about what went on at Mercy House over the years and when I make it public, it's going to cause quite a stink."

Iris continued to fix Dorothy with a steely stare. "And you're sure *this* chapter isn't a fabrication?" she asked.

Dorothy glared back. "Yes."

"So where do I come in?"

Dorothy paused again. There was something very

calculated, Iris thought, about the way she sipped her tea and then dabbed her lips with a paper napkin.

"I know you're very well connected," Dorothy said. "You've got friends in high places, you're always telling us. So I was wondering, if I gave it to you, would you be able to pass it on to someone important, someone who could *do* something about it?"

Iris was just starting to feel a faint stirring of excitement when Dorothy added sharply, "Only on condition we don't hear another *word* about the Russian princess of course."

Summer

THE SECOND CHANCE CENTRE

Summer Term 2013 Register

Course: Life Story Writing			Day: Thursday Time: 2pm			
Instructor: Dorothy Woodward			Room Number: G3			
Student Name						
Pearl Barter						
Iris Bennett						
Enid Harkin						
Sabine Moreton						
Esther Solomon						
Edgar Whistler						
NOTE LOW NUMBERS						

Pearl

PEARL WAS AT the sink when she heard the front door open and, without turning round, she called, "Hi Kai, did you remember to get the stuff for the washing machine?"

She heard Kai answer something she couldn't make out and she asked, "Well, did you?"

Behind her, she heard Kai in the kitchen doorway saying, "Nan —" and she turned round, ready to scold him for having forgotten.

There were two people in the doorway: Kai and a small bony girl. Pearl stood still. A girl. She asked, "Who's this then, Kai?" and Kai answered – she thought, "Neem."

The girl said, "Hi" in a small voice and gave just a bit of a smile.

Pearl stood frozen. There hadn't been a girl in here since Tracy and the sight of one, so close to Kai, spooked her.

She made herself smile welcomingly and offered tea but Kai said vaguely, "We got stuff to do," and they disappeared into his room. Pearl was left in the kitchen to get over the shock.

Of course she was pleased, in a way. Who wouldn't be? It was another step forward like the first tooth or the first word. Oh yes, she was pleased enough – in a way – but she was also scared stiff. Kai was only 17 and he didn't know which way was up. He was a dear but a dozy dear, a dear who – as far as Pearl was aware – didn't know anything about girls and so on. And now – out of the blue – here was a girl, it was true, not a terribly scary-looking girl – no make-up, not much chest – but a girl who could, without even meaning to, derail Kai's young life. The instant Neem had appeared in the doorway, Pearl had foreseen it in a flash: history repeating itself, Kai in his innocence getting this young girl pregnant and everything Pearl hoped for him going by the wayside.

She had to sit down. What were they doing together even now, dead quiet in Kai's room? And this girl, with her funny name, where had she sprung from? How long had this been going on? Kai could be a dark horse when he chose; maybe he and this girl had been hanging out together for some time already and no one any the wiser.

Pearl considered the girl. She was a scrap of a thing but she had a quantity of hair. It stood out around her head like an Afro but it was light brown. When she turned to go with Kai to his bedroom, her hair seemed to turn a moment later as if it were following her. Pearl supposed that she must have a bit of mixed race in her somewhere. Not that Pearl cared about that. It was the inside which mattered. The girl had to be a good girl, who wouldn't lead Kai up the garden path. Still, she thought, still, a titchy girl in scruffy clothes with weird hair; couldn't Kai have done a bit better?

She waited and waited. It was evening already, the clocks had gone forward, it stayed lighter later but even so it was starting to get dark. Still the pair of them didn't come out of Kai's room. What should she do? Should she knock? Should she barge in? Should she call Mavis and ask what Mavis would do? Not that Matt had ever had much in the way of girlfriends. It was long past time to make the tea. Pearl decided to start cooking very noisily, banging the pans and the cupboard doors in the hope that it would remind them it was getting late. She made such a racket she must have missed hearing the front door go and when Kai came into the kitchen, she asked "Where is she?"

Kai said, "She had to get back. What you cooking Nan?"

Pearl said, "Spaghetti" and then, "Where did you meet her Kai?"

Kai grinned. "At Mr Robinson's party."

"Did you not know her before?"

"I mean," Kai said, "she was in my class but we kind of lost touch, you know? I mean just Facebook friends and that. Like, we never really hung out together or anything. But we kind of met up again at the party." He laughed.

"What's she up to?" Pearl asked. "Is she still at school or at college or what?"

"Still at school," Kai said. "She's doing A levels. She's clever Nan."

Pearl wondered whether a clever girl was more or less dangerous than a slow one. "What A levels she doing then?"

Kai said, "DT and drama and something else. I can't remember. She's brilliant at drama and DT. She wants to make puppets."

"Puppets?" Pearl said. "Is that a job – making puppets?"

Kai said, "Ye-es."

"Well, you're quite a pair, aren't you?" Pearl said. "You with your music and her with her puppets?"

Then, wondering suddenly if she hadn't got the wrong

261

end of the stick after all, she asked straight out, "Is she your girlfriend or just a friend?"

And Kai gave one of his vague answers she couldn't stand. "A bit of both."

While they ate, Pearl wondered how to put it. There was no getting round it; she had to come out with it. As usual, she regretted the total absence of men in the family, a father figure to do this awkward job for her.

"D'you know about taking precautions?" she asked Kai.

"What Nan?"

"Condoms." Pearl said. "I'm assuming you know about using condoms?"

Kai looked appalled. "For God's sake Nan," he exclaimed. "Why are you suddenly talking about that?"

Pearl fixed him with a hard stare. "Use them. We've had enough babies come by mistake in this family."

"God Nan," Kai said. "You're so *rude*. I come home with a girl *once* and right off you start talking about condoms."

"Once is enough," Pearl said. "You'll thank me."

Kai looked outraged. He got up from the table and was about to leave the room when Pearl said, "Washing up."

Kai did the washing up without saying a word.

Pearl tried to put things right by adding, "I'm not just talking about Neem Kai, I mean generally."

But Kai didn't utter another word and in the morning he went out without saying goodbye to her.

Pearl supposed she could have handled things better but she didn't regret one bit what she had said. It had to be done and if Kai sulked for a while, then so be it. So long as he stopped by Boots while he was about it.

During the Easter break, Pearl missed the life story group. Her feelings about the lot of them had not gone away. But you wouldn't want to miss the next instalment of all their stories, would you, once you had listened this far.

Renée – and Renée's interrupted story – still preyed on her mind. Kai had found Renée's address in an instant online: Flat 7, Wesleyan Court, 24–26 Larkvale Gardens. You could find out pretty much everything it seemed online: Renée's age (70–74) and who else lived with her at the same address (Malcolm Thorpe).

Pearl knew which one was Wesleyan Court. It was that new block of luxury flats where the Methodist church used to be. Renée was obviously well off. Pearl felt a pang of envy; Renée was well off, she presumably still had a husband too, Malcolm and she had grown up with a father. She had everything which Pearl had missed out on. So in fact she *owed* Pearl the one thing which she could give her: the truth.

But the thought of confronting Renée, of perhaps having a scene put her off. What if her idea about why Renée had run away was simply wrong? What then? What if Renée refused to talk to her?

Pearl mulled it over. She walked past shiny new Wesleyan Court a couple of times and wondered which windows were Renée's. Maybe she had one of those big balconies? On the Larkrise Estate, the balconies were all tiny and always strung with washing.

Pearl thought about visiting Renée for a good few weeks. She imagined ringing the bell and Renée answering and herself saying – what? How would she put into words the reason why she had come? When Kai went into his strop and stopped speaking to her, she decided to go for it. She reckoned that if, by chance, she came up with something really amazing to tell Kai, he would forgive her and start talking to her again.

On a particularly bright and optimistic April morning, Pearl set out. She had dressed up really smartly. Whatever happened, she would be looking good. It was a bit of a trek all the way up to Larkvale Gardens so she took the bus. She didn't want to arrive already tired out for the moment of truth.

The bus set her down just around the corner and, as she turned into Larkvale Gardens, she half expected to see Renée coming towards her with a big smile. But of course she wasn't. Pearl crossed over to Wesleyan Court which was on the nicer side, away from the railway line and climbed the couple of broad, clean steps to the glass double doors. She looked at the door bells. Next to number 7 in neat black type was THORPE. Pearl stood there for a long time. No one came in or out. It would be so much easier if Renée just happened to appear and Pearl could talk to her directly face to face. Maybe this was a crazy idea? Maybe she should just go home? Almost without intending to, she rang the bell. After a moment or two, Renée's voice came through the intercom, querying, suspicious, "Hello?"

Pearl cleared her throat.

Edgar

OVER THE EASTER weekend, Madeleine pointed out to Edgar that summer would be coming along soon. He nodded absently, thinking she was just passing the time of day. They were sitting together on his sofa, Madeleine more lying down in fact with her tired legs across Edgar's lap. He was absorbed in massaging her dear feet.

"So I was thinking," Madeleine said, "in the summer, why don't we go off on a little trip together somewhere?"

Edgar started. It was not long since he had read Joan's revelations about their trip to the Bay of Naples. A trip struck him as a very risky idea.

He played for time. "Where were you thinking of?"

And Madeleine answered immediately, "Venice."

Well, he was relieved it was somewhere he and Joan had never been. That would have felt just too uncomfortable. But Joan had never wanted to go to Venice; she found the idea of all the canals off-putting. Edgar remembered the way she used to shudder when something came up she didn't like the sound of.

He thought about strolling around Venice with Madeleine. How wonderful. How good it would feel too to reward such a deserving, hard-working woman with the luxury of a holiday. He thought about Madeleine smiling, relaxed, appreciative. He thought about candle-lit dinners, a nice hotel. He thought about Madeleine in a gondola and worried briefly.

"Were you thinking of any particular time?" he asked, careful not to reveal any suggestion of enthusiasm or agreement.

"Well," Madeleine said. "Well. At the end of June Luke's going off travelling with his friends and I believe Desiree's going for a week in Aya somewhere or other. They've both been working, they've saved. So I'll most probably have a week or so with no one at home to worry about and I thought why shouldn't I take a trip too? I've looked. It's not that pricey."

"Why not?" Edgar agreed. "Why not?"

"Come on," Madeleine said. "I can see you're not too keen. What is it?"

Edgar hesitated. What was it? It was partly a superstitious fear of too much happiness, he supposed; grabbing more than your fair share and everything coming apart. But it was also maybe a little bit to do with Joan's story. Madeleine seemed fond enough of him here in London, surprising as it was. But would she feel as fond of him in Venice? Or would she, like Joan, be carried away by the happy-go-lucky holiday mood and end up making eyes at someone else? Someone younger, more good-looking, more *educated*? There was no way he could come out with that so he just mumbled, "It takes a bit of getting used to."

Madeleine looked at him through narrowed eyes. "When did you last go on holiday Edgar?"

He thought. "Nine, ten years ago. Before Joan got ill."

Madeleine paused respectfully. "Where did you go?"

Edgar wasn't sure. After a while, they got jumbled together, those foreign holidays. Not that there had been so many of them. They had cost an arm and a leg. But they had all been a bit samey in the end. He wondered suddenly whether Joan hadn't found them all a bit samey too and that was why she had ended up wandering off with that chap – if indeed she really had, if it wasn't just some sort of *creative writing*.

He said, "Maybe Spain I think. Or Greece."

Madeleine smiled. "Not Venice."

"No," Edgar said, "not Venice."

Madeleine mischievously lifted her leg to nuzzle the soft underneath of his chin with her toes. "Think it over," she said gently. "We could have such a lovely holiday."

The next day Edgar went back to Joan's notebook. He supposed that teatime with Trevor in Sorrento was the sum of it. But what if there was more? What if Trevor, who sounded a decent sort, mind you, who hadn't pushed his luck, was just the tip of the iceberg? There were only two or three more chapters in Joan's book. It occurred to Edgar that wasn't much to show for three whole terms' worth of writing. Where was the rest of it? Was it still hidden away somewhere or had Joan got rid of the rest, leaving just the most needling reproachful bits for Edgar?

The next section was called "One of Life's Turning Points". Edgar didn't like the sound of that at all. As far as he was concerned, their life had not really had any turning points; it had been plain sailing. But he settled to read it grimly at the dining table, running his finger along beneath the lines so he didn't lose his place if he got a surprise.

Edward was the most loyal and loving husband. We enjoyed thirty-five years of happy marriage. But there was one year when he let me down. Now I know that I will most probably pass away this year or next, it seems all wrong to be writing about the bad bits when I should really be recalling the good times. But at nights when you can't sleep that's what comes back to haunt you: the one year out of the thirty-five when Edward let me down.

Edgar mopped his face and neck with his handkerchief. He was sweating with a mixture of anger and dread. What was Joan playing at? He hadn't done anything that terrible, had he? Most men got up to far worse. Strictly speaking, he hadn't even been unfaithful. True, he didn't come out of that bad patch too well. But what had Joan been thinking of, writing it all down, she, who rarely made a fuss, in the end making such a song and dance over nothing very much at all?

Of course he knew what he was about to read which, in one way, made it less shocking: the small unhappy details, the year Joan started with the change of life, her weeping, her moods and his frustration. Then there was the flirty young woman who had come to work in Menswear – bad timing. He could barely remember her name to be honest but Joan reminded him: Poppy. All he had done was chat, pay the odd compliment and have a quick drink with her once or twice – a few times – after work. One kiss. It was over almost before it began. Someone had said something. He had come to his senses. What upset him was the revelation of the grudge Joan had borne; all those years afterwards, when he thought all was forgotten and forgiven, it was anything but. Joan had gone on brooding, holding what he had done against him. He had thought she was perfectly content but in actual fact she was nothing of the sort. That was most probably why she had gone to the wretched creative writing class in the first place: to get it out of her system. She had left her notebook, meanly, so that she could have the last word.

Edgar read to the end. Nothing he didn't know there, just the details of the discovery: someone who worked with Joan passing by the same pub after work, catching sight of Edgar with Poppy, putting two and two together and making five. When he finished reading, he looked out of the window. He felt awfully sad but also somehow strangely detached as if he was floating away, floating away from Joan's creative writing and the house and the Larkrise Estate.

After a few moments, he wondered whether what he was feeling was that closure people talked about. He would call Madeleine when she finished work and tell her to look into tickets for Venice.

When the summer term started, he went back to the Second Chance Centre with a heavy heart. He really didn't want to but Madeleine, who of course had no idea why he had turned against it even more, insisted. Now he thought about Joan in her writing class, reading aloud what she had written to her group – how had she ever overcome her nerves to read aloud? – and everyone tutting and commiserating. Had Renée Thorpe realised that he was Edward, the less than perfect husband? Renée had never shown any sign of it; she had always been especially nice to him. But she had vanished – and maybe it was for the best.

The friendly chatty girl on the front desk had been replaced by a more severe one with blue hair. She called Edgar over and gave him a small plastic card. "We've got swipe cards now," she told him. "You'll need to touch in and out."

Edgar had no idea what she was talking about. He took the card, a nasty purple thing bearing the name Second Chance Centre in squat, chubby letters. He looked at it dubiously and the girl with the blue hair said carelessly, "Your teacher'll explain."

Dorothy seemed in her element with the swipe cards. They had been introduced at the library too, she told them, caused no end of trouble. Nonetheless she seemed to take great pleasure in explaining their workings over and over to everyone as they came in and it was well after 2 by the time they were all seated and ready to start.

Edgar looked round at the six women, none of whom did anything for him. Pearl was a good soul and Enid made him laugh but the others... What was he *doing* here? All along, he had gladly done Madeleine's bidding but now enough was enough. If in future Madeleine insisted he kept coming to classes, he would take up something useful instead.

Dorothy

DOROTHY PASSED CHRISTOPHER and Martin in the front hall, looking all lovey-dovey. Since Martin had moved in downstairs, she saw much less of Christopher and, while she had previously considered him a bit of a nuisance, now she found she missed him. Everything seemed to be working out very well for everyone else, she reflected rancorously. The most galling thing had been Gerald's MBE for inter-faith services. It was going to be announced in the Queen's Birthday Honours apparently but already everyone knew it was in the offing. It made Dorothy's blood boil. Gerald's library was a shambles. How could you reward someone whose cataloguing was such a mess and whose stock was in such a sorry state? Some of his inter-faith volunteers barely even spoke English. "The world's gone mad," Dorothy told Whittington. "Stark raving mad."

It made her even more determined to go public with her account of the goings-on at Mercy House despite her misgivings. Let someone finally suffer for their actions instead of everyone just waltzing away, scot-free, to enjoy their ill-gotten gains. It occurred to her with a pang of guilt that *she* probably didn't deserve to get away scot-free with her plagiarism of the Russian Princess. But no one had been harmed by her little criminal act had they, only the dead? She had cheated the group but that barely bothered her, not now she understood that they were *all* cheating.

Dorothy did worry about Iris though. She thought she had got the better of Iris but she wasn't absolutely sure. She guessed that most probably Iris knew full well she wasn't telling the truth but had no means of proving it. What Dorothy needed, she resolved, was some way to gain a hold on Iris, some piece of information about Iris which she wouldn't want made public either. Only that way could Dorothy guarantee that Iris would shut up about the dratted Russian princess. She turned to her new accomplice in crime, Google.

There were so many Iris Bennetts, it was hard to know where to start: 150 people in the UK with the name Iris Bennett. Dorothy looked for Iris Bennetts in London – still no end of them – and then Brondesbury. Here she straightaway struck gold: she found an Iris Bennett and an Iris Bennett-Ahmed both listed at the same address. Curious. She pondered for a moment and then googled Iris Bennett-Ahmed. She could barely believe her eyes: up came a whole string of items going back nearly fifteen years referring to Iris Bennett-Ahmed and a Yusuf Ahmed who seemed, oh joy, to have a criminal record.

Dorothy bent over her laptop. She was thrilled. As far as she could remember, Iris had told them she had been married twice: her first husband, Richard Galpin (Gilpin?) was a cad, her second, Maurice Bennett, a saint. But, apparently, she had been married three times and her third husband, who had slipped her mind, Yusuf Ahmed, seemed a rotter. Avidly, Dorothy read on: some sort of immigration fraud, a court case, accounts from the archives of the local paper of an unscrupulous character who had tricked a local woman, Mrs Iris Bennett, into marrying him in order to obtain a British passport and then set up a criminal ring to enable other foreign men to do the same. Dorothy was astounded when she came upon a photo of Yusuf Ahmed. At that time, Iris must already have been well into her sixties but the photo showed a devastatingly handsome man, not a day over forty. Dark, Mediterranean-looking, he looked out from the photo with a seductive smile. No wonder Iris had been swept off her bunion-ridden feet. Though how come she hadn't asked herself what Yusuf saw in her? Delighted, Dorothy copied down all the details and put them somewhere safe. Another quiet cup of tea with Iris should guarantee that the Russian Princess was never mentioned again.

Dorothy still felt herself drawn back to Mercy House even now the house was gone. Now that the days were getting longer, she sometimes went up there in the early evening when the workmen had finished for the day. The park was empty and quiet. The old spreading cedars of Lebanon still cast their dark shadows. But all around was a sad scene of devastation with the first poles rising up out of the foundations of the new building. It was the time of day when Dorothy often used to leave the library, walking down the curving drive with the pleasant satisfaction of a day's work well done. It was the time of day when shady figures would sometimes appear, slipping furtively up the drive to transact their night time business at Mercy House. Sometimes, they would drive brashly up in expensive cars, park on the forecourt (even in the disabled bays) and let themselves in the front door with their own keys. Other times, they would sneak quietly round the back, past the library windows and let themselves in discreetly via the library entrance. On those evenings, Dorothy would often decide to work late so that she could snoop. She had imagined back then that she would never tell anyone what she had seen; it was a dark secret she would keep to herself. But now she found she was simply bursting to tell all and sundry.

She decided to raise the subject of Mercy House with her group and ask them if they had any recollections of the place.

Iris was, as usual, the first one to speak up. "I used to go to the library from time to time and to the concerts and the poetry recitals. My friends the Chatterjees sometimes came along too. They always felt it was such a shame the place was so run down."

Dorothy bridled. "We —" she began but Iris ploughed on. "It was all so ramshackle, wasn't it? The council couldn't afford the upkeep. They should have sold it years ago."

"Well," Dorothy started. "Well —"

Enid piped up. "I remember we used to have life drawing classes there once upon a time."

Dorothy flushed. She remembered the life drawing classes. She remembered the scandal one warm summer's evening when the teacher – now identified as Edith – had decided to recreate an apparently famous French nude scene on the lawn for the class to copy.

She asked, "Does anyone else have any memories of Mercy House?"

Sabine and Esther shook their heads. Edgar and Pearl looked vague and a little embarrassed; Dorothy supposed they were not library goers.

Iris added, "Nowadays I go to the Unitarian Church hall. The librarian there's a *gem*."

Dorothy gave Iris a hard look. Where was this heading?

Iris smiled. "Actually, a funny thing happened the last time I was there."

Dorothy cut her off. "First let's hear what everyone's brought along this week. You and I can have a word together afterwards."

Esther

ANYWAY SIDNEY WENT to the Records Office and made his enquiries and came back and told me that my name wasn't on the Adopted Children's Register. For about two seconds I thought that was the end of it. I had made the whole thing up (along with my make-believe memories of splashing fountains and tiled floors.) But I could tell from the look on his face that it wasn't. He explained to me gently that up until something called the 1939 Adoption of Children Act, it was possible for people to adopt children privately. That meant someone who was in the know, a GP say, could bring together a young woman who was in trouble and a childless couple and arrange for the baby to be adopted privately without the authorities knowing anything about it. My head spun. I imagined a whole world of secrecy, babies being privately swapped from one life to another and nobody any the wiser. If that was what had happened to me, did anyone even know anymore where I was originally from or who my original parents were?

I must have looked a bit strange because Sidney put his arm round me and said he knew it was a lot to take in. But, he said, he had been thinking a lot and there was something else he wanted to tell me. Well I braced myself for the worst. But what came next was actually like a fairy tale. I forgot to say we were walking in Golders Hill Park on a Sunday when all this happened. It was a perfect summer's day. Sidney said he understood now why I needed to find out even if at first he hadn't really. He wanted to find out too. It would be our quest. (He had said "our"!) But because I might be about to find out something upsetting, he wanted me to know first that there was a safe happy future waiting for me to step into if I wanted. Also, he wanted me to understand that it didn't make the slightest bit of difference to him whether I was properly Jewish or not. He loved me how I was and he didn't care about the rest. Then he fumbled in his jacket pocket. For a minute, I thought he was getting out a hanky. But what he got out was a little red plush box and when he opened it inside was the prettiest sapphire and diamond engagement ring. After he had cleared his throat a few times, he came out with it, "Rita, will you marry me?"

Well of course I said yes, yes like a shot and he put the ring on my ring finger and his hands were all sweaty. He kissed me, I remember we were just down the hill from the café near the bandstand and a few moments later a jazz band struck up with Nat King Cole's "Smile" and ever after that was "our" song.

I wish I didn't have to tell what came next. We got on the bus back to Hendon on cloud nine and Sidney came in to talk to my father. They were shut up together for an awfully long time. I started to get scared. What on earth was going on? My father couldn't have said no, could he? Meanwhile I was in the kitchen with my Mum and I told her what had happened and she started to cry. That wasn't the reaction I had hoped for either. But she hugged me tight and congratulated me and admired my ring as best she could through her tears and I supposed she was sad because now I was going to leave home.

Finally Sidney and Dad came out. Neither of them looked that happy and when I saw that I started to cry too. "What's wrong?" I begged them. "Tell me, what's wrong?"

Dad said, "Nothing's *wrong* Rita. We're very happy we're going to have Sidney in the family." But he still didn't look happy. He looked uncomfortable, queesy almost as if he had indigestion.

It was Sidney who spoke. "Your Dad's given us the go-ahead Rita. No worries on that front. But he's told me something else too."

Mum gave a strangled cry. "Morris!" She looked at Dad as if he had just gambled away the family fortune.

Dad said sternly, "Rachel, this is the right moment. We can't let the young couple go along to plan their wedding and find out for themselves."

"Find out *what*?" I screamed. "Find out what?"

Of course I already knew. But I needed to hear Dad say it. He just stood there, looking sick. In the end it was Sidney who explained.

Everything turned out to be just how he had told me. My parents couldn't have children of their own and because it was making my Mum so miserable and ill, eventually their doctor suggested adoption. It was a sort of sideline for him apparently, matching up childless couples with single mothers who couldn't cope or who believed they were giving their babies a better future. He knew of a young girl, Irish apparently, who had had a child by the father of the family she worked for. The family had wanted her to get rid of the baby but she wouldn't. As a result they had thrown her out. She was living locally hand to mouth, barely keeping her head above water because of course she had no job and she couldn't go out to work because of the baby. She had even been seen begging in the West End together with the baby. The doctor told my parents the baby was a charming little girl, by then coming up to two.

I interrupted, "Did she have a dog?"

Everyone looked at me as if I was mad. But actually for me suddenly everything made sense: the fountain I dimly remembered was maybe the big one in Trafalgar Square. The tiled floors may have been in railway stations and places where we had sat begging. But no one knew anything about a dog.

By now everyone — apart from Sidney — was in tears. Mum was sobbing hysterickly, I had tears pouring down my face and even Dad had to keep on blowing his nose. Only Sidney kept his cool.

He said politely but firmly we should all sit down and have a cup of tea. Even though she was in such a state, my mum made tea. Then my dad who had pulled himself together a bit finished the story.

My parents met the Irish girl — who I still couldn't think of as my mother — at the doctor's house. The baby,

I was there. Dad said I was so pretty and sweet they had both fallen for me straightaway. The Irish girl had dressed me up in a little flowery dress and put a bow in my hair. I seemed very placid and smiley though, he added, that had changed when they brought me home. Various matters had been discussed and both sides were given a fortnight to think things over. My parents made up their minds very quickly. "Your Mum knew the minute she set eyes on you," Dad said. But the girl couldn't bring herself to part with her baby and kept asking for longer to decide. In the end the doctor, not our present doctor, this one was called Dr Glaser, long retired, he had put his foot down: either the girl hand the baby over or he would look elsewhere. A week later they got the call. They could collect me from Dr Glaser's house on Sunday afternoon.

"What about *her*?" I asked. "The young girl?" (I still couldn't think of her as my mother.) "What became of her?"

"We don't know," Dad said firmly.

Mum added, "We think she went back to Ireland. To make a fresh start."

I had so many questions I didn't know where to start. I asked, "What was her name?"

My parents looked at each other. Dad said, "You're not going to go looking for her, are you? She's probably long married with a family of her own by now. Don't go making trouble."

Suddenly I wanted to scream. For years they had told me off for making things up while they had been making things up the whole time, in fact they had made up my whole life. I had to sit back in my chair and close my eyes for a minute, I felt so strange.

280

Then I heard Sidney's voice, calm and reasonable, saying, "Maybe it would be best to get this all over with in one go Morris? Why don't you just tell Rita the bare facts and be done with it?"

To my surprise, Dad did as he was told. "Jenny," he said. "Her name was Jenny. We weren't told her surname, Dr Glaser thought it was better that way. And the father was Stanley, I think, Stanley. Jewish."

It was that which sent me over the edge. Was it supposed to make things any better? Was *that* what Dad thought? That it was all ok because I was actually *half* Jewish? (Half Jewish like a mongrel kitten with marmalade and tabby patches.)

"Oh," I said in a stroppy voice I didn't know I had, "so I suppose that makes it all alright, does it? He had a family of his own, he got the poor maid pregnant, tried to force her to have an abortion even though she didn't want one and then didn't lift a finger to help her once the baby was born. But it's all just fine because he was *Jewish*?"

Sidney said, "Now Rita, your dad didn't say that."

Suddenly another horrible thought occurred to me. "Do we know him?"

My parents both said "No" so quickly I was sure it was another lie.

Dad added, "Well obviously we don't know for sure who he was. But Dr Glaser assured us he lived some way off and he didn't mix in our circles."

Even in the middle of that awful scene, I thought what a funny expression that was to use. Mum and Dad didn't really mix in any circles. Dad's turn of phrase somehow gave me to understand that this Stanley, whoever he was, was rather posh.

Not that I cared. The longer the awful conversation went on, the more I just wanted to turn my back on the whole mess and run off and start afresh with Sidney. I honestly wouldn't have blamed him if he had got cold feet after all that. But he didn't, bless him, he stood by me. Even when Dad came out with the most breathtaking thing of all. Our synagogue didn't consider me properly Jewish apparently so in order for us to get married there I would need to convert.

I asked, "Convert to what?" not believing my ears.

My mum said in a whisper, "To being Jewish."

Then Sidney lost it. He had been so good and so patient but that was the last straw. He exclaimed, "That's ridiculous. I'm not having Rita put through that. If they won't marry us, we'll find someone else who will."

When I was done gazing at him adoringly, I sneaked a look at my poor parents. They looked so distraught, so devastated, I couldn't help feeling sorry for them. To have their only daughter go off and not get married in their synagogue would be a whole scandal for them.

I realised that up till then I had only thought about myself. But the truth was it was all awful for my parents too. (When all was said and done, they were my parents.) Up till that day they had lived a normal family life. Now they were petrefied it was all going to fall apart. And unlike me they didn't have a lovely new future just waiting to walk into.

Iris

IRIS COULD NOT fathom why Dorothy, who obviously disliked her intensely and was frightened Iris might spill her dirty little secret, wanted to have tea with her a second time. What was she playing at? Why wasn't she giving her a wide berth? They had split the bill last time; it certainly wasn't a free pot of tea she was after. Iris doubted that Dorothy's revelations about Mercy House amounted to anything much. What of any significance could possibly have taken place in that decrepit backwater? It was probably all a fabrication anyway, like Dorothy's so-called life story. Still, that was what it must be about; Dorothy was going to hand over her little exposé and Iris would be expected, via her high-up connections, to make it public. The trouble was that Iris didn't really have any high-up connections anymore. Some of them had died and the rest had been via the Chatterjees. Without the Chatterjees, Iris couldn't really claim to know them. She wondered who on earth she could pass Dorothy's manuscript on to.

But when they sat down in the same seedy café on the High Road and ordered their pot of tea, Dorothy didn't say anything about Mercy House. She seemed to be having trouble coming to the point.

Iris asked testily, "What is it you want Dorothy?"

She so resented the way Dorothy had sidestepped her accusation of plagiarism. It was obvious that every word Dorothy had written was pure fabrication and it infuriated Iris that, due to the theft of the book – in which she was herself an innocent victim – she had no hard evidence to back herself up. She was tempted to tell the group anyway. Dorothy was still on thin ice, no doubt about it.

Dorothy gave Iris a curious look. She took a slow sip of tea and patted her mouth with a paper napkin.

Iris assumed she was playing for time. She drummed her fingers on the table impatiently.

She was appalled when Dorothy said, "Does the name Yusuf Ahmed mean anything to you?"

Iris asked sharply, "Where have you come across Yusuf? What's he up to now?"

After all, she wasn't going to deny knowing Yusuf, was she? Despite what had happened, the man had been, for better for worse, her husband.

"I happened to come across his name online," Dorothy said. After a moment, she added, "Linked to yours."

Iris seethed. Computers were a closed book to her and she was well aware that Dorothy was flaunting her own expertise.

"Did you now?" she said. "And what did you find out?" She couldn't resist adding, "Miss Nosey Parker."

Dorothy flushed but carried doggedly on. "Using the internet isn't really being *nosey*, Iris. The information is *there*, publicly available, for everyone to find."

"Is it?" Iris asked in alarm. "What information?"

"Well," Dorothy said, "correct me if I'm wrong. I understood that you and he were married. You told us you had two husbands but you must have forgotten about this one. He got himself into some sort of trouble with the law, I believe..."

"All true," Iris said, not faltering. "All true. Yusuf was, I'm afraid, a lovable rogue."

Dorothy paused and, as she paused, Iris added witheringly, "It must be hard for you to understand that sort of thing. Your experience has been, if I'm right, rather limited in that respect."

Dorothy looked hurt. She retaliated, "It sounds as if this Yusuf was an experience best avoided."

Iris laughed. She raised her eyebrows suggestively and she said, "Well, in some ways, yes but in other ways, no." She looked archly at Dorothy.

Dorothy seemed to squirm. "Is it true he tricked you into marrying him?" she asked. "I read something along those lines."

"My," Iris said, "you *have* been doing your homework, haven't you?"

She considered Dorothy for a moment with her haughtiest expression and then she answered, "Yes, in a way he did but, in another way, I tricked him." And then, feeling quite suddenly a lot the worse for wear, she added, "Was there anything else? Because I really should be on my way."

Dorothy looked crestfallen.

Iris said, "Love all."

Dorothy didn't seem to understand.

Iris added, "A tennis term?" But that didn't seem to help either. Dorothy might know about computers but she obviously knew nothing at all about tennis.

Taking advantage of Dorothy's embarrassment, Iris asked,

"Was there anything else? Did you want to show me what you wrote about Mercy House?"

Dorothy scrabbled in her bag. She produced a few handwritten pages, closely folded. But she didn't hand them over to Iris; she held them in front of her.

"Well?" Iris said.

Dorothy clasped her papers. "I warn you," she said, "this is shocking reading. I know what you're thinking but every word of *this* is true. All I ask is that when you tell people about it, you don't say it came from me."

"So where am I supposed to say it came from?" Iris asked. "People will want to know."

Dorothy sat very straight. "Say a secret source," she said, "otherwise I will fear for my life."

Iris refrained from laughing; what *nonsense*. She took Dorothy's papers and humoured her by making a show of putting them away safely in her bag.

"Hang onto that bag," Dorothy said tactlessly, "like grim death."

They parted coldly. On the bus home, Iris wracked her brains as to who on earth she could possibly tell about Dorothy's supposed revelations.

Her memory let her down, not for the first time and when she got home she forgot all about Dorothy's papers. She was distracted by an imperious message from Joanna on her call minder; Joanna was informing her mother that she had signed her up for Gay Grandparenting classes. Whatever next? A chance, Joanna said, speaking slowly and purposefully, for Iris to become better informed on the issues around same-sex parenting. As a final kick in the teeth, she added that Nat's mother, Grandma Rox had already enrolled.

Iris fumed: the nerve. She didn't need any lessons on how to be a grandmother, gay or otherwise. If her granddaughter was, very unfortunately, going to have two mothers but no father, it was up to Joanna and Nat to deal with the consequences. There was no way she was going to classes.

Only much later in the evening did her thoughts wander back to her tea with Dorothy. She hadn't thought about Yusuf for a long time but now the hurt of the whole fiasco had long subsided, she enjoyed recalling the brief idyll which had preceded the scandal.

Right from the start, Yusuf had seemed too good to be true. He had sat down next to Iris in the park on a day when she was feeling particularly bleak and alone. He had asked her what the English word was for rhododendrons – he had pointed – and when she told him, he had laughed. He had a wonderful laugh, deep and rich and rolling. He had asked her what her name was and when, after a split second's hesitation, she had told him, he had laughed again and said, "So you are a flower too." Iris had wondered if that was a linguistic point or a compliment. For, after all, she couldn't fail to notice that Yusuf was a good bit younger than she was. But she knew there were men who were drawn to older women and she still considered herself an attractive woman. So when Yusuf suggested a coffee and an English lesson, she went along. It had gone from there.

Dark eyes which seemed to bore deep into her, luscious long black lashes and strong, even white teeth which he bared when he laughed. The caress of his bushy black beard against her skin. His magical way of undressing her, so skilled, barely perceptible, no fumbling, no violent urgency; it reminded Iris of nothing more than an accomplished waiter filleting a fish. And then. Oh then. His strong, capable hands taking her and his warm hairy arms holding her and his glorious body close against hers. Iris shut her eyes and shivered. For the delights she had experienced in bed – and elsewhere – with Yusuf, she could forgive him almost everything.

She sat in her armchair and relished the details of her reverie. Here she was, eighty years old and the memory of Yusuf still made her yearn.

It was getting dark outside. She loved the long June evenings and she left the curtains open as late as possible. But now it was time to draw them before she turned on the lights and wicked people could snoop in. She stood up with what felt like even greater difficulty. She noticed her new handbag sitting on the side table where she had left it when she came in. It was only then that she remembered Dorothy's papers.

Sabine

SABINE WONDERED WHO in the end would actually read her memories. Early on, she had made the decision not to tell Michael what she was writing and she had stuck to it. Obviously, she could not share it with her children, Anne and Luke. Or at least she supposed she could but she really didn't want to. They would understand why they had always seen so little of jolly Uncle Laurent and Uncle Charles. But they would then see everything in a different light too: not only their mother of course but their whole lifelong belief in her storybook Belgian childhood. She could not bear that. So had she really only written it for the group, for strangers? That made no sense at all. As she finished her last chapter and fretted over what to do, she thought of little Sage, her strangely named first grandchild, Anne's daughter, born last year. She imagined little Sage forty, fifty years from now, a mature woman with a developing interest in family history. By then, of course, everyone involved would be long gone: her dear grandmother Sabine, the mysterious great uncles. Sabine imagined a grownup version of Sage – as yet impossible to imagine – reading her grandmother's "Memories of my Belgian Childhood" which would by then be history and finding it fascinating. So, before hiding the manuscript away, Sabine dedicated it to Sage and, for the first time in years, she allowed herself to cry.

6. The Last Chapter

Childhood was drawing to an end, adolescence approached. When she was twelve, Sabine left Bois Joli and went to secondary school, to the local *Athenée*, a short tram ride away. Only Josette went there with her, Annick and Geneviève went instead to the local *collège* which was a less academic technical school. At the *Athenée* you learnt Latin and philosophy, at the *collège* you learnt more practical skills.

Sabine was happy at the *Athenée*. She liked the independence of taking the tram with Josette in the morning, comparing their homework en route, she liked to enter the grand gates of the *Athenée* and she liked many of her classes (which was not true at Bois Joli). She liked stopping sometimes in a café on the way home with a group of school friends to drink hot chocolate, to chat and laugh. Her universe began to grow and for the first time Woluwé Saint Pierre began to seem a little narrow.

At home things were different too. Charles and Laurent were at university now, studying medicine (Laurent) and dentistry (Charles). Although they still lived at home, they were almost never there. They spent their days at the faculty, they usually ate in the university canteen with their friends. When they came home, they paid no attention anymore to Sabine. Perhaps they were ashamed or perhaps they no longer remembered that they had performed their first medical procedures on her.

Her mother changed too. With the twins at university and her youngest child in secondary school, Bernadette began to devote more time to her mystic paintings. She joined a women's art group in Knokke and sometimes stayed up there for a week or two with the women artists.

During those weeks Sabine and her father were left to manage alone with meals cooked by an old Portuguese lady called Maria who did not speak a word of French. In the evenings, the doctor sat in his armchair and read medical journals or local history papers. Sabine did her homework in her bedroom and later read the forbidden teenage magazines which the doctor disapproved of secretly in bed.

It was the beginning of the 1960s. It seemed everyone's horizons were starting to open out. Even in Belgium, my dear slow Belgium, things were beginning to change. Only Dr Mertens stayed exactly the same.

At the *Athenée* Sabine began to learn English. She much preferred it to Flemish. For all Belgian schoolchildren in those years, English was the language of London, not so much the language of the US as now. It was the time of the Swinging Sixties, the epoch of the Beatles whose first hits we loved to sing with our terrible accents, "Please Please Me" and "Love, Love Me Do". It was the epoch of miniskirts and Carnaby Street, Twiggy and Mary Quant. Who would not want to learn English and visit London?

The distance between Brussels and London was much more in my youth than it is today. There was no tunnel under the Channel back then, no Eurostar. To travel from Brussels to London took a whole day: first an early morning train to the port of Ostend, then several hours on a turbulent ferry and finally another so slow train through the countryside of Kent to Victoria station. To travel to London in 1962 for a Belgian schoolgirl of just 15 was an incredible adventure!

Sabine had never been abroad (unless you count a short trip without interest to Luxembourg). So when they were told in their third year at the *Athenée* that there would be a school trip to London at Easter, the whole class was screaming. London seemed to us a fantastic paradise. Having now lived in London for fifty years, of course today I know better.

I remember almost every instant of that trip with pleasure. The school group took the early morning train to Ostend, their teachers greeted them in English at the station, "Good Morning, Good Morning" as if they were already in London. They were not too sick on the ferry. From the moment they disembarked in Dover, everything was different, strange and fascinating, to some – maybe the most chauvinistic – ridiculous but to Sabine exotic and attractive. She loved the sound of English spoken everywhere, even the announcements on the train seemed exciting. She loved the cosy little houses next to the railway line, each one with its own small garden.

When they arrived at Victoria Station, there was a moment of panic: it was so big, so dirty, so noisy. They had to take the Underground (which they knew already to call "the Tube") to their small hotel in Bayswater and they were all terrified to get separated from the group and lost in that dirty black labyrinth. But after that bad quarter of an hour, all was "fab". They spent three crazy days in London, they did not stop walking, they saw all the tourist sights, I do not think they slept one wink. They went to Carnaby Street and the Kings Road as well as to Buckingham Palace, Westminster Abbey and the Houses of Parliament which were of course de rigueur. The only problem was the English food. They were Belgian, they enjoyed good food but the food in London in the 1960s was execrable. For some of the children this was an insuperable problem, they swore they would never come back. But it did not matter to Sabine. On the way home, she told her classmates in the train that when she was grown up, she would live in London.

She told this to her parents too when she returned home. They laughed and her father said, "No, my silly Sabine, you will marry a good Belgian and live your life right here in Brussels." Like all *Bruxellois*, they thought their cosy capital was a paradise on earth and they could not understand why anyone would want to leave it. Especially with the European Community developing and Brussels acquiring the status of an international capital.

Sabine kept her dream. She worked hard at school and she counted the years, first five then four then three until she could escape.

When she was seventeen, she had her first boyfriend, Jean-Yves, a boy in her class who was the son of a prominent local piano dealer. She was fond of Jean-Yves, she liked his blue eyes and his exploring hands. But she stopped liking him the day she overheard her parents discussing what a good match he was and how marriage to Jean-Yves would put a stop to Sabine's foolish ideas of living in London. Poor boy, I do not think he ever understood why Sabine abruptly dropped him. But ten years later he married the prettiest girl in the school, Florence Sepulchre, settled in a grand house in Uccle and had four children so I guess that was a happy ending for him.

Sabine continued to pursue her plans in secret. She passed her final school exams and went to secretarial college. She knew her parents were surprised that she agreed so easily to their chosen path. They did not realise that they were helping her to achieve her ultimate objective. In 1968, as Brussels was growing, there was a high demand for bilingual secretaries and a secretary who spoke good English could earn much more than one who spoke only French and a little rusty Flemish. So there was nothing Sabine's parents could say when she announced, having completed secretarial college and about to celebrate her 21st birthday, that she was going to live in London for a year. She had found a job as an au pair, she would take English classes and yes, in a year's time she would come back and get a well-paid job as a smart PA in a Brussels firm.

Well, I expect you can guess how Sabine's story ended. She went to work for the Finch family who lived rather comically in Finchley. She looked after their two small children, Richard and Melanie and she attended English classes at a language school near Regent's Park. In her free time, she had more fun than she had ever had before. With the young people from the language school she went to pubs and clubs, dancing, drinking. But she was drunk not so much with alcohol but with London. She changed her hairstyle and her clothes, her make up. She did not look like little Belgian Sabine Mertens anymore; she looked like a swinging young girl from London in a short short miniskirt with exaggerated big black eyes and as thin as Twiggy. When the end of the year approached, she could not bear to go back to Brussels and her family. All year she had been listening to the constant music of the times, she could not bear for the music to stop. Two months before she had to go home, she met a nice young man in a pub. He was a cabinet maker, his name was Michael Morton. There was a whirlwind romance. Michael said if they got engaged, she could stay with his parents until they could afford a place of their own. At the time it seemed like a perfect solution. They got married three months later.

I would like to say here that they lived happily ever after. But in the real life of course things are not so simple. They had two healthy children, they did not divorce. But Sabine learnt that changing countries does not always mean an adventure. In London she ended up living almost the same life as if she would have stayed in Belgium. Only her name changed from Mertens to Morton. As she desired, she did not go back to Belgium but during the many years she regretted it always.

Pearl

WHEN RENÉE OPENED the door to Pearl, she said, "I know why you've come."

In Pearl's dreams, Renée had rushed forward and hugged her. But that wasn't what happened. Renée looked scared. She said, "Come in" but not enthusiastically, more as if she was afraid Pearl might make a scene in the passage.

Pearl followed her into a beautiful sitting room, twice the size of her own and decorated like a room in a magazine with everything perfectly in its place. Pearl made an admiring noise.

Renée said, "Do sit down."

From another room a man's voice called out. He sounded upset.

Renée looked uncomfortable. "That's my husband. He's not well."

She seemed to hesitate for a moment and then she said, "D'you mind just waiting a second while I go and tell him I've got a visitor?"

"No of course not," Pearl said, wondering whether Renée suspected she might nick something.

While she waited, she took a good look around. She had her eye out for photographs, especially of anyone who could conceivably be Renée's Dad but she couldn't see any. There were only a few photos on display and they all seemed to be of young couples on their wedding day or sweet little children.

Pearl was taking a good look at them when Renée came back in.

Pearl asked quickly, "Is he ok?"

Renée seemed at a loss for words. Eventually she said, "He's got dementia."

"Oh," Pearl said, "oh that must be so hard for you dear."

Renée said, "You get on with it."

She stood and looked at Pearl with a deeply worried look on her face and still she didn't say anything.

"Listen," Pearl said, "I haven't come to make trouble if that's what you're thinking. I just need to know."

Renée opened her mouth and then shut it again. She reached for the back of the nearest armchair and, for a moment, Pearl feared she was about to have another turn. Then she looked directly at Pearl and she said, so quietly Pearl had trouble hearing, "Neville Cheevers was my dad too. We're sisters."

They stared at each other, frozen. Even though it was what Pearl had dreamt about, she felt as if she might keel over.

She didn't mean to say, "Bloody hell." It just slipped out.

They stood and looked at each other. The woman across the room from Pearl no longer looked the same. Pearl stared at her. It felt like that moment when they were testing your eyes in the optician's and they slipped the right lens into the metal frame on your nose and suddenly you could see properly. She saw Renée's soft cheeks and familiar small

297

chin. She saw her nice peach cardy. She saw Renée's hands clutched anxiously together with their knuckles swollen by arthritis, Renée's legs with their familiar thick ankles and comfy mules on her feet that were an upmarket version of Pearl's.

She asked, "Why did you run away?"

Renée said, "I thought you would hate me."

"*Hate* you?" Pearl repeated. "Why ever would I do that?"

Renée shifted. "I had a father and you didn't. He stuck by my mother and me, not by your mother and you. I thought…"

Pearl snapped, "Don't be daft. That's not *your* fault."

Renée said, "He wasn't much of a husband and father to us either you know. He was a real swine."

Pearl said, "I suppose he's long dead?"

Renée looked even more worried. She shook her head. "He's still alive," she said, "but he's in a bad way. He's into his nineties, he has the district nurse coming in. I know I should see him more often but I can't bring myself to. Not after all he put us through."

Pearl asked, "You mean there were others? It wasn't just my Mum and me?"

Renée burst out, "I didn't even *know* about you until you played your recording. When I heard my Dad's name on your tape, it was the biggest shock of my life. I knew he was unfaithful to Mum, I knew he had loads of affairs, everyone knew. But I had no idea it had gone on the whole time, right from the start. I didn't know he'd had a child. I don't even know if Mum knew. How old are you exactly?"

Pearl answered, "71."

Renée cried out, "Despicable! I'm just 72. So he was carrying on with *your* Mum while *my* Mum was having me." She shuddered, "Horrible."

Pearl said quietly, "I think *you're* angry with *me*."

Renée looked across at her. "I'm sorry dear. It's just all a bit much, isn't it? And what am I supposed to tell the children? Suddenly there's this whole other branch of the family no-one knew anything about?"

Pearl said, "And not posh either."

Renée blushed. "I didn't mean that."

Pearl said, "Well, I'm really pleased I found *you* Renée. I can't wait to tell my grandson."

Maybe disturbed by their voices, Renée's husband called out again. Renée looked towards the open door and said, "Excuse me a minute."

She went over to the door but in the doorway she turned. "When I've settled him, would you like a cup of tea?"

Pearl nodded. "Yes please."

Renée said, "Milk and two sugars, I'm guessing?" and they both smiled.

While Renée was out of the room, Pearl tried to stop shaking. She tried to organize in her mind the questions she needed to ask, so many of them. A whole lifetime of questions. She thought what an idiot she was to have waited so long to do this. She remembered, as if it were yesterday, the day her mother had told her about Mr Cheevers and his secret wife and child. Pearl was sixteen, she was starting to hang around with boys, her mother wanted to warn her of the dangers. Why had Pearl put it out of her mind for ever after?

She had thought about her Dad, often, bitterly but she had barely ever given a thought to the woman, somewhere in the world, who was her sister. Why not? In her heart of hearts, Pearl had to admit Renée was right; she had imagined Neville Cheevers' other, legitimate daughter must be a stuck- up cow. She had not imagined Renée. Now she had found her, she was overcome by remorse. She had not imagined someone with the same chin, the same hands, someone who wore the same colour nail varnish, who took their tea with milk and two sugars. She could weep now for all the years of lost sisterhood.

When Renée came back in, after quite a long time, Pearl was still crying. It was all too much, the idea that through all the terrible years and the loneliness, she could have had a sister. Kai could have had a lovely aunt, cousins. But she had been too proud to go looking. And she wept because Tracy would never know she had had an auntie.

Renée set down the tea tray. In spite of the emotion, she had set it beautifully with biscuits and everything. She sat down on the sofa next to Pearl and, gingerly, she reached over and took her hand.

"Don't cry dear," she said. "We'll work this out."

Pearl sniffed and dabbed her eyes and felt ashamed. Here was Renée, looking after a husband with dementia; she had no business sitting crying on her sofa.

"I'm sorry," she said.

"Don't be sorry," Renée said. "How would you have found me anyway even if you'd gone looking? I've been Thorpe not Cheevers for forty-four years. In any case, I'm just as much to blame as you. I've known since Christmas, haven't I and I didn't do anything."

Pearl tried to get a grip. Weakly, she said, "We're a pair of ninnies."

Renée said, "Seventy-year-old ninnies."

Pearl turned towards Renée. For a long time, they searched each other's faces for reflections and then, at last, they hugged.

Pearl was sure it had been morning when she arrived at Renée's but by the time they finally stopped talking, it was well into the afternoon. Renée had to take care of her husband who was calling out more and more, Pearl had to be getting home.

On their way out, Renée hesitated in the hall and asked Pearl to say hello to her husband. She went in first and Pearl went after.

A gentle-looking old man with a vacant expression but a full head of silky white hair was sitting watching television. At least, the television was on, Pearl couldn't tell if he was watching it. It was a cooking show.

Renée said to him, "Guess who this is Malcolm?"

Malcolm's blank blue eyes turned to Pearl. After a moment or two, he said, "It's your cousin Angela."

Renée turned to smile at Pearl. "Not quite."

Malcolm looked crestfallen.

"You'll never guess," Renée said. "It's my *sister*."

Malcolm's gaze swivelled back to Pearl. He looked at her without surprise and nodded and smiled vaguely.

Renée murmured, "Nothing surprises him."

Before Pearl left, they swapped phone numbers, carefully reading them back to each other, no more missed opportunities.

At the door, it seemed they didn't know whether to hug and kiss or just pat. They compromised on a sort of half-hug, cautiously taking hold of each other but not squeezing

Outside, it had clouded over since the morning and Pearl walked back up Larkvale Gardens in her own cloud. Whoever would have thought that her story, the story of Pearl Barter who lived in a grotty flat on the Larkrise Estate, whose only daughter had died of a drug overdose, would turn out to have a better ending than anyone else's? She could barely wait to get home and tell Kai and Neem.

Edgar

EDGAR SAT ON the bench outside the Second Chance Centre and thought about his holiday packing. He wanted to be well turned out for the Venice minibreak; he didn't want Madeleine casting her eye around the hotel dining room for someone more sophisticated.

The day was overcast but warm enough to wait outside for 2 o'clock, for the last but one class of term to begin. It was silly to have come early when he lived so close but sometimes these days he suffered tormenting feelings when he sat for too long on his own in the house. He had moments when he wanted to sweep all Joan's stuff aside and make a new home for Madeleine but then, right away, he would feel dreadfully troubled and guilty. He had expected this time of life to be dull; he had never expected it to be such a rollercoaster.

Pearl Barter appeared out of nowhere and, with a pleasant smile, sat down beside him.

Edgar doffed his hat automatically and smiled back. Pearl was the best of a bad bunch.

After exchanging a few routine remarks about the weather, on the spur of the moment Edgar asked Pearl, "So d'you feel you've got anything out of this class then?"

Pearl looked taken aback. She seemed to hesitate and

then she answered, "Yes I have. But not what I expected."

"Me too," Edgar said, "not at all what I expected." He added in a rush, "Mind you, I'm not too sure what I *did* expect. I was pushed into it, truth be told. This centre's caused me no end of trouble."

Pearl said, "How's that?"

Edgar thought there was no way he could explain to Pearl. As he struggled to answer, he was saved by the sight of Enid Harkin in the distance, carrying some sort of banner, which caused them both to get up simultaneously and start to move towards the front door.

Edgar held the heavy door open for Pearl – it was an effort – and, in the doorway, they swapped glances. "In the nick of time," Pearl mouthed and Edgar grinned.

In that instant, he understood why Joan had kept coming back to the Centre; it must have been *friends*, all the friends she had made in all her classes.

Even though he knew he was running a risk, he said to Pearl, "You know that woman Renée who stopped coming? I found out she used to be in a class here a few years back with my late wife. I noticed you two seemed to know each other? I don't suppose you could put me in touch with her, could you?"

Pearl looked flustered but she said she thought she could.

After the class, Edgar returned home, relieved there was only one more to go. Enid's banner had been a piece of her artwork. It showed another nonsensical scene: a spindly girl with a magnifying glass peering through a giant keyhole almost as big as herself. You could not exactly make out what she could see. Edgar would enjoy telling Madeleine about it. She was coming over for dinner and he needed to tidy the place up. He needed to make some headway too with the Venice guidebook Madeleine had given him.

"You got more time than me for reading," she had instructed him. "You read it and you can tell me all about it."

He didn't want to let her down.

As they ate dinner, Madeleine mentioned, in passing, that one of her patients, old Mr Cheevers had passed away. What was lucky was that his neglectful daughter had apparently shown up just the day before, for one of her rare visits. Perhaps he had died from the surprise of seeing her.

Edgar knew it was foolish, old Mr Cheevers had been well into his nineties but he couldn't help feeling glad that at least one rival for Madeleine's attention was out of the way.

Before the last class of term, he decided to steel himself and read to the end of Joan's exercise book. There were a couple of shortish pieces, one called "A Memorable Meal" about Edgar's retirement dinner. They had done him proud. He wished Joan had written a little more about him and a little less about all the courses and the table decorations – but there you go. There was one about Joan's work at the Health Centre and what it felt like to be a patient when she had spent her whole life dealing with people who were ill. Then, right at the end, there was a letter.

He found himself breaking out in a sweat. It was a muggy evening.

Dear Edgar

Now the end is near there are a couple of things I have to tell you. Firstly thank you for everything, for the good years and the companionship. What you did with P is forgiven if not forgotten. You may notice after I am gone and you have to take care of everything that there are a few things missing. They are the things I made for you over the years in my classes (embroidered hankies, cufflink box, table runner, cushion with E and J etc.) I am afraid I got in the habit of doing away with them now and again when I was feeling fed up and now I am truly sorry. It was silly and I regret it because when I am gone you won't have them to remember me by. I know I wasn't perfect either, I had my moments, I left it out of what I wrote but Trevor and I had a big kiss behind a palm tree one night in Sorrento. So you see, I am no better than you. I hope you will be alright on your own, you've not got many friends but maybe you will sign up for some classes and, who knows, maybe you will find happiness again?

With love and kisses
Your loving wife
Joan

When Edgar had composed himself, he got up and put the exercise book away in the cupboard. He locked it and put the key away. He went and got the Venice guidebook and sat down to read some more.

It was getting late, Madeleine would be over soon and, after a page or two, his concentration lapsed. He drifted into a reverie about how he would buy Madeleine a beautiful glass necklace on the island of Murano and how stunning it would look on her dear dark neck. They would take a boat back to Venice across the lagoon. If it wasn't too blowy, they would sit out on the deck, maybe hold hands. Madeleine would admire her necklace in her little handbag mirror and plant a warm appreciative kiss on Edgar's lips. Back at their hotel, they might have a little lie down before supper.

Iris

SURELY, IT COULD not have been Dorothy's revelations which had made Iris feel so strange. It was true they had been shocking, delightfully shocking, far more titillating than anything Iris had imagined. But it could hardly be that which was making her feel so peculiar, could it? After all, most of what Dorothy had written about was history, it had taken place years ago. Iris doubted that the culprits could now be identified and brought to book as Dorothy hoped. The best she could hope for, Iris supposed, was a flurry of attention in the local paper, probably followed by a letter or two denouncing the writer's lurid imaginings. Of course, Dorothy was a proven fabricator. Who was to say all this wasn't more of the same?

Iris wondered who she could possibly tell. Mina and Subhamoy would have been upset by the sexual content, (that was what Iris had enjoyed the most) but they would have known who to turn to. As pharmacists, Iris supposed, they must have had to deal with all sorts of unpleasant things. Without the Chatterjees, Iris was at a loss. She wondered whether Joanna and Nat might have a clue. They always seemed to have an answer for everything. But should she bother them with this with the baby less than two months away?

She couldn't remember whether she had eaten any supper. Was that why she was feeling so wobbly, so light-headed? She decided to go and make herself a cup of tea, maybe something with it but when she tried to get up, nothing seemed to work. She struggled for a moment or two and then she sat back in her armchair. Not to panic. Maybe what she needed was a little rest.

Dorothy's revelations had begun in a low key. Iris assumed that it was as she thought; there was nothing much to them. It was all in Dorothy's over-active imagination. People running all sorts of dodgy businesses had supposedly used Mercy House as their company address. Post came for them, deliveries were made at odd hours of day and night. Dorothy had kept a painstaking list of all the company names on the packages and a log of the vehicles which came and went. But without knowing what was actually going on or who those supposedly shady people were, Iris couldn't really make head or tail of it. She supposed it was even possible that it was all completely innocuous.

But then, three or four pages in, she had a colossal shock.

"Worst of all," Dorothy had written – and heavily underlined – "were the porn movies."

Apparently, some years back, someone at the Council had given permission for Mercy House to be used for filming. It was a nice little earner. But instead of the costume dramas they had been given to expect – with the backdrop of Mercy House and the park and the cedars of Lebanon – the company turned out to be a prolific producer of porn movies, some of them what Dorothy described euphemistically as "specialist".

These films were made at night – deliberately of course

so that there was no one around to see what was going on. But Dorothy was, she explained, in the habit of working late. She often used her evenings to catch up on all the little jobs there was no time for during the day. So she was still there when the film crew first arrived with all their paraphernalia and the young good-looking actors. Because she was expecting a costume drama, on her way out she slipped round to the side of the building where they were filming and took a look in through a window. What she saw horrified her. In fact, she was sick in the flower bed. She could barely bring herself to spell it out but it was obvious to Iris that what Dorothy had seen was two of the young actors simulating sex doggy style while wearing animal masks.

Iris chuckled, as much at the image as at the idea of prim little Dorothy peeping in and getting the shock of her life. Iris read on eagerly. This was far better than anything she had anticipated. Dorothy had overcome her revulsion enough to keep a record of what was going on. She had dates and times and, more interestingly, clear details of what she had seen during the filming. Occasionally they would film out in the garden too if the weather was fine. It was harder to spy on them there because, for discretion, they put up a big screen around what they were filming. But once or twice Dorothy had hidden behind a tree and seen things which even Iris found illuminating.

In fact, Iris had thoroughly enjoyed reading Dorothy's papers. It couldn't be that which was making her feel so unwell. Could it be Dorothy's mean reminder about Yusuf? Thinking about Yusuf still had the power to churn her up although not only because of the hurt he had caused her.

Thinking about Yusuf reminded Iris of all the lost pleasures. Reading Dorothy's papers reminded her of that too. Not that any of her three husbands had ever been *that* inventive. Still, that sort of thing was all long gone now and how very sad it was.

Iris sat in her armchair and waited to feel well enough to get up again. It seemed her legs had gone to sleep. She had spent too long sitting reading Dorothy's papers. She really must get up and walk about a bit to get things going. But, no matter how hard she tried to lever herself up, her legs weren't cooperating. She began to feel scared. Was this the beginning of something serious? Should she call Joanna? But how could she call her if she couldn't get over to the phone? She didn't even have a glass of water within reach. She would be found in her armchair after several days. But who would find her? And how? Busy preparing for the baby, Joanna and Nat hardly ever came round these days. Joanna just rang and left a message now and then and if her mother didn't ring back, would she worry? No, she wouldn't. She would put it down to Iris's meanness and not give it a second thought. Iris was done for. Next Thursday, when she didn't show up for the life story group, they would realise something was amiss. But that was a whole week away.

She wondered whether she should slide onto the floor and drag herself over to the phone. Would that work? She thought she would just about be able to reach up to the phone on its small table from the floor. But could she even drag herself?

All this would be a frightful nuisance for Joanna and Nat. But Iris couldn't help wondering, as she debated the floor route to the phone, whether Joanna might not be kinder to her if she fell seriously ill. Maybe a stroke or a heart attack or whatever this was would finally bring the two of them closer? Was such a thing even possible?

Iris tried to imagine Joanna tending to her on her deathbed, stricken with remorse for her long years of hostility. In her mind, she ran through a little scene between them: Joanna weeping and saying, "Mummy, Mummy, please forgive me," and she weakly reaching out a feeble hand to caress her daughter and murmuring, "Of course, my darling, of course." No, that certainly wasn't going to happen.

But what about the baby? Even though the baby – conceived by Nat with a sperm donor chosen from a catalogue – was biologically nothing to do with Iris, she would still be her grandchild. Might the baby, especially if she was pretty, be able to weave her spell and draw them all together? It was possible, wasn't it?

Encouraged, Iris let herself slip gently onto the floor. She thought she would be able to make it over to the phone but it was such a relief to be lying down, even on the floor, that she let herself have a little rest first. It must have got dreadfully late because the room had grown very dark. As Iris lay there, a pale wisp of a thought crossed a corner of the deepening darkness. Oh, she did hope she wasn't going to die and miss seeing the —

Esther

SIDNEY AND I could probably have got married in a Reform synagogue. But we did something very brave and modern, we got married in a registry office. I wore a cream satiny suit with a corsage of little crimson carnations and ferns. Sidney wore a charcoal grey suit with a crimson tie which matched my flowers. It was the happiest day of my life.

My parents were devastated because in their eyes it wasn't a proper wedding, in Jewish law we weren't really properly married. I pretended I didn't care because I wanted to try and be as modern as my darling Sidney. Also it was my way of getting back at everyone. We do these things blindly when we are young, don't we and we don't realise how they will come back to haunt us. Privately of course I cared terribly. In fact I went on being upset about it in secret all the rest of my life. But if I ever mentioned it to Sidney, he always said, "Stuff and nonsense" and got quite cross. In his prime, being a partner at his firm and everything, my lovely Sidney could be a bit pompous.

It wasn't the only thing which tormented me as the years went by. Not knowing more about my real origins and knowing I would most likely never know tormented me too. Dr Glaser was long dead, his practice closed, his records gone (even if there ever was any record of me). Remember this was all long before the internet. I suppose I could have put an ad in the papers but I did not dare or hired a private detective. But that would have cost loads and I would have felt bad spending Sidney's hard-earned money on what might turn out to be a wild goose chase. Besides Sidney wasn't that keen. Even though he had said it would be our quest to find out the truth, once we had found out he thought that ought to be the end of it. He felt there was no point going looking for trouble. Most likely I would never find my birth mother (and to be honest I wasn't that keen on finding my birth father after what he had done). Sidney thought I couldn't possibly have anything in common with my birth mother anymore and if by some chance we did meet up, it would only be dreadfully distressing for all concerned. Maybe he was right. I will never know. All I know is that it is hard to be happy if you don't belong anywhere.

My life should have been perfect. I was married to the man of my dreams, we lived in a lovely little house in Swiss Cottage. But I was tormented. Even though I had everything, I felt all the time like I didn't deserve it, it was too good to be true and it would turn out not to be true too. I must have driven poor Sidney round the bend. All the time I was anxious and fretting, frightened my happiness would turn out to be made up like my life before had. Sometimes I was convinced Sidney had only married me because he felt sorry for me. Poor Sidney, what he had to put up with.

Six months after we got married, I fell pregnant and even though I was really happy that was when my nightmares started. I was scared I wouldn't know how to be a proper birth mother and, silly as it sounds, I imagined the baby I would give birth to would actually be me. When I imagined her (and for some reason I always imagined a *her*) I saw the Irish girl's baby sitting on her mother's knee in a little flowery dress, all placid and smiley with a big bow in her hair. I know it doesn't make any sense but that is how it was.

It was a difficult pregnancy. Along with my nightmares, I suffered from morning sickness which went on all day and later on terribly swollen legs and feet. At the end my blood pressure went so high I had to go into hospital and have the baby delivered two weeks early. They say that is the most painful labour of all when they bring you on before your time. My labour lasted two days and two nights. By the time my little Esther was born, I was so weak I couldn't even hold her.

I stayed in the hospital for a week. (There was no rushing home straight after giving birth in those days.) I loved my little Esther right away, she was a gorgeous baby and Sidney doted on her from the word go. But a few days after she was born I had the first of my bad spells. I was scared to pick the baby up in case I hurt her. I got the weird idea the nurses and Sidney were in a conspiracy to catch me out doing something wrong. I got so scared I didn't dare do anything at all, not even touch little Esther or cuddle her. That was when they carted me off to the House on the Hill for the first time.

They pumped me full of drugs to make me better and as a result I couldn't even breastfeed my baby.

Samson asked, "So now you've finished your Mum's story, are you going to write yours?"

Esther exclaimed, "God no!"

Samson grinned, "What you hiding?"

"I'm not hiding anything," Esther said. She sat back in her chair and spread her hands. "Who'd want to hear about all *my* hang-ups? And nothing that dramatic has ever happened to me."

Samson considered. Smiling, he said, "You could write about me."

Dorothy

CHRISTOPHER AND MARTIN told Dorothy they were going to hold a summer garden party. She could barely believe it; Christopher, the recluse, partying. It was the last straw.

Two weeks before the end of the summer term, Dorothy had been summoned to Lavonda's office. Triumphantly, Lavonda had told her that the life story group would not be running next year. The numbers were not economical and, besides, the Second Chance Centre management felt it did not cater to their client base.

"Whatever do you mean?" Dorothy asked. Not that she was entirely sorry to hear the group would be closing down. It had got her into deeper water than she had ever imagined and she would certainly not be sorry to see the back of Iris or Enid. As for the rest of them, she might miss their weekly instalments but she certainly wouldn't be heartbroken to see them go. Still, thrown on the scrap heap again in her sixty-second year; what would her future be? She glared at Lavonda and waited for an answer.

Lavonda flipped through the Centre's small mauve prospectus. "We thought we'd try it out the once. But if you take a look at our *other* courses, you will see that they are all geared to personal development, acquiring skills, attaining *goals*. Look," she said, "physical activity, healthy eating, literacy, numeracy.

We don't feel that, going forward, life story writing really belongs here Dorothy."

"Aromatherapy?" Dorothy snapped. "Chocolate cookery? Palm reading? What *goals* are people attaining there?"

Lavonda smirked. "Those classes can enable people to set up their own small businesses, you see. A single mum could do aromatherapy or whatever from home. Those classes are *enabling*, they create *pathways*. Yours doesn't."

"How do you know?" Dorothy asked shrilly. "How do you *know* telling your life story doesn't create a pathway?"

"Dorothy," Lavonda said, shaking her head and apparently suppressing mirth. "How *could* it? Most of your students are well on, aren't they? What sort of pathway could it *be*?"

Dorothy considered Lavonda. She knew she must choose her words carefully. "With all due respect, Lavonda," she said, "you are rather young and I'm not sure how much you understand older people."

Lavonda looked outraged. Her shaped eyebrows shot up. She opened her mouth but Dorothy silenced her with a swiftly raised hand. To tell the truth, she was amazed by her own audacity.

"Telling your life story is not just wallowing in nostalgia you know," she said. "It gives people the opportunity to pass on the version of their life *they* want. It gives them a chance to right wrongs, to set down burdens they've been carrying around for years: secrets, horrible things. You wouldn't believe what's come out in my group. No doubt you think we're just a bunch of old fuddy-duddies. Left-over people. But we've lived through terrible things. And some of my group," she faltered, then drew breath for a final assault, "I think some of them will live the rest of their lives more easily thanks to the stories they've told here. You think it's all just self-indulgence —"

"I never said," Lavonda interrupted, "I never said."

But Dorothy, carried along on the wave of her own eloquence, could not stop. "Sweep us aside," she declared. "Get rid of me. Cancel the class. But don't you *dare* suggest it's worthless. It's the stuff of life, Lavonda, the stuff of life."

"Fine," Lavonda said curtly. "But it's got to stop. We're going to do Zumba instead."

On the bus home, Dorothy felt proud of her stand. But something was niggling her still. Everything she had boasted about to Lavonda she had failed to do herself. *She* hadn't set down any burdens or shared any secrets. Her life story was a fraud. She had done what she always did, what she had done her whole life in fact; she had hung back, stayed at the margins. She had never engaged with life, she had only ever run away from it. When Peter Gentry with the bad teeth had asked her to marry him, she had taken fright and hidden away at Mercy House for the next twenty-seven years. She had not even dared to write her real life story. She had told someone else's instead.

So Christopher's party invitation, pronounced painfully in the front hall as she came in, was the last straw. Even hopeless Christopher, it seemed, had managed to launch himself at last on the current of life. Only Dorothy was left at the edge, limited to taking notes on others.

"Thank you Christopher," she said haughtily. "I do hope I'll be free."

Christopher looked hurt. "Oh, I h-hope so t-t-too."

"The thing is Christopher," Dorothy said, "I'm awfully busy nowadays."

It seemed to her that Christopher gave her a rather funny look but she might have imagined it.

Over the final two weeks of term, she tried to gear herself up to do something extraordinary. She wondered if she might not own up in the last class of term, tell them all what she had done and throw herself on their mercy. The very thought of it gave her palpitations but still she hoped she might be brave enough to do it. As justification, she would tell them her real life story and, hopefully, they would all feel so sorry for her that they would forgive her. It would take the wind out of Iris's sails too, deprive her of the pleasure of ever denouncing Dorothy. The only thing was, would she dare?

The weather in that last fortnight was unusually fine. From her window, Dorothy watched the preparations for Christopher and Martin's party and reflected sourly how well everything seemed to have turned out for them since that miserable Christmas night; even the weather was cooperative. Garrulous Martin was out in the garden at all hours, stringing up multi-coloured lights and planting curious cartoon characters on stakes in the flower beds.

Dorothy could hear him calling all the time to Christopher indoors, asking him what he thought of the decorations and whether he should trim back some of the bushes. He called Christopher "Kitty" which irritated Dorothy no end. She wondered whether this was what the rest of her life was going to be like; just eavesdropping on other people's. She would have to swallow her pride and join Gerald's volunteers; it was all she could think of. Probably no one would employ her anyway once her revelations about Mercy House were made public.

The day of the party dawned overcast but Dorothy's mean

hope that it would rain was dashed when the sun came out after lunch and a warm afternoon turned into a mellow golden evening. Dorothy had not committed herself to going, she kept hinting at another engagement she would need to get out of first. Christopher had been very easy-going, offhand almost and told her just to show up if she could make it.

When the noise of the party began to be audible in her flat and the garden started to fill up with Christopher and Martin's medley of guests, curiosity got the better of Dorothy. She changed into a flowery frock, considered and rejected a hat and applied a little lipstick. She took out the bottle of chilled white wine she had had ready in the fridge all week and left her flat. As she stood on the landing, locking her front door and checking she had what she needed, she began to have second thoughts. It was several years since she had been to a party and she wasn't sure she was up to one. But an unfamiliar urgency made her go downstairs. However frightening it felt, however horribly it went wrong, this was what you had to do, wasn't it? You had to launch yourself on the current of life. This was what she had never managed to do but what she was determined to do now. Better late than never. At the door of Christopher's flat, which was standing open, she allowed herself a last moment of hesitation. Inside, people were talking at the top of their voices and laughing hilariously. Dorothy breathed deeply and then she swept into the party.

Enid

"ARE YOU TELLING me," Enid demanded, "that art is not enough?" She glared around the semi-circle.

In the silence which followed, Edgar cleared his throat.

"Frog?" Enid asked sharply. "Or are you trying to tell me something? Out with it."

"Art," Dorothy volunteered, "does wonders but it leaves gaps."

"And words," Enid retorted, "don't words leave gaps too?"

Really, she was fed up to the back teeth with the lot of them. Iris, whom she could not abide, had not even deigned to show up for this last class. Doubtless she was off on holiday somewhere frightfully posh and frightfully expensive. Iris's absence made Enid particularly angry because she had decided to give them all a piece of her mind today and she was disappointed that Iris was not there to hear it.

Enid had had more than enough of their idiotic reactions to her drawings. Every time she brought one along it was the same: the raised eyebrows, the barely polite puzzled faces and the silly questions.

"Who is that supposed to be in the picture Enid?"

"Did it actually really happen like that?"

"What does it mean?"

Oh, Enid would gladly put a rocket under the lot of them. She was working on a new piece at home, a collage which depicted the seven remaining members of the life story group as seven assorted chairs. Renée was represented by a gap. Each chair, made up of an assortment of glued-on scraps of fabric, conveyed the character of its owner. Iris's chair was a high-backed faux leather armchair, Enid's own a wonky three-legged stool.

As she glared at them, Sabine, a vintage rocking chair, answered tentatively, "Yes Enid, words leave gaps. But the gaps are part of the story too."

"I get that," Enid said. She had no reason to be cross with Sabine. In fact, she had had a soft spot for her ever since Sabine had read out about how much she loved her childhood art classes with that heroic teacher. "It's the same with my drawings. If you look, you can make out a lot of what's been left out along with what's actually there."

"How?" Esther asked. "How can you make out something which isn't there?"

Enid turned on her. "I would have thought you of all people would understand that Esther. I mean you left yourself out completely, didn't you?"

"I wasn't writing about me," Esther said, "I was writing about my Mum."

"Yes!" Enid said. "Yes! But why? Why did you decide to leave yourself out? The rest of us, our stories begin

325

with our birth, right? Why does yours stop at your birth? Surely you must see that's extremely unusual. And we ask ourselves **why**. Why this odd decision, why the gap?"

Dorothy murmured, "Enid —"

Esther was starting to look upset.

"Look," Enid said, "look, I don't mean to pry. But it drives me round the twist when you all go on about my drawings not telling the whole story. You've all of you left things out, big things: Iris has only ever told us about her la-di-dah family history, hasn't she, precious little about her actual life and you, Edgar, we've heard no end of funny stories about your department store - which is great - but next to nothing about your home life. I feel there's a double standard here: one rule for the written word and another for my art. I'm not the only one here who's left stuff out."

Esther appeared to boil over. "Why ever would I want to write about my life? It was awful, awful growing up with a mother with mental health issues, a mother who spent the whole time obsessing about herself. She never had time for me, growing up, it was always all about **her**. All that mattered was her own drama, the being adopted, the was she, wasn't she. You know what, it was a relief the times she had to go into hospital. It was just me and my Dad without her non-stop crises. We went on holiday together once, just me and my Dad, when she was getting treatment, it was the best week of my life. Sometimes I wonder if it was the best week of his life too? Except he did love her, that was the thing, however awful she was, he always stood by her, he didn't like it when I said stuff about her."

"But you wrote about her very lovingly too," Sabine said.

There was a murmur of agreement.

"Well of course I did!" Esther exclaimed. "I was trying to make up for being angry with her my whole life. I thought if I wrote it all down, I might feel better about it. My counsellor suggested it. She thought it might help me let go of my anger. I'm not sure it worked." She shuddered. "My Mum messed up my life, you know. She made me feel bad about being me. Because she felt she didn't fit in, she wasn't sure who she was, she passed it all on to me. If it wasn't for her, I could be a completely normal person."

Pearl said, "We could all say that, dear."

Surprisingly loudly, Dorothy agreed, "Hear, hear."

Esther looked around. "Look, I'm not trying to make out I had it worse than anyone else. I know you've all had issues. It's just, you know, just because I said I loved my Mum, it doesn't mean I did. And I didn't write about my life because, you know what, there's nothing much to say."

"You've got time," Edgar said, "loads of time still."

"Yes," Sabine said, "you are our baby, aren't you" and Enid thought with delight of Esther's pink highchair in her collage.

"Look," Esther said, "look, I don't want today to be all about me. It's our last class. Can I ask you something Enid? You know what you said about finding out your Mum was alive from a bit of blotting paper? When you thought she was dead? What was all that about?"

"So I see," Enid said indignantly, "you're still expecting me to resort to words?"

"Well," Dorothy said, "this isn't a painting class, is it?"

Enid waved her latest drawing, of a thin knight in armour charging forward brandishing an outsized paintbrush. "I think this says it all," she said, "if you have the eyes to see it."

"Maybe we don't?" Pearl said. "I dare say it's our fault. We don't have your artistic background."

Enid sighed.

"Just tell us about your mother and the blotting paper," Esther begged, "just that."

Enid frowned at the floor. She hummed for a minute or two and then she looked up and said, "Ok, the bare bones. I'll tell you just the bare bones. My Mum walked out when I was six. She left my Dad for another man, a bit strangely an undertaker. My Dad told me she was dead. I suppose he meant she was dead to him but I was six, you don't get that sort of thing. So I believed she was literally dead and, who knows, maybe it was better than the truth and me thinking she had left me because I was such an awful child. Maybe, in his weird and wonderful way, my Dad was trying to protect me? Anyway. We carried on together, me and Dad, muddling through but doing ok until I was eleven. That was when I made a shattering discovery.

I found out my Mum wasn't dead after all, she was alive and corresponding with my Dad. About money doubtless.

"I needed a sheet of blotting paper for my homework which was a mess. So I took it over to Dad's big blotter on his table where he did his invoices and estimates. He was a locksmith. And I was about to lay my homework face down on the blotter when I saw something which made me freeze: my Mum's name. Coral. I hadn't heard of any other Coral so I knew it must be my Mum. Anyway, what other Coral would there have been on my Dad's blotter? There were the words, back to front, but perfectly legible: 'Dear Coral'. I stared at them. I felt faint. 'Dear Coral'. Then I thought how stupid I was; Dad never changed his blotter, that I knew of, it must be a bit of really old writing from five years back, from before Mum died. But hang on a minute, why would Dad have been writing to Mum then, when they lived under the same roof? I peered closer at the blotter and my heart stood still. A little way away from 'Dear Coral', up and to the left (remember, back to front writing) there was a date and the date was only two weeks before: 20 October 1952. It must be the beginning of a letter, written in the formal old-fashioned way, the way Dad wrote his invoices. Somewhere or other, my Mum was still alive.

"When Dad came home from work, I showed him what I'd found and, poor man, he broke down in tears. He told me the whole story, how my Mum had left and how he had tried to hide her wicked behaviour from

329

me. He kept saying, 'Don't be angry Enid, it was for the best.' But I had no time to be angry; all I wanted to know was where was my Mum?"

Enid paused and Esther asked, "Well, where was she?"

"I'm coming to that," Enid said. She drew breath and said, "Berwick-upon-Tweed."

The questions came from all sides: "Why such a long way away?" "Did you get to see her?" and "Why was your Dad writing to her anyway?"

Enid frowned. "I'll answer just one question," she said, "and then that's it."

She was infuriated – even more infuriated than she already was – to be interrupted at that point by a knock at the door. It was Lavonda, Lavonda with her advanced certificate in self-righteousness.

She was looking especially self-important.

"Sorry to interrupt," she said, addressing the semi-circle, Enid noticed, rather than Dorothy. "I waited until you were nearly done because I didn't want to upset your last class. But I have a piece of sad news to share, I'm afraid. Iris Bennett passed away at the end of last week. Her daughter called the Centre to let us know."

Of course everyone was instantly distracted from Enid. She didn't know whether to feel relieved or put out at being upstaged by Iris. There were gasps and exclamations and questions to Lavonda about the circumstances of Iris's death and the arrangements for the funeral.

"She passed away peacefully," Lavonda said. "Her daughter said it was mercifully quick. She was reading, I believe."

Enid commented, "A dangerous activity obviously," and Lavonda threw her a dirty look.

"The funeral's tomorrow," Lavonda added. "At the crematorium at 11. If any of you want —"

"Oh, I do think we should," Dorothy said. "Don't you all?"

There were shufflings and mutterings. It was true, Iris had not been popular. Only Sabine said, "Yes, I'll come."

Edgar said, "I would but I'm off on my hols tomorrow."

Enid and Pearl exchanged looks, Esther squirmed.

"Ok, I'll come," Pearl said, "to pay my respects."

That let Enid off the hook, she thought. Three going from the class was more than enough. "I'm working flat out on a big piece of artwork," she said. "I'm hoping you'll display it here at the Centre, Lavonda. Students' work."

Lavonda raised her eyebrows and didn't answer Enid. Instead, she said to all of them, "I'm sorry to end your last class like this," and then she left, checking her watch busily.

When Lavonda had gone, none of them seemed to know quite what to say. Dorothy shuffled her papers ineffectually. To Enid's relief, no one seemed to feel like asking her any more questions.

They said their goodbyes and, afterwards, Pearl followed Esther out into the corridor.

"You won't believe it," she said quietly, "but I met your Mum's old boyfriend, Peter Robinson."

Esther exclaimed, "No!" She clutched Pearl's arm. "Where? How? What's he like?"

"Turns out he's the headmaster of my grandson's school," Pearl said, "Larkrise School. He's lovely. But, you know, I don't think the story your Mum told you is the whole truth."

On her way home, Enid wondered what to do about Iris's armchair in her collage. Should she unstick Iris's chair and leave a second gap like Renée's? Or should she sketch in with some black embroidery thread, standing behind the chair, the silhouette of the grim reaper?

Dorothy

A FULL MOON hung low over the ravaged park. Dorothy supposed that it was not appropriate to call it a harvest moon in NW6 but that was what it was. It was late August, warm and close during the day, the first creeping doubts about summer faintly felt at night. Dorothy drew her light cardy closer as she walked silently up the once familiar drive. She wasn't sure if she was shivering from the cool of the night or from excitement. She had never done anything like this before.

The drive still curved but the gravel had been replaced by smooth oily tarmac which glistened repellently in the moonlight. When she reached the bend, Dorothy slipped behind a tree to see the lie of the land. The flats seemed to have shot up. They couldn't possibly be safe, having been built at such a pace. In any case, their inhabitants were not going to have peace of mind. Dorothy waited behind the solid old cedar of Lebanon and took stock. She put her hand to the mighty trunk and tried to draw strength from its silent presence.

The flats were an absolute eyesore. In fact, they weren't finished yet; she could see a lot of bits were still missing. But the windows were in on all three floors, huge display windows more suited to a department store than homes. She imagined flashily dressed mannequins in the windows; that was what the people who came to live here would be, strutting around their showcase homes, with their ultra-modern kitchens and bathrooms, but probably not a book between them.

From her safe spot behind the tree, Dorothy considered the building. It was charmless and featureless and, to add insult to injury, its big flashy entrance stood exactly where the front door of Mercy House had been. As she scowled at it, a gleam of something silver in the moonlight caught her attention; to the side of the double glass front doors, an array of stainless steel letter boxes was set in the wall. Letter boxes already! Dorothy's spirits rose for this was even better than she had imagined.

She slipped out from behind the tree and took a long look at the security guard's cabin a little way off. There was a light on inside but Claw, her unexpected new ally, had sworn the guard went off every night between 11.30 and 12 to get a late kebab on the High Road. Dorothy crept closer – no sound of music or radio from the cabin. Barely breathing, she got close enough to peer in at the window and to see that what Claw had told her was true; the guard was not there. How shameful and irresponsible, Dorothy thought, to abandon his duties like that.

Now she knew she had to act quickly. It was already a quarter to. Darting across the newly tarmacked forecourt, she made a beeline for the letter boxes. It occurred to her, as she hurried, that maybe it was just as well they had done away with the gravel; you could always hear someone walking on gravel from yards away, especially at night.

She fished in her shopper bag for the printed pages and quickly and methodically, left to right, first the top row and then the bottom, she posted one in each letter box. That still left quite a few over; what should she do with them? She decided she still had time to walk briskly round the building and see if there were any more letter boxes anywhere else: the estate agents who were promoting the show flat maybe or a management office. She could also take a look at Claw's latest work of art.

Dorothy had made Claw's acquaintance at Christopher and Martin's garden party. She had enjoyed the party much more than she had anticipated; the extravagantly decorated garden was full of fascinating young men, some in elaborate fancy dress. Apart from strange Suzy, the top floor tenant and Martin's sister, a large and loud woman with shocking pink hair, there were hardly any women guests. It was an all-male gathering and they were enjoying themselves with an energy and a gusto that was contagious.

Dorothy circulated, sipping sparkling white wine and congratulating herself on being there. But she knew she had to do more to join the current of life; she had to plunge in. So when Christopher came near her, refilling glasses, she took a big swallow of her wine and asked him to introduce her to some of his lovely friends.

Christopher asked, "B-b-b-bookish pee-people?"

Dorothy shrugged. "Anyone Christopher. Up to you," and Christopher led her over to a small gaggle of young men at the bottom of the garden who weren't dancing or hooting with laughter but just standing around chatting and the chattiest one was Claw.

He was a graffiti artist. Claw was not his real name but since he liked to remain anonymous, he went by Claw.

He said, "It's my tag."

Dorothy smiled politely. "You're going to have to explain that I'm afraid," and all the young men grinned.

Claw looked amazed. "You don't know what a tag is?"

335

"Do *you*," Dorothy retorted, "know what the Dewey Decimal Classification system is? Each to his own."

Claw, who was small and slight and looked to Dorothy no more than sixteen, scowled in concentration. "Your tag," he said slowly, as if he were speaking to someone really very simple, "is how you write your name. It's like how you sign your work." He scrubbed at his head vigorously as if trying to stimulate his thought processes.

"I see," Dorothy said. "And this work, what is it exactly?"

"It's art," Claw said. "It's art and it's protest." He looked pleased with himself but Dorothy was none the wiser.

Claw became eloquent. "People are oppressed," he said. "Right? And this is how we fight back. Not with like guns and stuff but with spray paint – and *ideas*. We're anti-capitalist and that. We do banks and big business places, you know, McDonald's, Starbucks. We spray stuff on their walls, like messages, like a *warning*."

"What about property developers?" Dorothy asked. "Do you ever target them?"

Dorothy would be the first to admit they formed an unlikely alliance: she, a sixty-one year old librarian with an extensive vocabulary and young Claw with his glottal stops. He had been enthusiastic about targeting the new block of flats. He had suggested HOMES FOR THE HOMELESS using non-permanent paints to get round a charge of criminal damage if they were caught. Dorothy said she would prefer "Desecration" and "Philistines" but Claw said there was no way he could spell those. They argued a bit, Claw pushing the issue of young people priced off the housing ladder, Dorothy more concerned about aesthetics and barbarianism.

The day after the party, Claw took Dorothy on a covert tour of his local work. It was an eye-opener. All around Brondesbury, multi-coloured messages on walls and hoardings, which Dorothy had taken to be just vandalism, turned out to be mysterious art. Big ballooning messages which you could at first barely decipher were designed by Claw and his friends. They said BANKERS ARE WANKERS, KEEP WARM BURN THE RICH, FUCK MONEY and OUT FASCIST SCUM.

Afterwards, Dorothy took Claw to tea and, even though it was four o'clock in the afternoon, he hungrily ate a full English breakfast.

"If you can't manage 'philistines,'" Dorothy suggested, "what about 'ugly' or 'vulgar'?"

"Spell those?" said Claw. He thought for a few moments, polishing off the last of his breakfast. "Uh-huh," he said. "I think I could do 'em." He added, "Though it'd have more impact you know if you just put SHIT HOLE."

He had managed UGLY in lurid orange and purple right across the featureless front façade. (That was how he had found out about the security guard's habits.) It had been swiftly cleaned off with high pressure hoses and special scouring products but not before Claw and his friends had taken loads of pictures on their phones and the graffiti had, he said, become quite famous online.

A few nights ago Claw had gone back – during the kebab break – and sprayed a new message at the entrance to the block's underground car park. He wouldn't tell Dorothy what it said, he told her it would be a nice surprise for her.

That had helped Dorothy to screw up her courage. She had been planning to deliver copies of her shocking revelations about Mercy House for some while but until now her nerve had failed her. The fact that puny little Claw was doing something so much worse, risking a prosecution for criminal damage, made it easier. After all, beyond possibly trespassing, what was the harm in putting flyers, socially responsible flyers into letterboxes? But Dorothy was still overwhelmed by the enormity of her act and, as she tiptoed round the back of the building seeking the entrance to the garage, she felt herself trembling.

When she saw Claw's new artwork, she was beside herself. She had rehearsed the spelling of several words with him so why did the bright pink graffiti which sprawled across the garage door read VULGER? Dorothy felt herself flush with annoyance and embarrassment as if the spelling mistake reflected badly on her too. She stood there for a few moments seething before remembering that she really shouldn't dawdle; time was running out.

She supposed she had lingered a little too long. As she hurried back down the drive, a forceful smell of grilled meat and onions assailed her. The security guard was back.

She could make him out, ambling in through the gates. (Oh, of course they had kept the gates to give themselves a false air of class.) She told herself not to panic. The guard, a bulky chap, hadn't seen her yet; he was concentrating on his kebab. For a fanciful moment, Dorothy wondered if she could just pass him and wish him good evening and nothing would happen at all. She did not look like a burglar – or a graffiti artist.

"Oy!" His cry rang out across the silent park. "What you doin' here?"

Dorothy was amazed by her own presence of mind. "I'm looking for my cat," she replied.

"You can't look here," the guard called, hampered by the kebab. "This is private property."

"Is it?" Dorothy asked. "It used to be council."

"Well it's private *now*," the guard said angrily. "You've got no right coming in here."

He glared at her.

Dorothy repeated, "I'm just looking for my cat."

"Oh, for Christ's sake," the guard said, visibly annoyed both by Dorothy and by the prospect of his kebab getting cold. "You can't just walk onto someone else's property 'cos you're looking for a cat. You're old enough to know that."

Dorothy bridled. But everything would be alright, she reckoned, provided he didn't ask to search her shopper bag. His fingers would be greasy too.

She asked indignantly, "Don't you care about animal welfare?"

The guard said, "No I don't." He added, "Just get out ok. And don't come back." He took a big bite of the kebab to make up for lost time and, with his free hand, gestured towards the gates. "Just count yourself lucky I'm not calling the police." He shook his head. "Fucking *cat*."

Dorothy walked briskly away down the drive. Her heart was pounding. Her mission had succeeded. She supposed no-one would think to look in the letter boxes until the new inhabitants moved in and by then the nocturnal visitor looking for her cat would be long forgotten. She had dared to do something extraordinary, she had confronted danger and she had got away with it. Happily, she imagined the trouble, the harm she had caused. Some of the new people would crumple up her article and throw it away without bothering to read it. But some of them would read it, horrified and worry ever after that their new homes were jinxed.

Smiling radiantly, Dorothy walked out of the gates. The night bus loomed into view just as she approached the bus stop. Everything was going her way. Aboard the bus, she breathed deeply and tried to compose herself. Then she sat and wondered what her next chapter might be.